PAUL TEMPLE AND THE SULLIVAN MYSTERY

Francis Durbridge

WILLIAMS & WHITING

Applications for performance or other rights should be made to The Agency, 24 Pottery Lane, London W11 4LZ.

Cover design by Timo Schroeder

9781912582846

Williams & Whiting (Publishers)

15 Chestnut Grove, Hurstpierpoint,

West Sussex, BN6 9SS

Titles by Francis Durbridge published by Williams & Whiting

1   The Scarf – tv serial
2   Paul Temple and the Curzon Case – radio serial
3   La Boutique – radio serial
4   The Broken Horseshoe – tv serial
5   Three Plays for Radio Volume 1
6   Send for Paul Temple – radio serial
7   A Time of Day – tv serial
8   Death Comes to The Hibiscus – stage play
     The Essential Heart – radio play
     (writing as Nicholas Vane)
9   Send for Paul Temple – stage play
10 The Teckman Biography – tv serial
11 Paul Temple and Steve – radio serial
12 Twenty Minutes From Rome – a teleplay
13 Portrait of Alison – tv serial
14 Paul Temple: Two Plays for Radio Volume 1
15 Three Plays for Radio Volume 2
16 The Other Man – tv serial
17 Paul Temple and the Spencer Affair – radio serial
18 Step In The Dark – film script
19 My Friend Charles – tv serial
20 A Case For Paul Temple – radio serial
21 Murder In The Media – more rediscovered serials and
     stories
22 The Desperate People – tv serial
23 Paul Temple: Two Plays for Television
24 And Anthony Sherwood Laughed – radio series
25 The World of Tim Frazer – tv serial
26 Paul Temple Intervenes – radio serial
27 Passport To Danger! – radio serial
28 Bat out of Hell – tv serial
29 Send For Paul Temple Again – radio serial

30 Mr Hartington Died Tomorrow – radio serial
31 A Man Called Harry Brent – tv serial
32 Paul Temple and the Gregory Affair – radio serial
33 The Female of the Species (contains The Girl at the Hibiscus and Introducing Gail Carlton) – radio series
34 The Doll – tv serial

Murder At The Weekend – the rediscovered newspaper serials and short stories

Also published by Williams & Whiting:
Francis Durbridge : The Complete Guide
By Melvyn Barnes

Titles by Francis Durbridge to be published by Williams & Whiting

A Game of Murder

Breakaway – The Family Affair

Breakaway – The Local Affair

Farewell Leicester Square (writing as Lewis Middleton Harvey)

Five Minute Mysteries (includes Michael Starr Investigates and The Memoirs of Andre d'Arnell)

Johnny Washington Esquire

Melissa

Murder On The Continent (Further re-discovered serials and stories)

One Man To Another – a novel

Operation Diplomat

Paul Temple and the Alex Affair

Paul Temple and the Canterbury Case (film script)

Paul Temple and the Conrad Case

Paul Temple and the Geneva Mystery

Paul Temple and the Gilbert Case

Paul Temple and the Jonathan Mystery

Paul Temple and the Lawrence Affair

Paul Temple and the Madison Mystery

Paul Temple and the Margo Mystery

Paul Temple and the Vandyke Affair

Paul Temple: Two Plays For Radio Vol 2 (Send For Paul Temple and News of Paul Temple)

The Man From Washington

The Passenger

Tim Frazer and the Salinger Affair

Tim Frazer and the Mellin Fforrest Mystery

INTRODUCTION

Those not familiar with the career of Francis Durbridge (1912-98) might welcome a brief résumé. He began as a prolific writer of sketches, stories and plays for BBC radio in 1933, mostly light entertainments, but a talent for crime fiction became evident in his early radio plays *Murder in the Midlands* (1934) and *Murder in the Embassy* (1937). The *Radio Times* (11 February 1938) mentioned that Durbridge had by then written some one hundred radio pieces, and Charles Hatton commented in *Radio Pictorial* (28 October 1938) that "He is one of the very few people in this country who have succeeded in making a living by writing for the BBC."

Durbridge continued to write plays and serials for BBC radio for many years, using his own name and the pseudonyms Frank Cromwell, Nicholas Vane and Lewis Middleton Harvey, while capitalising on a particular brainwave. In 1938 he created the dream team of novelist/detective Paul Temple and his wife Steve, and the audience reaction to his radio serial *Send for Paul Temple* was to lead to sequels over several decades that built an impressive UK and European following. Later in 1938 Durbridge responded to his fan mail with *Paul Temple and the Front Page Men*, and from 1939 to 1968 there were another twenty-six Paul Temple cases, of which seven were new productions of earlier broadcasts.

Then in 1952, while continuing to write for radio, Durbridge embarked on a run of BBC television serials (without the Temples) that attracted huge viewing figures until 1980. And additionally, from 1973 in the UK and even earlier in Germany, he crafted intriguing stage plays in the style of Frederick Knott (of *Dial M for Murder* fame) and Ira Levin (of *Deathtrap* fame).

Paul Temple and the Sullivan Mystery was the tenth outing for the Temples, broadcast on the BBC Light Programme in eight thirty-minute episodes from Monday 1 December 1947 to Monday 19 January 1948, with all episodes repeated on Saturday each week. Temple was played for the fourth time by Kim Peacock (1901-66), whose tenure began in 1946 with *Paul Temple and the Gregory Affair* and ended in 1953 with the one-hour play *Paul Temple and Steve Again*. He was then replaced by Peter Coke (1913-2008) for *Paul Temple and the Gilbert Case* (1954) and all subsequent serials until the concluding *Paul Temple and the Alex Affair* in 1968.

As Steve Temple, Marjorie Westbury (1905-89) partnered both Peacock and Coke in all their appearances, and before Peacock she had played opposite Barry Morse in *Send for Paul Temple Again* (1945) and Howard Marion-Crawford in *A Case for Paul Temple* (1946). In total she was Steve on twenty-two occasions until the final serial *Paul Temple and the Alex Affair* (1968) – which coincidentally was a new production of her debut as Steve in the 1945 *Send for Paul Temple Again*. But mention must also be made of Sir Graham Forbes of Scotland Yard, the role in which Lester Mudditt appeared nineteen times from the original serial in 1938 until *Paul Temple and the Spencer Affair* (1957-58).

The Temples, renamed Paul and Ina Vlaanderen, had become popular in the Netherlands, and in this case the Dutch radio version was *Paul Vlaanderen en het Sullivan* mysterie (6 November – 22 December 1949, eight episodes), translated by J.C. van der Horst and produced by Kommer Kleijn, with Jan van Ees as Vlaanderen and Eva Janssen as Ina.

Much later, from 2006 to 2013, the BBC revived Paul Temple by taking surviving radio scripts and re-creating five of the original serials, all produced by Patrick Rayner and featuring Crawford Logan and Gerda Stevenson. *Paul Temple and the Sullivan Mystery* (1947-48) was the first, followed by *Paul Temple and the Madison Mystery* (1949), *Paul Temple and Steve* (1947), *A Case for Paul Temple* (1946) and *Paul Temple and the Gregory Affair* (1946). The new production of *Paul Temple and the Sullivan Mystery* was broadcast from 7 August to 2 October 2006 and marketed on audiocassettes and CDs (BBC Audio, 2006), later included in the CD set *Paul Temple: The Complete Radio Collection: Paul Temple Returns 2006-2013* (BBC, 2017).

Like many of Durbridge's radio and television serials, *Paul Temple and the Sullivan Mystery* was novelised. It was, however, some years after the radio serial that the book appeared, with certain features that must have made it difficult to detect its origin. Firstly, there was a change of title to *East of Algiers* (Hodder & Stoughton, February 1959); and secondly, it was published under the pseudonym "Paul Temple" and written in the first person. The popular crime novelist Douglas Rutherford (James Douglas Rutherford McConnell, 1915-99) collaborated with Durbridge, having worked with him previously on *The Tyler Mystery* (Hodder & Stoughton, September 1957), which was an original story rather than a radio spinoff and written by "Paul Temple" in the third person! The paperback editions of *The Tyler Mystery* (Hodder, November 1960) and *East of Algiers* (Hodder, January 1962), incidentally, were both credited to Durbridge only and not to "Paul Temple".

East of Algiers was later marketed as an audiobook – in five audiocassettes and six CDs, read by Michael Tudor Barnes as *East of Algiers* by Durbridge and Rutherford (ISIS Audiobooks, 2006); and on two CDs there was an abridged reading by Anthony Head as *Paul Temple East of Algiers* by Durbridge (BBC Audio, 2009). In Germany the book was published as *Die Brille*, in the Netherlands as *Paul Vlaanderen ten oosten van Algiers*, in Portugal as *A Leste de Argel* and in Slovenia as *Očala*.

A nice point on which to end is that the original broadcast of *Paul Temple and the Sullivan Mystery* provided a notable landmark, as its first episode on 1 December 1947 saw the introduction of Vivian Ellis's *Coronation Scot* as the Paul Temple signature tune. While a snatch of Rimsky-Korsakov's *Scheherazade* suite had been used since the first serial in 1938, it was *Coronation Scot* that became synonymous with Paul Temple from 1947 until the final serial in 1968.

Melvyn Barnes
Author of *Francis Durbridge: The Complete Guide* (Williams & Whiting, 2018)

This book reproduces Francis Durbridge's original script together with the list of characters and actors of the BBC programme on the dates mentioned, but the eventual broadcast might have edited Durbridge's script in respect of scenes, dialogue and character names.

PAUL TEMPLE AND THE SULLIVAN MYSTERY

A Serial in Eight Episodes

By FRANCIS DURBRIDGE

Broadcast on BBC Radio

1st December 1947 – 19th January 1948

CAST:

Paul Temple . . . . .Kim Peacock
Steve . . . . .Marjorie Westbury
Joyce Raymond . . . . Margaret Inglis
Victor Armstrong . . . . Laidman Browne
Inspector Fowler . . . . .Stanley Groome
Harold Darwin . . . . .Cyril Gardiner
Miss Fraser . . . . .Vivienne Chatterton
Mr Constantine . . . . .Sidney James
Olaf Schreider . . . . .Olaf Olsen
Signor Rossetti . . . . .Ian Sadler
Sidney Jeans . . . . Tucker McGuire
Hakim . . . . .Leo de Pokorny
Colonel Marquand . . . . .Tommy Duggan
Zoltan Bahri .Leslie Perrins
Tom Durant . . . . Richard Williams
Sir Graham Forbes . . . . .Lester Mudditt
Charlie . . . . .Kenneth Morgan
Gustav Valkerie .Fritz Krenn

Other parts played by

Frank Atkinson, Betty Baskcomb, Frederick Bell,
Beryl Calder, Andrew Churchman, Peter Claughton,
Peter Creswell, Harry Hutchinson, Basil Jones,
David Kossoff, Charles Leno, Paul Martin, George Owen,
Frank Partington, Eddy Reed, Arthur Ridley, Alec Ross,
Joan Clement Scott & Norman Webb

NEW PRODUCTION
Broadcast on BBC Radio
7th August – 2nd October 2006
CAST:

Paul Temple . . . . Crawford Logan

Steve . . . . Gerda Stevenson

Charlie . . . . Greg Powrie

Joyce Raymond . . . . Lucy Paterson

Receptionist . . . . Nick Underwood

Receptionist 2 . . . . Lucy Paterson

Victor Armstrong . . . . Michael Mackenzie

Maid . . . . Lucy Paterson

Hall Porter . . . . Nick Underwood

Inspector Fowler . . . . Greg Powrie

Harold Darwin . . . . Richard Greenwood

Customs man . . . . Greg Powrie

Elderly lady . . . . Eliza Langland

Customs man 2 . . . . Michael Mackenzie

Baker, the Journalist . . . . Nick Underwood

Passenger . . . . Nick Underwood

Flying Officer . . . . Greg Powrie

Passenger 2 . . . . Michael Mackenzie

Miss Fraser . . . . Eliza Langland

Flying Officer 2 . . . . Nick Underwood

Steward . . . . Greg Powrie

Steward . . . . Nick Underwood

Mr Constantine . . . . Angus MacInnes

Italian Girl Receptionist . . . . Lucy Paterson

Man at Desk (Wilton) . . . . Nick Underwood

Man (Thompson) . . . . Nick Underwood

Buggy Driver . . . . Michael Mackenzie

Colonel Marquand . . . . Angus MacInnes

Waiter 1 . . . . Angus MacInnes

Olaf Schreider . . . . Nick Underwood
Waiter 2 . . . . Michael Mackenzie
Signor Rossetti .Greg Powrie
Steward . . . . Gareth Thomas
Passenger 1 . . . . .Nick Underwood
Passenger 2 . . . . Eliza Langland
Passenger 3 . . . . Greg Powrie
Passenger 4 . . . . .Wendy Seager
Egyptian Telephone Operator . . . . Wendy Seager
Clarence Sullivan . . . . Greg Powrie
Egyptian Barman . . . . .Michael Mackenzie
Patrick Quinn . . . . Gareth Thomas
Sidney Jeans . . . . .Wendy Seager
Egyptian Hotel Clerk . . . . .Nick Underwood
Commandant Hakim . . . . .Gareth Thomas
Egyptian Waiter . . . . Richard Greenwood
Egyptian Hotel Clerk . . . . Gareth Thomas
Egyptian Street Salesman . . . . . . Michael Mackenzie
Monsieur Flambert . . . . .Gareth Thomas
Egyptian Taxi Driver . . . . .Michael Mackenzie
Zoltan Bahri . . . . .Angus MacInnes
Tom Durant . . . . .John Paul Hurley
Sir Graham Forbes . . . . .Gareth Thomas
Zilla, the Head Waiter . . . . .John Paul Hurley
Gustav Valkerie . . . . .Gareth Thomas
Man in car park . . . . .Michael Mackenzie
Buggy driver . . . . Angus MacInnes
Egyptian Man in Street . . . . Gareth Thomas
Egyptian Hotel Clerk . . . . Michael Mackenzie
Steward 1 . . . . Michael Mackenzie
Steward 2 . . . . .Richard Greenwood
Mr Delaney . . . . Nick Underwood

EPISODE ONE

HAVING A WONDERFUL TIME

OPEN TO:

SCENE 1:   The TEMPLES' London Sitting Room
FADE UP on CHARLIE singing as he packs a suitcase.
CHARLIE is a young man of about thirty, he is a cockney:
bright and cheerful.
TEMPLE calls from the bedroom.
TEMPLE: Charlie!
CHARLIE: (*Crisply*) Yes, sir?
TEMPLE: Did you pack the flask?
CHARLIE: It's in the zip, sir.
STEVE enters the room and joins CHARLIE: she is faintly in
a dither.
STEVE: Have you nearly finished, Charlie?
CHARLIE: (*Closing the suitcase*) Yes, everything's packed,
           Mrs T. – I've only got to close this case an' then
           you're all set. (*Snapping the lock into position*)
           There you are ...
STEVE: Where's the hatbox?
CHARLIE: It's in the bedroom.
The Flat buzzer can be heard.
STEVE: And Mr Temple's valise?
CHARLIE: (*Amused*) There's the hatbox in the bedroom, the
           brown leather case in the hall, the small ...
CHARLIE hears the buzzer and stops as TEMPLE enters.
TEMPLE: Wasn't that the doorbell?
CHARLIE: Sounded like it.
TEMPLE: See who it is, Charlie!
CHARLIE: (*Moving off*) O.K.
We hear the sitting room door open as CHARLIE goes into
the hall.
TEMPLE: Did you pack my diary, dear?
STEVE: Yes, it's in the valise.

TEMPLE: Good! Well, we're nearly ready, Steve! (*Laughing*) At last!

STEVE: This case seems awfully heavy, Paul. Do you think it'll be all right on the plane?

TEMPLE: Of course it'll be all right! (*Laughing at STEVE*) Don't worry! Don't fuss so much!

STEVE laughs.

TEMPLE: By Timothy, what a woman! (*He takes STEVE by the arm*) Excited?

STEVE: Nervous.

TEMPLE: (*Faintly surprised*) What are you nervous about?

STEVE: (*A little laugh*) What do you think I'm nervous about? Flying of course!

TEMPLE: My dear Steve, you'll enjoy every minute of it. And once we get to Cairo, you'll have the – the time of your life.

CHARLIE returns.

CHARLIE: There's a Miss Raymond would like to see you, sir.

TEMPLE: Miss Raymond?

CHARLIE: Yes, sir.

TEMPLE: To see me?

CHARLIE: That's what she says.

TEMPLE: (*To STEVE*) Do you know anyone called Raymond?

STEVE: No …

TEMPLE: What does she want, Charlie?

CHARLIE: I've told you, she wants to see you!

TEMPLE: (*Faintly irritated*) Yes, I know that but …

STEVE: (*Thoughtfully*) There used to be a girl Raymond on the Daily News. Don't you remember? She did the Society gossip – tall, rather good-looking, blonde.

CHARLIE: That's the party!

4

TEMPLE: All right, Charlie. Ask her in.

CHARLIE: O.K.

TEMPLE: Joyce Raymond … Yes. Yes, I remember her. (*Casually*) What on earth does she want, I wonder?

CHARLIE returns.

CHARLIE:Miss Raymond, sir.

TEMPLE: (*Pleasantly*) Come in, Miss Raymond.

JOYCE RAYMOND is a sophisticated woman of about thirty-five.

JOYCE: It's awfully sweet of you to see me! Hello. Mrs Temple! How are you? It's ages since we met.

STEVE: I'm very well, thank you.

JOYCE: I'm awfully sorry to drop in on you like this. I'm sure you must be frantically busy.

STEVE: (*Laughing*) Well, as a matter of fact we are! We're leaving for Bournemouth in half an hour and on Thursday morning we're off to Cairo.

JOYCE: Yes, I know. I saw the write-up about you both in last night's paper. As a matter of fact that's why I'm here.

TEMPLE: (*Amused*) I'm afraid there's no mystery attached to our trip, Miss Raymond. I'm simply going to Egypt to get data for a new book I'm writing.

JOYCE: (*Laughing at TEMPLE*) But I'm not here for a story, Mr Temple. I left Fleet Street ages ago.

TEMPLE: Then why …?

JOYCE: I want you to do something for me. I hope you won't consider it a colossal impertinence but …

TEMPLE: Not at all, but what is it exactly?

JOYCE: I have a cousin in Cairo. His name's Richard Sullivan. He works for the Trans-Eurasian Oil Company. Richard was over here about six weeks ago and … (*Amused: frankly*) Look! To

5

be perfectly frank we had rather a night out together before he sailed and the poor darling lost his glasses.

STEVE laughs.

TEMPLE: (*Amused*) And now I suppose you've found them and you want us to take them to him?

JOYCE: (*Laughing*) You're a thought reader, Mr Temple! Yes, I found them this morning and I'd be terribly grateful if you would take them. I keep getting the most frantic cables.

TEMPLE: We'll do that with pleasure.

JOYCE: It's really most awfully kind of you.

STEVE: If you give me the glasses, Miss Raymond, I'll put them in my handbag.

MISS RAYMOND removes the glasses from her own bag and hands them over.

JOYCE: Here you are.

STEVE: Thank you.

JOYCE: I'll send Richard a cable: he'll probably meet the plane.

TEMPLE: Well, we're staying in Bournemouth for two days so we shan't be in Cairo until sometime on Friday, but don't worry, we'll see Mr Sullivan gets them all right.

JOYCE: It's really most awfully kind of you. I'm terribly grateful.

TEMPLE: Think nothing of it.

JOYCE: Well, bon voyage! Hope you have a wonderful time! (*Laughing*) And thanks again!

FADE UP music – gay and swift in tempo.

SCENE 2:	The TEMPLES' Bournemouth Hotel. Reception Desk.

Guests are coming and going. As the RECEPTIONIST greets the TEMPLES, a little to one side his female colleague is dealing with MR ARMSTRONG.

RECEPTIONIST:	Now let me see, sir – Mr and Mrs …?
TEMPLE:	Temple. (*Searching his pockets*) I've got your letter here somewhere … (*He finds the letter and passes it over*) Here it is.
RECEPTIONIST:	Oh, yes, sir! You're staying two nights. Leaving on Thursday morning … Would you register, please, sir?
TEMPLE:	Yes, of course.

As TEMPLE signs the register, the SECOND RECEPTIONIST leans across from a little way down the desk.

RECEPTIONIST 2:	Mr Armstrong's arrived, sir.
RECEPTIONIST:	Mr Armstrong? Oh, yes. Room 321.
RECEPTIONIST 2:	(*To ARMSTRONG*) Room 321, sir.
ARMSTRONG:	Thank you.
RECEPTIONIST 2:	You get the key from the hall porter, sir. I'll have your things sent up straight away.
ARMSTRONG:	Thank you. (*He turns and bumps into STEVE*) I beg your pardon!
STEVE:	That's quite all right.
RECEPTIONIST:	Room 322, Mr Temple.
TEMPLE:	Thank you.

SCENE 3:	A Corridor in the Hotel.

TEMPLE and STEVE are passing along the corridor, checking the room numbers.

TEMPLE:	319 … 320 … 321 …
STEVE:	Here we are, darling … 322 … I'll take the valise …

TEMPLE puts the key in the lock and opens the door. They step inside, then STEVE gives a little start of surprise.

STEVE:	Why, this can't be right! It's a single room!
TEMPLE:	Well, it's 322 …
STEVE:	They've probably given that other man the double room by mistake.
TEMPLE:	Yes, they must have.
STEVE:	There's someone coming …

VICTOR ARMSTRONG arrives. He is a man of about fifty-five, prosperous and well-dressed. He has a very slight north country accent which becomes slightly more pronounced when he is excited.

ARMSTRONG:	(*Pleasantly*) I beg your pardon, but the young lady in the office at the desk told me to tell you she's made a mistake. Apparently I'm in 322 and you're in 321.
TEMPLE:	(*Laughing*) We thought something like that has happened.
ARMSTRONG:	(*Handing it over*) Here's your key.
TEMPLE:	Thank you. Yours is in the door.
ARMSTRONG:	Oh, thanks. You're next door …
TEMPLE:	Yes … Come along, Steve.

SCENE 4:   Hotel Lounge

In the background, an orchestra is playing a quiet, sophisticated type of dance music.

TEMPLE:	Would you like some more coffee, Steve?
STEVE:	No, thank you.
TEMPLE:	Tired?
STEVE:	M'm. A little. (*She yawns*) Still, we can sleep in tomorrow morning.
TEMPLE:	Yes, and make the most of it! We shan't be able to sleep in on Thursday.

8

STEVE:	Where do we go through the customs, at Poole?
TEMPLE:	Yes. It shouldn't take very long.
STEVE:	And then what happens?
TEMPLE:	Well, after the customs and the currency check-up they take us out to the flying-boat.
STEVE:	And then we really start!
TEMPLE:	Yes, and then we really start!
STEVE:	What would you like to do tomorrow?
TEMPLE:	Well, if it's a decent day, I thought we might have a ride over to Sandbanks and go for a sail.
STEVE:	Yes, that would be rather nice.
TEMPLE:	Ready, Steve?
STEVE:	Yes, I'm ready.
TEMPLE:	Right, let's go up!

SCENE 5:   The Hotel Corridor.

TEMPLE and STEVE approaching their room. Further down the corridor we can hear the voice of VICTOR ARMSTRONG. He is extremely angry.

TEMPLE:	Have you got the key?
STEVE:	Yes, it's in my handbag. (*She takes the key from her handbag and passes it over*) Here …
TEMPLE:	Thanks. I do hope it's a decent day tomorrow, it'd be quite a change to take a boat out again … (*He stops, having noticed ARMSTRONG*) Our friend next door seems to be pretty het up!

MIX CLOSER to ARMSTRONG during the following:

ARMSTRONG: It's not a bit o' damn use telling me that now the damage has been done! Send for the manager!

MAID: I've sent for the manager, sir. He should be here any minute –

ARMSTRONG: Well, send for him again! Just look at the place! Good heavens, it's fantastic! I wouldn't have believed this could have happened in a respectable hotel!

TEMPLE and STEVE walk up.

TEMPLE: (*Pleasantly*) Hello, what seems to be the trouble?

ARMSTRONG: (*Boiling over with anger, yet not without a touch of humour*) My goodness, you've had a narrow squeak, my friend! You can thank your lucky stars an' no mistake!

TEMPLE: What do you mean?

ARMSTRONG: Just look in here! Just look at my room!

ARMSTRONG throws open the door and leads TEMPLE and STEVE into the room.

ARMSTRONG: Look at it!

TEMPLE: By Timothy!

STEVE: (*Astonished*) What happened?

ARMSTRONG: What's happened? What's happ …? Why, the room's been ransacked, that's what's happened! Just look at it! Look at that suitcase! Look at that trunk.

TEMPLE: When did this happen?

ARMSTRONG: It must have happened while I was having dinner. The room was perfectly all right when I left it. Just look at that suitcase! They must have ripped the thing open with a razor!

STEVE: Have they taken much?

ARMSTRONG:	They haven't taken a thing, that's the extraordinary part about it. I just can't understand it! I left a pair of cufflinks on the dressing table – gold cufflinks – they're still there … Look!
STEVE:	You don't think it's a practical joke –
ARMSTRONG:	A joke! Well, it's certainly not my idea of a joke!
TEMPLE:	(*Quietly: seriously*) No, nor mine either, Mr …?
ARMSTRONG:	Armstrong, Victor Armstrong.
TEMPLE:	How long are you staying here?
ARMSTRONG:	Only for one night, thank the Lord! As a matter of fact, after this muck-up I'm not so sure I shall stay here the night.
TEMPLE:	(*Casually*) Are you quite sure they haven't taken anything?
ARMSTRONG:	I've told you! They haven't taken a blessed thing! Not so much as a pocket handkerchief. I just can't understand it!
STEVE:	(*Suddenly*) Paul! I wonder if our room's all right?
TEMPLE:	Good Lord, yes! Hadn't thought of that!
STEVE:	(*A little laugh*) We'd better go and have a look!

SCENE 6:	The TEMPLES' Bedroom.

A key is inserted in the lock, the door opens and the TEMPLES enter.

TEMPLE:	Ah – well, that's all right. Everything's just as we left it.
STEVE:	Thank goodness. … It's rather odd, isn't it – about that room, I mean?

TEMPLE:	(*Thoughtfully*) If Armstrong was telling the truth and they didn't take anything, then whoever broke into that room must have been looking for something in particular, something which Armstrong either knew nothing about or –

TEMPLE is interrupted by the ringing of the telephone. He lifts the receiver.

TEMPLE:	Hello?
HALL PORTER:	(*On the other end*) Mr Temple, sir?
TEMPLE:	Yes?
HALL PORTER:	This is the hall porter; there's a gentleman to see you, sir. Inspector Fowler.
TEMPLE:	Inspector Fowler? To see me …?
HALL PORTER:	Yes, sir.
TEMPLE:	A police inspector?
HALL PORTER:	Yes, sir.

A moment.

TEMPLE:	Where is he?
HALL PORTER:	I've asked him to wait in the lounge, sir.
TEMPLE:	(*Thoughtfully*) Yes, all right, tell the Inspector I'll be down straight away … Oh – do you know Inspector Fowler – personally, I mean?
HALL PORTER:	Yes, sir. He's been to the hotel several times, sir. He's from the Bournemouth C.I.D.
TEMPLE:	Oh … Oh, thank you.
HALL PORTER:	Thank you, sir.

TEMPLE replaces the receiver.

STEVE:	Who was it, darling?
TEMPLE:	Well, apparently there's an Inspector Fowler wants to see me. He's in the lounge.

STEVE:	Do you know him?
TEMPLE:	(*His thoughts elsewhere*) No, I've never even heard of him.
STEVE:	Well, what does he want?
TEMPLE:	M-m?
STEVE:	I said: What does he want?
TEMPLE:	(*A little laugh*) Your guess is as good as mine. (*Brightly*) Let's ask him!

SCENE 7: The Hotel Lounge

The orchestra plays in the background.

INSPECTOR FOWLER is a man of about fifty, solid and reliable and quite well spoken.

FOWLER:	I'm sorry to disturb you at this time of the night, Mr Temple.
TEMPLE:	That's all right, Inspector. Oh – this is my wife.
FOWLER:	How do you do?
STEVE:	How do you do, Inspector?
TEMPLE:	(*Briskly*) Well, what can I do for you?

A tiny pause.

FOWLER:	About half an hour ago, I had a telephone message through from Scotland Yard – from Superintendent Cleaver.
TEMPLE:	I know Cleaver; he's an old friend of mine.
FOWLER:	Yes, sir. He asked me to contact you and to make inquiries concerning a Miss Raymond.
STEVE:	(*Surprised*) Miss Raymond?
FOWLER:	Yes.
TEMPLE:	What exactly is it you want to know about Miss Raymond?
FOWLER:	(*Drily*) We want to know everything, sir.
TEMPLE:	(*A little laugh*) Yes, I know, but …

FOWLER: We've reason to believe that Miss Raymond visited you this afternoon at your flat in Half Moon Street. Is that correct, sir?

TEMPLE: Quite correct.

FOWLER: Had she an appointment?

TEMPLE: No, the visit was, to say the least, unexpected. Look here, has something happened to Miss Raymond?

FOWLER: (*Ignoring the question*) What do you mean, sir – the visit was unexpected?

TEMPLE: I mean that both my wife and I were very surprised when she turned up at the flat. Miss Raymond isn't a friend of ours – she's barely an acquaintance.

STEVE takes the spectacles from her bag.

STEVE: She'd read that we were flying to Cairo and she asked us if we'd deliver these spectacles to a friend of hers. Apparently he lost them in London about six weeks ago.

FOWLER: What was the name of this friend?

STEVE: (*To TEMPLE*) What was it, darling?

TEMPLE: Richard Sullivan. He's with the Trans-Eurasian Oil Company.

FOWLER: I see. (*Politely*) May I see the glasses, Mrs Temple?

STEVE passes them over.

FOWLER: Thank you. M'm. They appear to be a perfectly ordinary pair of spectacles.

TEMPLE: (*Watching FOWLER*) Is there any reason why they shouldn't be?

FOWLER: Mr Temple, shortly after she left your flat this afternoon, Miss Raymond was murdered.

STEVE gives a quick gasp of surprise.

14

FOWLER: She was shot dead just as she was getting into a taxi on the corner of Half Moon Street.

TEMPLE: Who shot her?

FOWLER: We don't know. The person who did it got clean away. Frankly, we haven't the slightest idea whether it was a man or a woman.

TEMPLE: Motive?

FOWLER: There doesn't appear to have been a motive. Miss Raymond didn't ask you to deliver anything else to Mr Sullivan – a letter perhaps, or …?

TEMPLE: No, nothing else.

FOWLER: Was there a case for the glasses?

TEMPLE: No.

STEVE: Inspector, you surely don't think that these spectacles have got anything to do with –

FOWLER: (*Rather sharply: interrupting STEVE*) With what, Mrs Temple?

STEVE: Well – with why she was murdered?

FOWLER: (*A moment: then quickly*) What's your opinion, Mr Temple?

TEMPLE: Well, as you said yourself a moment ago – (*He is examining the glasses*) – they appear to be a perfectly ordinary pair of spectacles.

FOWLER: M'm. (*Suddenly: a decision*) Look here, we've got a man down here called Warrender, who was with the M.I.5 during the War. I'd rather like him to see these glasses. If there's anything peculiar about them he'll ferret it out.

TEMPLE: Well, that's all right by me. As a matter of fact I should prefer it.

FOWLER: When are you leaving?

TEMPLE: We're leaving from the B.O.A.C. base at Poole on Thursday morning.

15

FOWLER: (*Business-like*) Good. I'll get these to Warrender tonight and contact you tomorrow. If the report's negative there's no reason why you shouldn't deliver the spectacles to Mr Sullivan as arranged.

TEMPLE: Right. Now – would you like a drink, Inspector?

FOWLER: (*Pleasantly surprised*) That's very kind of you, sir. May I have a whisky and soda?

SCENE 8: The TEMPLES' Bedroom.

FADE UP on TEMPLE snoring. He is fast asleep. The snoring continues for some little time and then stops.

After a moment, and from the next room, we hear a low, soft cry: it is almost a moan, a cry of anguish.

There is a pause and then the cry is repeated.

STEVE: (*Tense whisper*) Paul ...

TEMPLE grunts and turns over.

STEVE: Paul ...!

TEMPLE: M'm ...

STEVE: Paul, wake up.

TEMPLE: What is it?

STEVE: Listen.

TEMPLE: Steve, what the Dickens is the idea waking ... (*He stops*)

STEVE: (*Quickly*) Did you hear it?

TEMPLE: Yes ... what is it?

STEVE: I don't know ... I've heard it before ... several times ...

The cry is repeated: a definite, low moan.

TEMPLE: Listen!

STEVE: Paul, what is it? Where's it coming from?

TEMPLE: It sounds to me as if ... Wait a minute!

TEMPLE climbs out of bed.

TEMPLE: Put the light on!

16

STEVE switches on the bedside light. The cry can be heard again. It is repeated several times.

STEVE: Paul, someone's in pain, terrible pain.

TEMPLE: Yes. Pass me my dressing gown.

STEVE: Where's it coming from?

TEMPLE: Next door – from Armstrong's room. You stay here, Steve.

STEVE: No!

TEMPLE: Don't be silly, darling, I'll be back in a minute.

STEVE: I'm coming with you.

The cry is heard again.

TEMPLE: Sh! Listen …

STEVE: You're right – it is from next door.

The cry is repeated: almost a final cry of anguish.

TEMPLE: Come on, darling!

TEMPLE opens the door and he and STEVE pass out into the corridor.

STEVE: I don't know what you think, Paul, but I've got a feeling that … (*She stops*) There's someone coming out of the room!

TEMPLE: No, it's the room on the other side of 322 …

STEVE: Oh, yes, so it is! They must have heard it too …

HAROLD DARWIN arrives. He is a man of about thirty-eight. As a general rule HAROLD DARWIN is a bright, almost facetious, sort of person. At the moment he appears a little bewildered.

DARWIN: I say – I beg your pardon – but do you hear that noise coming from 322?

TEMPLE: Yes, as a matter of fact we've been listening to it.

DARWIN: So have I. Whoever it is, the poor devil's obviously pretty ill. I don't know what you feel, but I really think we ought to do something about it.

17

TEMPLE: Well, the room's occupied by a man called Armstrong.

DARWIN: Oh, do you know him?

TEMPLE: No, not exactly. I've spoken to him, that's about all.

DARWIN: Well, I really feel we ought to see if he's all right, don't you?

TEMPLE: Yes, I do.

They move to the door of Room 322.

DARWIN: Shall I knock?

TEMPLE: Yes.

DARWIN knocks on the door.

There is a pause.

DARWIN knocks again.

A pause.

DARWIN: That's odd …

TEMPLE: What's that you've got, Steve?

STEVE: H'm? Oh – I just picked it up, it was near the door.

DARWIN: It looks like a lozenge of some sort – a peppermint.

STEVE: Yes, that's what it is, a peppermint.

DARWIN knocks again.

DARWIN: I say, this is rather odd, isn't it? You think he'd at least answer …

TEMPLE tries the door.

TEMPLE: The door's unlocked.

TEMPLE slowly opens the door and they enter the room.

DARWIN: Where's the light?

STEVE: It's all right, I've got it …

STEVE switches the light on.

DARWIN: Why – there's no one here … The room's empty!

STEVE: But there must be someone here, we heard them …

18

TEMPLE interrupts STEVE.

TEMPLE: The bed hasn't been slept in.

DARWIN: I say, I just don't understand this. If the bed hasn't been slept in, then how the devil … (*He stops: tensely*) What are you looking at?

A moment.

STEVE: Paul, what is it?

TEMPLE: (*Quietly*) The wardrobe … Look at the door of the wardrobe …

STEVE gives a sudden start of surprise.

STEVE: It's blood!

TEMPLE: (*Springing to life*) Get it open! Get the wardrobe open! Quickly!

TEMPLE and DARWIN throw the wardrobe door open and the body of a girl slumps forward. STEVE gives a terrified shriek.

DARWIN: Good Lord, it's a girl! And look at her … Look at her face! She's been beaten up!

STEVE: (*Covering her face with her hands*) Oh, Paul …

TEMPLE: (*After a tiny pause: quietly*) Steve, do you see who it is?

STEVE: What – (*A horrified gasp*) – why, it's the girl who came to the flat – Joyce Raymond!

FADE UP of music.

FADE DOWN of music.

SCENE 9: The Hotel Dining Room. Next Morning.

TEMPLE and STEVE are having breakfast. There is murmured conversation in backgrounds from other guests.

TEMPLE: Pass the marmalade, Steve … (*A moment*) Look here, Steve, you mustn't be silly about this business. You've got to eat some breakfast.

STEVE: I can't. I'm not hungry.

TEMPLE: Well, drink your coffee. Come on!

19

A moment.

STEVE drinks.

STEVE: What happened to Armstrong – did you find out?

TEMPLE: Yes, he apparently checked out last night soon after we spoke to him. I rather gather he had a row with the manager. He was certainly all set for one.

STEVE: Then he never actually stayed here?

TEMPLE: No; the room was supposed to be empty. Oh, by the way, that young fellow we met last night. He's in the same boat as us – or rather the same flying boat. He's on the way to Egypt.

STEVE: Oh. (*Suddenly*) Paul, is this business going to make any difference to us?

TEMPLE: In what way, dear?

STEVE: I mean: are we still going to Cairo?

TEMPLE: But of course we're going to Cairo! I've got to go, you know that, darling!

STEVE: But what about the inquest?

TEMPLE: I've been on the phone to Sir Graham. Don't worry about the inquest. In any case, we've made a detailed statement to Fowler, there's nothing else we can do. (*Gently*) Come along, darling, eat some of that toast.

STEVE: (*Thoughtfully, as she takes a bite*) You know, I still don't understand about Joyce Raymond. The Inspector said that she'd been shot.

TEMPLE: Joyce Raymond had a sister called Lydia. Lydia was apparently watching our flat yesterday afternoon when Joyce delivered the spectacles. After her sister had left the flat, and we'd departed for Bournemouth, Lydia made her way to the end of Half Moon Street and hailed a taxi. It was then it happened.

STEVE: You mean that it was Lydia Raymond that was shot in Half Moon Street?

TEMPLE: Yes. The police checked all the houses in the street and naturally when Charlie told them that a Miss Raymond had paid us a visit they jumped to the conclusion that it was Lydia. Actually they knew nothing about Joyce.

STEVE: I see. (*A moment*) Paul, why do you think they were murdered like that, both of them? Do you think those glasses have got anything to do with it, or is it simply a coincidence that – (*She stops: aside*) Here's the Inspector.

INSPECTOR FOWLER walks up.

FOWLER: Good morning, sir.

TEMPLE: Good morning, Inspector.

FOWLER: Good morning, Mrs Temple.

STEVE: Good morning.

FOWLER: I'm sorry to interrupt your breakfast, but … I've brought these back.

TEMPLE: Oh, the glasses.

FOWLER: Yes. Warrender's examined them, sir. He's made a pretty thorough examination of them.

TEMPLE: Well?

FOWLER: He's quite convinced that they're just an ordinary pair of spectacles.

TEMPLE: You mean they haven't been tampered with?

FOWLER: (*Emphatically*) No, sir. Not in any way at all, sir.

TEMPLE: Well – in view of what's happened – what do you want me to do with them?

A significant pause.

FOWLER: We'd like you to deliver them to Mr Sullivan, sir.

FADE UP of music.

FADE DOWN of music.

SCENE 10: TEMPLE and STEVE at sea in a small sailing boat.

A calm sea, seagulls.

STEVE: Paul, I think you're wonderful!

TEMPLE: Why?

STEVE: I never knew you could handle a yacht.

TEMPLE: This is only a glorified dinghy. I'm very ignorant – Look out! Don't touch that rope or you'll have us over!

STEVE: Aye, Aye, Captain!

TEMPLE: (*Laughing*) Enjoying it?

STEVE: Enormously.

TEMPLE: And you're the girl that didn't want to come! Remember?

STEVE: Yes, I know, but I felt so depressed. That business last night upset me.

TEMPLE: You're supposed to be steering …!

STEVE: (*Laughing*) I'm sorry!

TEMPLE: I just can't believe we're in Bournemouth today and we shall be in Cairo on Friday.

STEVE: What time do we get there?

The sound of an approaching motor launch can be heard.

TEMPLE: Well, we leave here tomorrow at eight o'clock, spend the night in Augusta – we should be in Cairo about teatime on Friday.

STEVE: It seems so awfully quick.

TEMPLE: Don't worry. It's all very luxurious and as safe as houses … (*He stops*) Hello …

STEVE: What is it?

TEMPLE: There's that launch again …

STEVE: Which one do you mean?

TEMPLE: You know: the chap with the binoculars.

STEVE: Oh, yes! (*A moment*) He's still using them.

22

TEMPLE: We must look a very edifying couple! I don't believe the blighter's taken his eyes off us.

STEVE: (*Nervously*) I say, he's coming awfully near!

TEMPLE: (*Watching the launch*) Why the darn fool! What's he trying to do?

The launch draws nearer.

STEVE: (*A little alarmed*) Darling!

TEMPLE: It's all right, Steve! Just stay still! Don't move!

The launch speeds past the sailing boat which is tossed from side to side by the wash.

TEMPLE: The darn fool nearly had us over!

STEVE: He did it deliberately! Paul, he must have done it deliberately!

TEMPLE: Are you all right?

STEVE: Yes, but ... (*Gets her breath back*) Phew!

TEMPLE: By George, I thought we'd had it! If he'd been a yard nearer we should have ... Mind that rope, Steve! Change over to the other side, dear. (*Crossing the boat*) I'll take over.

In the distance the launch turns and starts to approach again.

STEVE: He's turning ...

A pause.

TEMPLE and STEVE watch the launch nearing.

STEVE: He's coming back!

TEMPLE: I should think if he's got any manners he'll come back and apologise!

STEVE: Paul, I don't like this.

TEMPLE: It's all right, Steve. Don't be silly; he won't do it again. He's probably pretty shamefaced about it ...

The launch is accelerating towards them.

TEMPLE: Lie down! Lie down!

STEVE: Paul!

TEMPLE: Lie down, Steve!

23

STEVE: He's trying to capsize us! He's doing it
           deliberately! Paul!

The motor launch flashes by close to the sailing boat.

STEVE: (*Screaming*) Paul!!!!

The boat is thrown against the heavy wash and capsizes.

*As the motor launch roars away, TEMPLE and STEVE are
left struggling in the water, desperately fighting for breath.*

TEMPLE: Steve! Steve! Where are you? Where are you,
           darling?

STEVE: I'm ... I'm ... I'm over here.

TEMPLE: Where?

STEVE: Over the other side ... I've got hold of the boat
           ...

TEMPLE: Hang on! I'm coming ...

TEMPLE swims round to the other side of the capsized boat.

TEMPLE: Oh ... Oh, good girl!

STEVE: Here ... get hold of the rope.

TEMPLE: It's all right. Can you hold on?

STEVE: Yes, I think so ...

TEMPLE: Don't let go, Steve!

TEMPLE and STEVE fight to regain their breath.

STEVE: He did it deliberately! He saw what happened ...
           If he hadn't done it deliberately then he'd have
           come back!

TEMPLE: Yes ... Yes, don't talk, Steve.

A pause.

STEVE: Did you see him – the man in the boat, I mean?

TEMPLE: I couldn't see his face. He held the binoculars up.

STEVE: (*A note of desperation creeping into her voice*)
           Paul, what's behind all this? Why should we
           suddenly ...

The boat starts to bob up and down in the water.

TEMPLE: Steve, watch out! Do be careful ...

STEVE: What are we going to do?

The sound of a second motor launch is heard in the distance.

TEMPLE: We'll either hold on here until someone comes and rescues us or … try to swim for it. (*Suddenly*) There's a boat! There's a boat, Steve!

STEVE: Where?

TEMPLE: Over there! Look!

STEVE: He's seen us! He's seen us!

TEMPLE: Has he? (*A tense moment*) Yes! Yes, you're right! Oh, good man! Good man!

SCENE 11: A short while later.

The launch is now by the sailing boat, its engine idling.
TEMPLE is partly climbing and partly being dragged by DARWIN out of the water.

DARWIN: Come on! Come on! Come on! One more … one (*Then TEMPLE is out of the water*) That's it!

TEMPLE: Phew! Thank you! Are you all right, Steve?

STEVE: (*Breathless*) Yes, thank you, dear …

DARWIN: (*Amused*) These little tubs are pretty tricky to handle you know. You shouldn't go out in them unless you know how. (*He stops: staggered*) I say, you're the people I bumped into last night in the hotel!

STEVE: (*Suddenly: recognising DARWIN*) Why, yes, of course!

DARWIN: Well, I'm dashed! (*A short laugh*) Ah! I'm afraid I didn't recognise you.

TEMPLE: That's not surprising.

DARWIN: Look here, in view of the fact that we're going to see quite a bit of each other, I think it's about time we introduced ourselves, don't you? My name is Darwin. Harold Darwin.

FADE UP of music.

FADE DOWN of music.

SCENE 12: Customs Hall

A small crowd of passengers for the flying boat are making their way through customs. The atmosphere is quite informal.

CUSTOMS MAN: Would you mind opening the case, madam?

ELDERLY LADY: The small case?

CUSTOMS MAN: If you please, madam. (*The case is opened*) Thank you. Yes, all right. Pass along, please – thank you. (*After a moment*) Are these yours, sir?

TEMPLE: Yes.

CUSTOMS MAN: I'd like to see in this one, sir.

TEMPLE: Have you got the key, darling?

STEVE: Yes, but there's absolutely nothing in it …

TEMPLE: (*Smiling*) Have you got the key, Steve?

STEVE hands the key over.

TEMPLE: Thanks.

TEMPLE opens the case.

CUSTOMS MAN: Is this a camera?

TEMPLE: Yes, it's a cine: 16mm. I've got the receipt for it if you'd like to see it.

CUSTOMS MAN: No, that's all right.

TEMPLE: Thanks.

At another customer's table nearby …

CUSTOMS MAN 2:	Is this your case, sir?
DARWIN:	Yes.
CUSTOMS MAN 2:	Is there anything in it, other than personal belongings?
DARWIN:	Pound notes.

Several people laugh.

CUSTOMS MAN 2:	Yes, well we'll have a look at it.
DARWIN:	It's all right – it's only a gag, old boy!

The case is opening and its contents emptied onto the table.

DARWIN:	I say, look out! You're emptying everything all over the place!
CUSTOMS MAN 2:	It's all right – it's only a gag, old boy.

Back at their customs table, STEVE and TEMPLE are about to move away when BAKER approaches.

BAKER:	(*Anxiously: quickly*) Mr Temple?
TEMPLE:	Yes?
BAKER:	My name is Baker, sir – Bournemouth Despatch. I'm covering the Raymond murder, sir, and I was wondering if you'd be good enough to –
TEMPLE:	I'm sorry, Mr Baker.
BAKER:	I realise you're in a hurry, sir, but if you could just give me a brief outline of the –
TEMPLE:	(*Moving quickly away*) Sorry, Mr Baker. Come along, Steve – the launch is waiting …

SCENE 13:	A large Motor Launch en route to the Flying Boat.

The hum of conversation from about twenty passengers.

DARWIN:	Well, are you excited, Mrs Temple?
STEVE:	Yes, Mr Darwin, I am rather!

TEMPLE: We shall be alongside the flying-boat in a moment.

DARWIN: Yes. I say, these flying-boats are pretty impressive looking, aren't they?

PASSENGER: What class is this: Hythe?

FLYING OFFICER: No, sir, it's a Plymouth … I wouldn't light a cigarette now, sir.

PASSENGER 2: Oh? Can't we smoke on board?

FLYING OFFICER: Not until we're airborne, sir. Then it's o.k.

PASSENGER 2: (*Pleasantly*) Oh, oh, I see, thanks.

MISS FRASER: Always best to be on the safe side.

FLYING OFFICER: Yes, ma'am.

MISS FRASER is a Scots lady: a spinster: about fifty.

FRASER: It's quite choppy on the water, isn't it? I'm really surprised, it looked so calm. Is this your first trip, my dear?

STEVE: Well, in a flying-boat, yes.

FRASER: Mine too. As a matter of fact I've never been up before.

FLYING OFFICER: (*Pleasantly*) Well, there's no need to be nervous, ma'am.

FRASER: Oh, I'm not nervous! I'm a wee bit anxious perhaps …

They all laugh: the launch slows down.

FRASER: Did you read about that murder in Bournemouth, the night before last?

STEVE: (*Almost interrupting MISS FRASER: curtly*) Yes, I … saw something about it.

The launch has reached the side of the flying-boat; there is an atmosphere of activity.

FRASER: I was staying in the same hotel. In the same hotel, mark you!

28

TEMPLE:	Here we are, darling!
DARWIN:	Give me your hand, Mrs Temple.
FLYING OFFICER:	(*Raising his voice: pleasantly*) Wait a moment, please!

The steel entrance door of the flying-boat is opened. The SECOND FLYING OFFICER (RAF type) calls from the flying boat.

FLYING OFFICER 2:	Hello, Perry! How's tricks?
FLYING OFFICER:	Can't grumble, old boy! (*To STEVE*) Watch your step!
TEMPLE:	Go on, darling!
FLYING OFFICER 2:	Give me your hand.

STEVE climbs into the flying-boat.

FLYING OFFICER 2:	That's it!
STEVE:	(*Laughing*) Thank you!
FLYING OFFICER 2:	Next please! Any more for the Skylark?

They all laugh.

SCENE 14:   The Passenger Cabin of the Flying-Boat a few moments before departure.

The engines are still silent.

FRASER:	Well, I must say it's really quite cosy. And there seems to be every possible convenience. Oh, is my handbag in your way at all?
STEVE:	No, no, that's quite all right. (*To TEMPLE*) Where's Mr Darwin?
TEMPLE:	There he is – further along – in the next cabin.
STEVE:	(*Laughing*) Oh!
DARWIN:	(*Calling to them*) Hello there!
STEVE:	(*Pleasantly*) Hello!

The engines begin to start up.

STEVE:	Are we off?
TEMPLE:	Not yet.
FRASER:	Hello! What's this?
TEMPLE:	Oh. It's your belt, Miss …?
FRASER:	Fraser.
TEMPLE:	It's your belt, Miss Fraser.
FRASER:	Belt?
TEMPLE:	Yes, you just put it round you and … That's it! They'll tell you when to fasten it.

The flying-boat starts to move, and begins to gather speed across the water.

STEWARD:	Fasten your belts, please!
STEVE:	Paul, we're off! We're leaving the water!
TEMPLE:	No, we're not – not yet.

A pause.

The flying-boat continues to gather speed.

FRASER:	(*Softly: to herself*) Oh dear, my tummy … Could I trouble you for my handbag, please?
TEMPLE:	Yes, of course!

TEMPLE passes it across, MISS FRASER opens it and nervously searches.

FRASER:	I've got some lozenges somewhere, I … Oh, here we are! Would you like a lozenge, my dear?
STEVE:	No, thank you, Miss Fraser.
FRASER:	No?
STEVE:	No, thank you.
FRASER:	(*After a tiny pause*) … They're peppermints.

The flying-boat roars into the air.

FADE UP of music.

END OF EPISODE ONE

EPISODE TWO

INTERLUDE AT AUGUSTA

ANNOUNCER: Paul Temple and Steve are on the point of leaving for Egypt when they receive an unexpected visit from a Miss Joyce Raymond. She has apparently read of Temple's proposed trip to Egypt and tells him that she has a cousin in Cairo.

SCENE 1: Flashback to Episode 1, Scene 1:
The TEMPLES' Sitting Room

JOYCE: His name's Richard Sullivan. He works for the Trans-Eurasian Oil Company. Richard was over here about six weeks ago and ... (*Amused: frankly*) Look! To be perfectly frank we had rather a night out together before he sailed and the poor darling lost his glasses.

STEVE laughs.

TEMPLE: (*Amused*) And now I suppose you've found them and you want us to take them to him?

JOYCE: (*Laughing*) You're a thought reader, Mr Temple! Yes, I found them this morning and I'd be terribly grateful if you would take them. I keep getting the most frantic cables.

TEMPLE: Well, we're staying in Bournemouth for two days, so we shan't be in Cairo until Friday. But don't worry, we'll see Mr Sullivan gets his glasses all right.

JOYCE: That's awfully sweet of you. I'll send Richard a cable: he'll probably meet the plane.

FADE OUT.

33

ANNOUNCER: When Temple and Steve reach Bournemouth however, things begin to happen. Firstly, a guest at the hotel, Victor Armstrong, has his room ransacked. Secondly, Paul Temple and Steve make the acquaintance of a man called Harold Darwin. Thirdly, they discover the dead body of Joyce Raymond. Steve finds a small lozenge – a peppermint – near Miss Raymond's bedroom door. Because of the murder of Miss Raymond, Inspector Fowler of the Bournemouth C.I.D. insists on taking the spectacles down to Police Headquarters for detailed examination. He later reports that they are a perfectly innocent pair of spectacles – untampered with in any way whatsoever – and informs Temple that he can deliver them, as arranged, to Mr Sullivan. The next morning, Temple and Steve arrive at Poole and – together with Harold Darwin who is also flying to Egypt – proceed on to the B.O.A.C. flying-boat. On board the flying-boat they make the acquaintance of a Miss Fraser.

SCENE 2A: The Flying Boat Passenger Cabin.
The engines are starting up.
STEVE: Are we off?
TEMPLE: Not yet.
FRASER: Hello! What's this?
TEMPLE: Oh. It's your belt, Miss …?
FRASER: Fraser.
TEMPLE: It's your belt, Miss Fraser.

FRASER: Belt?

TEMPLE: Yes, you just put it round you and … That's it! They'll tell you when to fasten it.

The flying-boat starts to move, and begins to gather speed across the water.

STEVE: Paul, we're off! We're leaving the water!

TEMPLE: No, we're not – not yet.

A pause.

The flying-boat continues to gather speed.

FRASER: (*Softly: to herself*) Oh dear, my tummy … Could I trouble you for my handbag, please?

TEMPLE: Yes, of course, Miss Fraser.

TEMPLE passes it across, MISS FRASER opens it and nervously searches.

FRASER: I've got some lozenges somewhere, I … Oh, here we are! Would you like a lozenge, my dear?

STEVE: No, thank you, Miss Fraser.

FRASER: No?

STEVE: No, thank you.

FRASER: (*After a tiny pause*) … They're peppermints.

STEVE: (*Slightly taken aback*) Peppermints …

FRASER: (*Quite innocently*) Yes. Do have one, my dear.

STEVE: (*With a nervous laugh*) No, I … won't have one … thanks very much.

The flying-boat is on the last burst of speed before leaving the water.

TEMPLE: We're leaving the water …

FRASER: (*Quietly*) Oh, dear … Oh, dear …

A sudden, final burst of speed …

TEMPLE: There we are …

And the flying-boat rises from the water.

TEMPLE: … We're off!

The flying boat climbs steeply.

FRASER: Oh, dear, we seem to be going very high …

TEMPLE: (*Amused*) I'm afraid we shall go a lot higher, Miss Fraser!

The flying-boat continues to climb.

STEVE: What's that place, darling?

TEMPLE: Where? Oh, that's Brownsea Island.

A pause.

FRASER: Is that Poole I can see?

TEMPLE: Yes, that's Poole.

FRASER: What a tiny wee place!

TEMPLE laughs.

A pause.

FRASER: (*Faintly surprised*) You know, this is really quite pleasant.

TEMPLE: You can undo your belt now, Miss Fraser.

FRASER: Oh.

STEVE: How high are we, darling?

TEMPLE: I don't know. I'm not very good on heights. (*Turning*) How high are we, steward?

STEWARD: About five thousand feet, sir. You can unfasten your belt now, madam.

STEVE: (*Having forgotten the belt*) Oh, thank you.

STEWARD: Can I get you anything, sir?

TEMPLE: Not at the moment, thank you.

STEVE: Is there an observation cabin?

STEWARD: There's what we call the Promenade Deck, madam.

TEMPLE: (*To STEVE*) We'll have a look at that later, dear.

STEWARD: (*To MISS FRASER*) Anything I can get you, madam?

FRASER: No, thank you.

A moment.

FRASER: Are you travelling far, Mr Temple?

TEMPLE: We're going as far as Cairo, that's all.

FRASER: Oh, I've a much longer journey. I'm going to Port Darwin.

STEVE: Port Darwin?

FRASER: Yes. Fortunately, I'm staying a week in Cairo and almost a fortnight in Singapore so the journey won't seem quite so long.

TEMPLE: No.

FRASER: Is this your first trip to Egypt, Mrs Temple?

STEVE: Yes, I'm afraid it is.

FRASER: It's a fascinating country, really fascinating. The first time I visited Egypt was just over twelve years ago ... Yes, just over twelve years ago ... June, 1935 ... (*A sigh*) T't – t't ... My, things have changed a great deal since then, haven't they?

TEMPLE: Have you friends in Cairo?

FRASER: I've a brother – or rather, strictly speaking, a half-brother. Apart from a short spell in Indo-China, he's spent pretty nearly all his life in Egypt. I must say, he's done very well for himself. He's with the Trans-Eurasian Oil Company.

TEMPLE: (*Nodding*) Oh, yes.

FRASER: (*Faintly amused*) In many ways I suppose we're rather a curious family. I've a half-brother in Cairo, a sister in Singapore, two brothers in Port Darwin and a sister in Wellington, New South Wales.

TEMPLE: You certainly believe in spreading yourself out.

FRASER: Yes ... Yes, we do that. (*Thoughtfully: suggestion of a sigh*) I sometimes wonder whether it's a good thing or not ...

A pause.

STEVE: We seem to be climbing higher, Paul.

37

TEMPLE: Yes.

FRASER: My word, the sea's beginning to look rather rough.

TEMPLE: Would you like to see the Promenade Deck?

STEVE: Yes. Yes, I would.

STEVE rises and passes MISS FRASER.

STEVE: Excuse me, Miss Fraser.

TEMPLE and STEVE move off down the flying-boat.

SCENE 2B: The Observation Cabin on the Promenade Deck.

The door opens, and TEMPLE and STEVE enter.

TEMPLE: You'll get the best view over here, Steve.

STEVE shuts the door.

STEVE: (*Suddenly tense*) Paul, what do you make of that woman? Do you think she's mixed up in this business?

TEMPLE: Now, darling, listen! I don't know whether she's mixed up in this business or whether she isn't, but for the last five minutes you've been looking at her as if she was Dracula's favourite aunt and Frankenstein's kid sister rolled into one!

STEVE: But you saw what happened! You heard what she said!

TEMPLE: Steve, Miss Fraser stayed the night at the same hotel as Miss Raymond. Right. So did we, so did Harold Darwin, so did fifty or sixty other people.

STEVE: But the peppermints …

TEMPLE: Miss Fraser sucks peppermints. Agreed – but so do thousands of other people.

STEVE: And the fact that her brother …

TEMPLE: She has a half-brother who works for the Trans-Eurasian Oil Company.

STEVE: Does this mean you're not interested in this case?

TEMPLE: Case? What case? Joyce Raymond gave us a pair of spectacles and asked us to deliver them to a man in Cairo, called Richard Sullivan.

STEVE: But Joyce Raymond was murdered! And she was murdered because …

TEMPLE: Because what?

A moment.

STEVE: (*Quietly: facing TEMPLE*) She was murdered because of the spectacles, you know that as well as I do. (*A note of determination in her voice*) Why do you think we were nearly drowned yesterday afternoon? Do you think that was an accident or do you think it was done deliberately?

TEMPLE: (*Faintly amused*) I say, you're pretty determined about this business, aren't you?

STEVE: Someone intends to stop us from delivering those spectacles to Richard Sullivan. Well, I don't intend to let them stop us, I intend to deliver those glasses if it's the last thing I do.

TEMPLE: (*Politely*) Excuse me, darling, but – er – where are the glasses?

STEVE: Why, they're in my handbag.

TEMPLE: Are you sure?

STEVE: Of course I'm sure. (*She opens her handbag*) I put them … Why, they're gone! Paul, they've gone!

TEMPLE: It's all right. Don't get excited. I've got them.

STEVE: You've got them?

TEMPLE: Yes, I took them out of your handbag half an hour ago. (*A moment: smiling*) Just to be on the safe side.

STEVE: You know, I've got a hunch that you're not being
          straight with me about this business. I think that
          you think that I think that … (*She stops*)
TEMPLE: What do you think, darling?
STEVE: … I think I'm beginning to feel sick.
TEMPLE: Yes, I thought you were. Let's go back to our
          seats.

The door opens and DARWIN enters.

DARWIN: (*Brightly*) Hello! Everything shipshape?
STEVE: Yes, thank you.
DARWIN: Just going back?
TEMPLE: Yes. My wife …
STEVE: (*Rather quickly*) Excuse me …

STEVE leaves. DARWIN laughs.

DARWIN: Have a cigarette?
TEMPLE: No, I won't have one just now, thank you.

A moment.

DARWIN: Looks like being a nice trip.
TEMPLE: Yes.
DARWIN: Temple, I've been meaning to ask you … That
          girl we found …
TEMPLE: Joyce Raymond?
DARWIN: Yes. Was she a friend of yours?
TEMPLE: Hardly a friend.
DARWIN: But you'd seen her, quite recently, I mean?
TEMPLE: Yes, as a matter of fact I'd seen her that very
          afternoon.
DARWIN: In Bournemouth?
TEMPLE: No, in London.
DARWIN: (*A little surprised*) In London?
TEMPLE: Yes.
DARWIN: Did you tell the Inspector that you'd seen her in
          London?
TEMPLE: Yes, of course I did.

40

DARWIN: Oh sorry, I didn't mean to be rude.

TEMPLE: (*Laughing*) That's all right.

DARWIN: I'm not exactly used to this sort of thing, you know. I suppose it's only natural that I should be – well – rather curious.

TEMPLE: What exactly is it you're curious about, Mr Darwin?

DARWIN: (*Faintly surprised*) Well, the usual sort of things, I suppose.

TEMPLE: (*Watching DARWIN*) Why was she murdered? Who murdered her?

DARWIN: (*An uneasy little laugh*) Yes …

TEMPLE: (*After a moment*) I wish I could satisfy your curiosity. (*Casually*) How long are you staying in Cairo?

DARWIN: Six months – a year – perhaps even longer. I'm with Heinemann and Mervyn, the engineering people.

TEMPLE: Oh.

DARWIN: (*Laughing*) I can see Heinemann and Mervyn doesn't mean a thing to you! Drills, mining equipment. We deal with all the Middle East combines.

TEMPLE: Including the Trans-Eurasian Oil Company?

DARWIN: Good Lord, yes! I should say so! Without the good old T.E.O.C. we should go right under.

TEMPLE: You don't happen to know a man in Cairo by the name of Richard Sullivan? I believe he's with the T.E.O.C.

DARWIN: Sullivan? No, I'm afraid I don't. Always used to deal with a chap called Beklar. Ronnie Beklar. Nice chap, but drank like a fish. Pity. (*Suddenly*) Is this chap Sullivan a friend of yours?

TEMPLE: (*Offhand*) No, he's just a sort of friend of a friend.

DARWIN: (*Indifferently*) M'm. I see. If I can be of any help to you while you're in Cairo, just give me a tinkle. I shall be at the Cosmopolitan for the first week or so.

TEMPLE: That's very kind of you.

DARWIN: Not at all. Only too delighted.

A moment.

DARWIN: I say, look at that yacht! She's a beauty, isn't she?

A pause.

TEMPLE: See you later.

DARWIN: (*Turning*) Oh, yes. Rather!

SCENE 2C: The Flying Boat Passenger Cabin.

TEMPLE returns to STEVE.

TEMPLE: How are you feeling?

STEVE: Oh, I shall be all right. I just feel a bit giddy, that's all.

TEMPLE: (*A laugh*) Good.

FRASER: Did you see that yacht, Mr Temple?

TEMPLE: Yes.

FRASER: It really looked most attractive. Most attractive, I thought.

A slight pause.

STEVE: What time is it?

TEMPLE: It's just a quarter past ten. Would you like a drink?

STEVE: I think I would. I'd like a brandy and ginger ale. Might settle my tummy.

TEMPLE: That's a very good idea. How about you, Miss Fraser?

FRASER: Well, that's awfully kind of you, Mr Temple. To be truthful, I very rarely indulge, but … may I have the same?

TEMPLE: Yes, of course. Ring for the steward, darling.

SCENE 2D: The Flying Boat Passenger Cabin.

Several hours later.

Most of the passengers are asleep.

MISS FRASER is – gently – snoring.

TEMPLE: (*Quietly*) Would you like some more coffee?

STEVE: No, thank you.

TEMPLE: Did you enjoy your lunch?

STEVE: Yes, I did, darling.

TEMPLE: Tired?

STEVE: A little.

TEMPLE: Why don't you try and get some sleep?

STEVE: Yes, I think I will.

TEMPLE: You can adjust your seat, if you'd like to lie down.

STEVE: It's all right dear, I'm quite comfy.

TEMPLE: Miss Fraser's well away.

A slight pause.

STEVE: (*Dozing*) M'm? What was that?

TEMPLE: I said: Miss Fraser's … (*Seeing STEVE is nearly asleep*) It's nothing … You have a snooze.

STEVE makes a gentle little noise as if she is settling down into a doze

Pause.

MISS FRASER continues to snore.

STEWARD: (*Softly: not wishing to disturb anyone*) I beg your pardon, sir. Mr Temple?

TEMPLE: Yes.

STEWARD:	A gentleman in C Cabin asked me to deliver a message, sir.
TEMPLE:	Which gentleman?
STEWARD:	The dark, stout gentleman, sir.

A moment.

TEMPLE:	The one I can see through the door: the man smoking a cigar.
STEWARD:	Yes, sir. He'd like to have a word with you, sir – at your convenience.
TEMPLE:	Yes, all right. Tell him I'll see him on the Promenade Deck.
STEWARD:	Now, sir?
TEMPLE:	Yes – straight away.
STEWARD:	Very good, sir.
TEMPLE:	Oh – do you happen to know the gentleman's name?
STEWARD:	I think it's Constantine, sir.
TEMPLE:	Brazilian?
STEWARD:	Portuguese.

TEMPLE rises and moves out towards the Promenade Deck.

TEMPLE:	Right. Thank you, steward.
STEWARD:	Thank you, sir.

SCENE 2E: The Observation Cabin.

The door opens and TEMPLE enters.

TEMPLE: You wanted to see me?

CONSTANTINE: Mr Temple?

TEMPLE: Yes …

CONSTANTINE: It's nice of you to spare me a few minutes.

CONSTANTINE is a man of about fifty. He talks slowly and with a distinct accent.

TEMPLE: That's all right.

TEMPLE closes the door.

CONSTANTINE: Would you like a cigar?

44

TEMPLE: No, thank you.

CONSTANTINE: Perhaps I ought to introduce myself. My name is Constantine.

TEMPLE: Well, what can I do for you, Mr Constantine?

CONSTANTINE: I don't suppose my name conveys a great deal to you?

TEMPLE: To be frank, it doesn't.

CONSTANTINE: That is unfortunate. However … (*A shrug: pause: sharply*) What is your business, Mr Temple?

TEMPLE: (*Not caring for MR CONSTANTINE*) I'm a novelist. I write books, detective stories – amongst other things.

CONSTANTINE: Oh, yes. (*Faintly amused*) Detective stories.

TEMPLE: If you look me up in Who's Who, Mr Constantine, you'll find that I am the author of sixteen detective novels, three plays, four biographies and a very slim volume of verse. You will also find that I am married, that I have a flat in Town, a country house near Evesham, and that my hobbies are reading, riding and criminology. For your private information, Mr Constantine, I have a pet aversion.

CONSTANTINE: And what is that?

TEMPLE: People who don't come straight to the point.

A moment and then CONSTANTINE starts to laugh.

CONSTANTINE: Apparently you also have a sense of humour, my friend. You may need it.

TEMPLE: What is it you want?

CONSTANTINE:	Two days ago a very charming lady by the name of Miss Raymond visited your flat in Half Moon Street. She handed over to you a certain … document. You were told, if my information is correct, to deliver that document to a certain Mr Richard Sullivan.
TEMPLE:	What about coming straight to the point?
CONSTANTINE:	Very well. I am a businessman, Mr Temple. I have a proposition to put to you.
TEMPLE:	What is your proposition, Mr Constantine?
CONSTANTINE:	Well, first of all, perhaps you might be interested to know that there is no such person as Richard Sullivan. He doesn't exist. He is a myth. He is a – what is the word? – a figment of the imagination.
TEMPLE:	Go on.
CONSTANTINE:	If you will hand over to me now the document that Miss Raymond gave to you, I will pay to you this evening – on arrival in Augusta – the sum of seven thousand pounds.
TEMPLE:	Go on.
CONSTANTINE:	(*A shrug*) That is all. So far as I am concerned, there is nothing more to say.
TEMPLE:	Well, so far as I'm concerned there's quite a lot to say. In the first place, Miss Raymond did not hand me a document. In other words the document, my dear Mr Constantine, does not exist. It's a myth. A figment of your apparently fertile imagination. I was asked to deliver a perfectly ordinary pair of horn-rimmed spectacles to a gentleman in Cairo by the

	name of Richard Sullivan. I intend to deliver those spectacles, Mr Constantine.
CONSTANTINE:	There is no such person as Richard Sullivan.
TEMPLE:	(*Moving away*) That, I shall find out for myself, when I get to Cairo.
CONSTANTINE:	Mr Temple, one moment, please ... These glasses: you say they are a perfectly ordinary pair of horn-rimmed spectacles. Not tampered with in any way at all?
TEMPLE:	No.
CONSTANTINE:	You were told by Miss Raymond to –
TEMPLE:	(*Correcting CONSTANTINE*) I was asked by Miss Raymond ...
CONSTANTINE:	... You were asked by Miss Raymond to deliver them to a Mr Richard Sullivan?
TEMPLE:	Yes.

A moment, then quite suddenly:

CONSTANTINE:	I will give you ten thousand pounds for the glasses.

There is a pause, then TEMPLE starts to laugh.

CONSTANTINE:	What is so funny?
TEMPLE:	Apparently, you also have a sense of humour, Mr Constantine.

TEMPLE opens the door and returns to STEVE.

SCENE 2F:	The Flying Boat Passenger Cabin.

MISS FRASER is still gently snoring.
STEVE moves and slowly wakes up.

STEVE:	(*Yawning*) Oh, dear ... oh, dear ... What time is it?
TEMPLE:	(*Softly*) Nearly half past two ...
STEVE:	What time do we reach Augusta?
TEMPLE:	About five.

STEVE:	Paul, what is it? Why the frown?
TEMPLE:	(*After a pause: even voice*) It appears that you were right about the spectacles, Steve.
STEVE:	What do you mean?
TEMPLE:	(*Quite simply*) I've just been offered ten thousand pounds for them.
STEVE:	(*Staggered*) Ten thousand pounds!

MISS FRASER suddenly wakes up.

FRASER:	Oh, good gracious! … (*Stretching herself*) Good gracious me now. I've been asleep …

FADE UP of music.

FADE DOWN of music.

SCENE 3: The Deck of a Motor Launch.

The launch is moored, the engine idling, to the side of the flying-boat. Passengers are climbing out of the flying-boat and into the launch. The water splashes against the side of the launch and the flying-boat.

There is a general atmosphere of noise and conversation.

FRASER:	(*Nervously*) I shall want my suitcase … (*Raising her voice*) I shall want my suitcase, young man!
FLYING OFFICER:	That's quite all right, madam. The luggage is taken off by the customs. It'll be handed over to you later.
TEMPLE:	Mind your step, Miss Fraser!
FLYING OFFICER:	Give me your hand!
FRASER:	Oh! (*She climbs into the launch*) Oh, thank you!
FLYING OFFICER:	(*To STEVE*) Can you manage, madam?
STEVE:	Yes. Yes, I'm all right. (*She slips*) Oh!
DARWIN:	Steady, Mrs Temple!

STEVE gives a nervous little laugh.

TEMPLE: Don't go and fall in the water, darling!

A little laughter from the passengers.

FLYING OFFICER: (*To the passengers*) Would you all mind moving a little further along, please? Thank you. (*Turning*) Give me your arm, sir.

CONSTANTINE: I can manage, thank you.

SCENE 4: The Reception Hall of a Small Hotel in Augusta.

The flying-boat passengers are registering at the hotel.

GIRL: (*An Italian: her English is not by any means good*) Miss ... Fraser?

FRASER: Yes.

GIRL: You are in room 24, please.

FRASER: 24?

GIRL: Yes, that is on the first floor. (*Taking a key from the board*) Here is your key.

FRASER: Thank you. (*Turning: pleasantly*) I expect we shall meet at dinner, Mrs Temple.

STEVE: Yes, I expect so.

DARWIN: Mr Darwin.

GIRL: Dar-Vin?

DARWIN: Darwin.

GIRL: (*Sees DARWIN's name on the list*) Ah yes! Dar-Vin ... Room 17, sir. (*Taking a key from the board*) Here is your key.

DARWIN: Thank you. (*To TEMPLE and STEVE*) Cheers!

TEMPLE: See you later. (*To the GIRL*) Mr and Mrs Temple.

GIRL:	Mr and Mrs … ok yes! Room 23, please … (*Taking a key from the board*) Here is your key.
TEMPLE:	Thank you.
GIRL:	Oh, Mr Temple …
TEMPLE:	Yes?
GIRL:	There was a telephone call for you about half an hour ago.
TEMPLE:	For me?
GIRL:	Yes, sir.
TEMPLE:	From London?
GIRL:	No, sir. The gentleman is ringing again later this evening.
TEMPLE:	Did he leave a name?
GIRL:	No, sir. No name: no message.
TEMPLE:	(*Puzzled*) Thank you.
MAN:	(*At desk*) Wilton …
GIRL:	Wilton? Oh, yes! Mr and Mrs Wilton … Room 14 …

SCENE 5: The TEMPLES' Hotel Room

STEVE is unpacking.

STEVE:	Here's your razor, darling.
TEMPLE:	Oh, thanks.
STEVE:	And your shaving soap.
TEMPLE:	Thanks.

A moment.

STEVE:	Who do you think telephoned?
TEMPLE:	(*Puzzled*) I don't know. I can't imagine. Unless of course the girl was mistaken and the call was for someone else.
STEVE:	I don't think she was mistaken; do you?
TEMPLE:	(*A moment*) No.
STEVE:	That man you told me about, the man on the plane, Mr …?

50

TEMPLE: Mr Constantine?

STEVE: Yes. Was he serious about the £10,000?

TEMPLE: Perfectly serious.

STEVE: And yet he knew nothing about the spectacles until you told him?

TEMPLE: No. He was apparently under the impression that Joyce Raymond had asked me to deliver a document to Richard Sullivan.

STEVE: Yes. Yes, that bears out what I thought.

TEMPLE: What do you mean?

STEVE: Those glasses contain a secret message.

TEMPLE: My dear Steve, whichever way you look at it those glasses are just a perfectly ordinary pair of horn-rimmed spectacles, so …

STEVE: Do you think Mr Constantine would have offered you £10,000 for a perfectly ordinary pair of spectacles?

TEMPLE: Well, you've seen them, you've examined them. Do you see any sign of a secret message?

STEVE: No, I must confess I don't.

TEMPLE: No, and neither do I and neither did the C.I.D. expert.

STEVE: You know, darling, I just don't understand your attitude over this business.

TEMPLE: Don't you? My attitude is really quite simple, Steve. There's something pretty important behind all this. And pretty dangerous. But in spite of that, when I get to Cairo I intend to hand the spectacles over to Richard Sullivan and go politely about my own business. There, so far as I am concerned, the matter ends.

STEVE: But supposing Mr Constantine was telling the truth and there is no Richard Sullivan?

TEMPLE: Then I shall take the glasses back to London and turn them over to the C.I.D.

STEVE: (*A note of determination in her voice*) Yes, well, I've got an intuition about all this.

TEMPLE: Oh, Steve, don't! Not that good old intuition!

STEVE: You can laugh! But do you know what I think? I think it's quite possible that we've already met the mysterious Mr Sullivan.

TEMPLE: Already met him?

STEVE: Yes.

TEMPLE: What do you mean?

STEVE: Hasn't it occurred to you that Harold Darwin might be Richard Sullivan?

TEMPLE: (*Surprised*) Harold Darwin?

STEVE: Yes.

TEMPLE: If he is then why hasn't he spoken to me about the glasses?

STEVE: He probably doesn't know you've got them, unless of course you've told him.

TEMPLE: (*Thoughtfully*) No, I haven't told him. But I spoke to him about Richard Sullivan and he said he'd never heard of him.

STEVE: He may have had a reason for saying that.

TEMPLE: M'm. Possibly. (*Suddenly*) I think I'll change this collar, darling. Where's the clean one – the blue one?

STEVE searches in the case.

STEVE: Oh dear, don't tell me I forgot to pack it!

TEMPLE: Don't tell me you forgot to pack it!

A slight pause.

STEVE: Darling, I'm afraid I have.

TEMPLE: Oh, well, it doesn't matter. I shall have to keep this one, that's all. (*Looking in the mirror*) I suppose it doesn't look too bad.

| STEVE: | Where's the bathroom, Paul – did you notice? |
| TEMPLE: | Yes. It's at the end of the corridor, on the right. |

STEVE moves to the door and opens it.

STEVE:	I shan't be a moment.
TEMPLE:	All right.
STEVE:	Don't unpack the large case, Paul. I packed everything we need in the small one.
TEMPLE:	Everything except my collar.
STEVE:	(*Laughing*) Yes, I expected that!

TEMPLE laughs.

STEVE closes the door and we go with her as she walks along the corridor.

CONSTANTINE:	(*Quietly*) Mrs Temple?
STEVE:	(*With a start*) Oh! Yes?
CONSTANTINE:	(*Politely: quite pleasantly in fact*) Forgive me, but I wonder if you would be so kind as to spare me a moment?
STEVE:	What is it you want?
CONSTANTINE:	I don't know whether your husband told you or not but we had quite a conversation together on the plane. Unfortunately he –
STEVE:	Oh! So you're Mr Constantine!
CONSTANTINE:	Yes. Mrs Temple, we can't talk out here – like this – in the corridor. I wonder, would you be so kind as to step into my room for a moment? (*Smiling, as he moves towards his room and opens it*) It's quite all right, I assure you. I will leave the door open.

A moment, then STEVE follows CONSTANTINE into the room.

| STEVE: | Thank you. |

A pause.

STEVE: Well?

CONSTANTINE: Your husband is carrying a pair of spectacles. I have offered him £10,000 for them. He has refused and insists that he is taking the spectacles to Cairo to a gentleman by the name of Richard Sullivan.

STEVE: Quite right.

CONSTANTINE: Mrs Temple, I hope you will use your influence with your husband. I hope you will, in fact, persuade him to accept my offer.

STEVE: But the spectacles don't belong to my husband. They were entrusted to him by –

CONSTANTINE: (*Interrupting STEVE: smiling*) They were given to him by a rather impetuous young lady. Yes, I know all about that.

STEVE: For your information that impetuous young lady was murdered, Mr Constantine.

CONSTANTINE: Murdered because she was stupid enough to interfere in something which … (*He is smiling*) … did not concern her. You see, Mrs Temple, the matter is really quite simple. If your husband persists in taking the glasses to Cairo he will discover – always providing of course that he reaches Cairo quite safely – he will discover that there is no such person as Richard Sullivan.

STEVE: Mr Constantine, those glasses appear to me to be just an ordinary pair of glasses;

54

> then why are you offering my husband
> £10,000 for them?

There is a pause.

CONSTANTINE: (*Ignoring STEVE's question: slowly,
pleasantly*) Mrs Temple, I am quite serious
– I am in fact speaking to you as a friend –
if you are fond of your husband, and do
not wish him to take unnecessary risks,
then please persuade him to hand those
glasses over to me here, in Augusta ...
now ... tonight ... before it is too late.

FADE UP of music.

FADE DOWN of music.

SCENE 6:   The TEMPLES' Hotel Room.

STEVE opens the door.

TEMPLE: (*Pleasantly*) Hello, you've been a long
time ... Steve, what is it?

STEVE: I've seen Constantine. He stopped me in
the corridor.

TEMPLE: (*Quickly*) Did he annoy you? Because if he
did then –

STEVE: No, he was really quite pleasant. He asked
me to use my influence with you, to try
and get you to hand over the glasses.

TEMPLE: I suppose he told you that Sullivan doesn't
exist, that when we get to Cairo –

The telephone rings.

STEVE: Here's your call ...

TEMPLE: Yes ...

TEMPLE lifts the receiver.

TEMPLE: (*On the phone*) Hello?

GIRL: (*On the other end of the phone*) Mr
Temple?

TEMPLE: Yes?

GIRL: There is a call for you. Wait a moment, please.

A tiny pause.

Some clicks on the line, then an Englishman speaks. He is fairly bright in manner.

MAN: (*On the other end of the phone*) Hello?

TEMPLE: Hello?

MAN: Mr Temple?

TEMPLE: Yes.

MAN: This is Richard Sullivan here.

TEMPLE: (*Taken aback*) Richard Sullivan?

MAN: (*Laughing*) That's right! I suppose this is rather a surprise? You didn't expect to hear from me …

TEMPLE: No, as a matter of fact I didn't. Not until we reached Cairo.

MAN: I got the cable from Joyce on Tuesday, just before I was leaving for Naples.

TEMPLE: Where are you now?

MAN: Where am I? I'm here, in Augusta. I'm staying with a friend of mine – Colonel Marquand. (*Suddenly*) But what about the glasses? Have you got them with you?

TEMPLE: Yes, I've got them

MAN: That's fine! Can I pick them up in about twenty minutes?

TEMPLE: Yes, of course.

MAN: Good! It's awfully decent of you to bring them.

TEMPLE: That's all right. I shall look forward to seeing you.

MAN: Thanks. Oh – how is Miss Raymond?

A pause.

TEMPLE: I'm afraid I've got some rather bad news for you, Mr Sullivan.

MAN: What do you mean? About … Joyce?

TEMPLE: Yes. (*Quietly*) I'll tell you when I see you.

MAN: All right. I'll be there in twenty minutes. See you in the lounge.

TEMPLE: Yes, all right.

MAN: Goodbye.

TEMPLE: Goodbye.

TEMPLE replaces the receiver.

STEVE: (*Staggered*) So that was … Richard Sullivan?

A moment.

TEMPLE: (*Thoughtfully*) Yes.

FADE UP of music.

FADE DOWN of music.

SCENE 7: The Hotel Lounge.

TEMPLE and STEVE are seated. There is a background hum of conversation.

STEVE: What time is it?

TEMPLE: It's nearly half-past seven.

STEVE: It's over an hour since he telephoned.

TEMPLE: I know. I've got a hunch he's not going to show up.

STEVE: Paul, do you think it really was Sullivan or …

TEMPLE: What do you mean?

STEVE: … Or could it have been Mr Constantine?

TEMPLE: Well, it certainly wasn't Constantine: for one thing, it was an outside call. Of course he may have got a friend to phone.

STEVE: That's what I thought.

TEMPLE: Yes. Well in that case why hasn't the friend turned up?

STEVE: (*Thoughtfully*) Paul, is Constantine on the way to Cairo?

TEMPLE: I gather he's booked through to Singapore, but of course that might mean anything.

STEVE: (*A moment: puzzled*) What did he sound like, – the man on the telephone, I mean?

TEMPLE: He seemed a bright, cheerful sort of chap. A bit too cheerful, perhaps.

STEVE: What do you mean?

TEMPLE: Oh, I don't know. He sounded just a little forced, I thought, as if the whole business had been rather carefully rehearsed.

STEVE: You asked him where he was speaking from: what did he say?

TEMPLE: No. I didn't ask him where he was speaking from. I said: "Where are you now?" And he said: "I'm here, in Augusta. I'm staying with a friend of mine – Colonel Marquand." (*To himself*) Colonel Marquand. That's an idea. (*Rising*) Let's have a word with the receptionist.

TEMPLE and STEVE move out of the lounge to the reception desk.

GIRL: (*Pleasantly*) Is there anything I can do for you, sir?

TEMPLE: Yes. Have you a telephone directory?

GIRL: Certainly, sir.

TEMPLE: I want to find the address of a Colonel Marquand.

GIRL: Colonel Marquand?

TEMPLE: Yes.

GIRL: But I can give you the address, sir. Villa Negara.

TEMPLE: Villa Negara. Where is that?

GIRL: It is about half a mile away, sir.

TEMPLE: Where, exactly?

GIRL: Towards Syracuse, sir. The villa stands in a small park on the hill overlooking the harbour.

TEMPLE: Well – how do we get there?

GIRL: If you wish to walk you take the road towards the harbour and bear right when you get to the bridge. It is a pleasant walk this time of the night.

TEMPLE: Thank you.

GIRL: Thank you, sir.

TEMPLE: (*Quietly*) Well, what do you say? Shall we go up to the Villa, or wait?

A pause.

STEVE: Let's go up to the Villa.

TEMPLE: Right. I'll go upstairs and get the torch, we might need it …

FADE UP of music.

FADE DOWN of music.

SCENE 8: Outside the Gates of the Villa Negara, on a hill overlooking a harbour.

The distant noise of the sea can be heard.

STEVE: (*Slightly out of breath*) Oh! Gosh, what a climb! I thought we should never get here.

TEMPLE: (*Laughing*) I was beginning to wonder if we should ever make it! Here's the gate …

STEVE: Where's the house?

TEMPLE: There it is, through those trees.

STEVE: (*Impressed*) What a lovely place. Let's open the gate.

They open the gate.

TEMPLE: I'll bet they've got a wonderful view from those windows.

STEVE: Yes.

They close the gate and continue up the drive.

TEMPLE: What's that, Steve … over there?

STEVE: (*A little laugh*) It's a lake! It's certainly a lovely garden.

59

TEMPLE: Yes, it's a pity it's getting dark, we could have
           … (*He stops*)
STEVE: What is it?
TEMPLE: Listen!

From the house in the distance we hear angry voices. Men shouting at each other in intense anger. The sound of a struggle.

Then there is a sudden smashing of glass as a man throws himself through a French window.

Voices reach an angry peak. The voices are louder.

Then a revolver shot is heard, followed by a second shot.

We hear a cry of pain; the man is hit.

STEVE: Paul … what is it?
TEMPLE: There's someone coming! Someone is running
           from the house …

We hear another revolver shot.

STEVE: Paul!
TEMPLE: Here he is! Look! He's coming down the drive!

The MAN who spoke to TEMPLE on the telephone is running down the drive. He is frightened, exhausted and badly hurt.

TEMPLE: (*Raising voice*) Hello, there!
MAN: (*Completely exhausted, in pain*) Who are you
           …? Who are …? Oh! Oh …
TEMPLE: Give me your arm and I'll help you to …
MAN: (*Desperately*) No! No, don't touch me … Oh!
           Oh …
STEVE: Paul, he's been shot! He's badly hurt, we've got
           to do something …
TEMPLE: I'll get hold of his arm. We'll try and help him
           towards the gate.
MAN: (*Desperately frightened*) No, don't touch me, just
           … (*Suddenly, suspicious*) Who are you? What
           are you doing here?

60

TEMPLE:	(*Quietly*) Just a minute, my friend ... You're the fellow that spoke to me on the telephone! Are you ... Richard Sullivan?
MAN:	(*Desperately*) No, I'm not but I had to speak to you, I was made to speak to you, I ... Oh ... oh, my back, I ...

Voices are heard: two men are approaching.

EMILE:	(*Off*) Potete vedere? (*Can you see?*)
MARQUAND:	(*Off*) Dore e andato? (*Where did he get to?*)
STEVE:	Paul, there's someone coming!
MAN:	Don't let them touch me ... please! Don't let them touch me! Oh ... Oh ...
STEVE:	He's falling!
TEMPLE:	It's all right, I've got him!
MAN:	Temple, listen! Listen! Whatever happens ... Get those glasses to Cairo ...

FADE UP of music.

END OF EPISODE TWO

EPISODE THREE

INTRODUCING
COLONEL MARQUAND

ANNOUNCER: Just before leaving for Egypt, Paul Temple receives a visit from a Miss Joyce Raymond, who asks Temple to deliver a pair of spectacles to a friend of hers in Cairo called Richard Sullivan. From the moment Temple takes possession of the spectacles, however, things begin to happen. Miss Raymond is murdered and the spectacles are taken down to Police Headquarters for a detailed examination. The police report states that they are a perfectly ordinary pair of spectacles and Temple can deliver them, as arranged, to Richard Sullivan. The following morning Temple and Steve arrive at Poole, and – together with Harold Darwin, an acquaintance of theirs – proceed out to the B.O.A.C. flying-boat. On board they make the acquaintance of a Scots lady, a Miss Fraser. Shortly before arriving in Augusta which is the overnight stopping place – a passenger introduces himself to Temple as Mr Constantine. Constantine offers Temple £10,000 for the spectacles. Temple treats the offer as a joke; when he arrives at Augusta, however, he receives a telephone call from a man claiming to be Richard Sullivan. The man states that he is staying with a certain Colonel Marquand. Temple discovers that Colonel Marquand lives at the Villa Negara. Late that night Temple and Steve visit the Villa Negara …

SCENE 1:   Flashback to and continuation of Episode 2, Scene 8: Outside the gates of the Villa Negara, on a hill overlooking the harbour.

The distant noise of the sea can be heard.

STEVE: Where's the house, darling?

TEMPLE: There it is, through those trees.

STEVE: (*Impressed*) What a lovely place. Let's open the gate.

They open the gate.

TEMPLE: I'll bet they've got a wonderful view from those windows.

STEVE: Yes.

They close the gate and continue up the drive.

TEMPLE: What's that, Steve … over there?

STEVE: (*A little laugh*) It's a lake! It's certainly a lovely garden.

TEMPLE: Yes, it's a pity it's getting dark, we could have … (*He stops*)

STEVE: What is it?

TEMPLE: Listen!

From the house in the distance we hear angry voices. Men shouting at each other in intense anger. The sound of a struggle.

Then there is a sudden smashing of glass as a man throws himself through a French window.

Voices reach an angry peak. The voices are louder.

Then a revolver shot is heard, followed by a second shot.

We hear a cry of pain; the man is hit.

STEVE: Paul … what is it?

TEMPLE: There's someone coming! Someone is running from the house …

We hear another revolver shot.

STEVE: Paul!

TEMPLE: Here he is! Look! He's coming down the drive!

The MAN who spoke to TEMPLE on the telephone is running down the drive. He is frightened, exhausted and badly hurt.

TEMPLE: (*Raising his voice*) Hello, there!

MAN: (*Completely exhausted, in pain*) Who are you …? Who are …? Oh! Oh …

TEMPLE: Give me your arm and I'll help you to …

MAN: (*Desperately*) No! No, don't touch me … Oh! Oh …

STEVE: Paul, he's been shot! He's badly hurt, we've got to do something …

TEMPLE: I'll get hold of his arm. We'll try and help him towards the gate.

MAN: (*Desperately frightened*) No, don't touch me, just … (*Suddenly, suspicious*) Who are you? What are you doing here?

TEMPLE: (*Quietly*) Just a minute, my friend … You're the fellow that spoke to me on the telephone! Are you … Richard Sullivan?

MAN: (*Desperately*) No, I'm not but I had to speak to you, I was made to speak to you, I … Oh … oh, my back, I …

Voices are heard: two men are approaching.

EMILE: (*Off*) Potete vedere? (*Can you see?*)

MARQUAND: (*Off*) Dore e andato? (*Where did he get to?*)

STEVE: Paul, there's someone coming!

MAN: Don't let them touch me … please! Don't let them touch me! Oh … Oh …

STEVE: He's falling!

TEMPLE: It's all right, I've got him!

MAN: Temple, listen! Listen! Whatever happens … Get those glasses to Cairo …

The MAN gives a sudden, desperate little cry and collapses.

STEVE: Paul, is he dead?

TEMPLE:	(*A moment*) Yes … Steve, listen! Take these glasses … take them, darling! Now go back to the gate and wait for me.
STEVE:	But, Paul –
TEMPLE:	(*With authority: determined*) Do as I tell you! Go back to the gate and wait!
STEVE:	But if you intend …
TEMPLE:	(*Tensely*) Darling, go back to the gate and wait, I don't want them to see you!
STEVE:	(*Softly*) Yes, all right.

STEVE departs.

A moment later COLONEL MARQUAND arrives, accompanied by EMILE. MARQUAND is an American, about forty-seven, tough and shrewd. EMILE is an Italian servant. He can speak very little English.

They are both out of breath, and EMILE is very excited. He bursts into a torrent of words on seeing TEMPLE.

EMILE:	Chi siete? Che cosa fa qui? (*Who are you? What are you doing here?*)
MARQUAND:	Be quiet, Emile. Be quiet!
EMILE:	(*To MARQUAND*) Chi e? Che fa qui? (*Who is he? What's he up to?*)
MARQUAND:	Non so. State tranquillo e lasciatemi parlare. (*I don't know. Be quiet and leave the talking to me*) (*To TEMPLE*) Who are you? What do you want?
TEMPLE:	(*Calmly*) What's more to the point, my friend – who are you?
MARQUAND:	(*Sharply*) My name is Marquand – Colonel Marquand. Is this man a friend of yours?
TEMPLE:	Well, judging from appearances he doesn't appear to have been on very friendly terms with anyone …
MARQUAND:	(*A moment*) Is he dead?

68

TEMPLE:	Yes.
MARQUAND:	Gee, that's unfortunate. But he asked for it. If these scoundrels make a habit of breaking into people's houses they must take what's coming to them.
TEMPLE:	Are you suggesting that this man broke into your house?
MARQUAND:	What do you mean – suggesting? He did! We caught him: we caught him red-handed. Didn't we, Emile?
EMILE:	Si. He very bad, try to steal everything.
MARQUAND:	There's far too much of this sort of thing going on. If the police won't take action then we've got to take the law into our own hands – that's all there is to it.
TEMPLE:	You appear to have taken the law into your own hands, Colonel Marquand.
MARQUAND:	(*Quietly*) What do you mean?
TEMPLE:	He's been beaten up.
MARQUAND:	(*After a slight hesitation*) Yeah, I know. That was Emile. You know what these wops are like, they're darned impetuous and ... Look, we caught the guy red-handed. Emile went for him, there was a struggle, he broke away, jumped through the French windows, and – well – I took a pot at him. I didn't mean to kill the guy. Frankly, I just meant to scare him.
TEMPLE:	You scared him all right.
EMILE:	(*Angrily*) Che e? Perche fa queste demande ... (*Who is he? Why's he asking these questions?*)
MARQUAND:	(*Turning on EMILE*) State zitto stupido! (*Be quiet, idiot!*)

69

TEMPLE:	I had a phone call about an hour and a half ago from a man called Sullivan. He said he was staying with you. My name's Temple.
MARQUAND:	Oh, you're Mr Temple! Gee, that explains it – that explains everything! Sullivan's up at the house, he's … waiting for you.
TEMPLE:	But he said he'd see me at the hotel.
MARQUAND:	At the hotel?
TEMPLE:	Yes. Over the phone he said, "I'll see you in twenty minutes". That was at six o'clock.
MARQUAND:	(*Apparently surprised*) Is that so? Gee, I guess there's been a misunderstanding. He gave me to understand that you were calling here. As a matter of fact he's been waiting for you. (*Suddenly*) Look, I think maybe we'd better go up to the house, then I can telephone the police and you can hand the spectacles over to Mr Sullivan.
TEMPLE:	(*Quietly*) Oh, so you know about the spectacles then?
MARQUAND:	(*With a laugh*) Yeah! And will he be glad to get them. (*To Emile*) Remanete qui finche arriciamo a casu poi conducete Thompson al cabino. Sapete cosa fare. (*Stay here until we get to the house, then take Thompson to the boat house. You know what to do*.)
EMILE:	Si, signor.
MARQUAND:	This way, Mr Temple.

FADE UP of music.

FADE DOWN of music.

SCENE 2:   A Room in the Villa Negara.

As a clock chimes eight, the door opens and MARQUAND enters.

MARQUAND: I'm sorry to have kept you waiting. I've been all this time on the telephone.

TEMPLE: That's all right.

MARQUAND shuts the door.

MARQUAND: The police have identified that fellow. Apparently they've been on the lookout for him for some time. I gather he's a pretty notorious character around here. (*Suddenly*) Oh, would you like a drink, Mr Temple?

TEMPLE: No, thank you.

MARQUAND: I have a very excellent port.

TEMPLE: Not at the moment, thank you.

MARQUAND: Mr Sullivan won't keep you long, he'll be down in a few moments. (*Pouring himself a drink*) How long are you staying in Augusta?

TEMPLE: Just for the night.

MARQUAND: Oh – you're leaving tomorrow then?

TEMPLE: Yes, I'm on my way to Cairo. As a matter of fact I expected to meet Mr Sullivan in Cairo. It came as quite a surprise to find that he was here in Augusta.

MARQUAND: Yeah … He arrived this morning, from Naples. (*Casually*) Are you sure you won't change your mind, and have a glass of port?

TEMPLE: Quite sure.

The door opens.

MARQUAND: Ah, here's Sullivan.

ARMSTRONG: I'm sorry to have been so long, Colonel, but –

ARMSTRONG stops speaking. He is staring at TEMPLE.

MARQUAND: What's the matter?

ARMSTRONG: (*Sharply*) What are you doing here?

71

MARQUAND: I've told you who he is. His name's Temple, he's got the … (*He stops, stares at TEMPLE*) Say, what is this?

TEMPLE: (*Slowly*) It's really quite simple. We've met before.

MARQUAND: Met before?

TEMPLE: (*Quietly, watching ARMSTRONG*) Yes …

MARQUAND: (*Sharply*) Where?

ARMSTRONG: We met at Bournemouth, two days ago.

TEMPLE: Only on that occasion, if I remember correctly, you called yourself Victor Armstrong.

MARQUAND: (*Intensely angry: to ARMSTRONG*) Why didn't you tell me you'd met him before? You fool, why did you tell me that he was –

ARMSTRONG: (*Also angry*) I didn't know! How could I know that this was the man you meant!

TEMPLE: There appears to be a certain amount of confusion. Do you mind if I clarify the situation?

MARQUAND: (*Sharply*) Well?

A moment.

TEMPLE: Two days ago a girl called Joyce Raymond gave me a pair of spectacles and asked me to deliver them to a man in Cairo called Richard Sullivan. Tonight, when I arrived in Augusta, I received a telephone call from this house: from a man claiming to be Richard Sullivan. That man was the person I met on the drive, the man that had been shot, the man that had been beaten up.

A moment.

MARQUAND: His name was not Richard Sullivan.

72

TEMPLE: (*Quietly*) All the same, he was the man that spoke to me on the telephone.

ARMSTRONG: For heaven's sake don't let's beat about the bush, Marquand. If he's got the glasses then …

MARQUAND: Be quiet! I'll handle this. I'll handle this in my own way. (*To TEMPLE*) Sit down.

TEMPLE: If you don't mind I should prefer to stand.

MARQUAND: Sit down!

TEMPLE: (*Lightly*) Well since you insist, I'll – sit down.

TEMPLE sits.

MARQUAND: Now listen. And listen, carefully. Before we go any further I should like –

TEMPLE: Before we go any further I should like that revolver of yours a little to the right; do you mind? I'm rather sensitive about … Ah, thanks, that's much better.

MARQUAND: (*Quietly; not unpleasant*) Mr Temple, I'm a businessman. Purely and simply a businessman. Therefore I'm going to play straight with you, put my cards on the table, and make you a proposition.

TEMPLE: Everybody seems to be making me propositions these days. What is yours, Colonel Marquand?

A moment.

MARQUAND: What did Miss Raymond tell you about the glasses: what did she say when she handed them over to you?

TEMPLE: I've told you what she said. She simply asked me to deliver them to a man in Cairo called Richard Sullivan.

MARQUAND: She said … nothing else?

73

TEMPLE: Nothing.

MARQUAND: (*Believing TEMPLE*) Right! Now, Mr Temple, for my proposition. You can either hand over the glasses to me now, in which case you can walk out of here Scot free, or you can refuse to hand them over to me, in which case, I shall take rather a delight in firing this revolver.

TEMPLE: Of course, I may be prejudiced, but that sounds rather a one-sided proposition for a businessman to make. For instance, I much prefer the proposition I received this afternoon from Mr Constantine.

ARMSTRONG: Who the blazes is Mr Constantine?

TEMPLE: He is a gentleman I met on the plane. Apparently he too is interested in the spectacles.

MARQUAND: What do you mean?

A moment.

TEMPLE: He offered me £10,000 for them.

ARMSTRONG: (*Staggered*) £10,000?

MARQUAND: (*Angrily*) Where are the spectacles? Where are they?

ARMSTRONG: (*Slowly: watching TEMPLE*) Did you sell them to this Mr Constantine?

TEMPLE: What would you have done, Mr Armstrong, under the circumstances?

MARQUAND: What Armstrong or anybody else would have done is quite beside the point. My guess is you've still got the spectacles or if you haven't got them you know where they are. Now start talking … (*A tense pause*) Mr Temple, I'm a pretty serious sort of guy, I

74

take things very much to heart. You saw what happened to Thompson …

TEMPLE: Thompson?

MARQUAND: He was the man you met on the drive.

TEMPLE: Oh, yes. I saw what happened to Thompson.

MARQUAND: Thompson was a nice fellow, but he started to get sentimental. I don't like sentimentality, Mr Temple, any more than I like stupidity. Now just at the moment you strike me as being very stupid. (*A pause*) I'm going to give you five seconds to tell me exactly where those glasses are. If you don't tell me, I shall pull this trigger … One … two … three … four … fi –

Outside in the hall the telephone starts to ring.

ARMSTRONG: It's the phone.

MARQUAND: (*Sharply*) O.K. Answer it.

ARMSTRONG goes out closing the door after him.

TEMPLE: If you've no objection I think I'll change my mind about the glass of port …

MARQUAND: Stay where you are!

TEMPLE: (*Laughing at him*) Very well … May I have a cigarette?

MARQUAND: There's a box on that table. You can reach it without getting up. Help yourself.

TEMPLE: (*Doing so*) Thanks.

MARQUAND: There's a lighter by the box.

TEMPLE: You don't believe in taking any chances, do you, Colonel?

TEMPLE lights the cigarette.

The door is thrown open and ARMSTRONG returns.

MARQUAND: (*Quickly*) Well? Who was it?

ARMSTRONG: You were wrong about this fellow, dead wrong!

MARQUAND: (*Angry*) What do you mean? Who was on the phone?

ARMSTRONG: It was the man he told us about – Constantine. The man on the flying-boat.

MARQUAND: (*Still angry*) Well?

ARMSTRONG: He wants to see you – now – tonight – at the El Passaro.

MARQUAND: (*Bewildered*) Why?

ARMSTRONG: He's got the glasses. Temple did sell them to him for £10,000.

A tense pause.

MARQUAND: (*Softly: but with a fierce determination*) Did you sell those glasses? Did you …? (*Slowly: the final threat*) I'm going to give you three seconds to tell me whether –

TEMPLE overturns the table.

ARMSTRONG: (*Sudden cry of alarm*) Look out! Look out!

MARQUAND: Get the revolver! Get the revolv –

There is a quick cry of pain from MARQUAND as TEMPLE strikes the revolver from his hand. Then TEMPLE catches him under the jaw.

MARQUAND: Argh!

And he falls like a log.

TEMPLE and ARMSTRONG both dash for the revolver, ARMSTRONG gets there first, TEMPLE grabs his wrist and they struggle.

ARMSTRONG: (*In pain*) My wrist …

TEMPLE: Drop it … Drop it …

ARMSTRONG: My wrist … my wrist … you're breaking it … you're …

TEMPLE: Drop it!

A moment's further struggle, then the revolver falls to the floor.

A tense pause.

Both ARMSTRONG and TEMPLE are breathing heavily.

TEMPLE: (*Quietly*) Now, stand over there ... Go on ...

ARMSTRONG: (*Frightened*) Don't shoot, Temple ...

TEMPLE: Go on, further away ...

ARMSTRONG: What are you going to do ...?

TEMPLE: (*With grim determination*) Now, Mr Armstrong, I want to know about the glasses.

ARMSTRONG: What ... do ... you mean?

TEMPLE: You know what I mean! Why did Mr Constantine offer me £10,000 for them?

ARMSTRONG: I ... don't ... know ...

TEMPLE: Why is our charming little friend down here so determined to get possession of them?

ARMSTRONG: I don't know! I tell you, I don't know!

TEMPLE: Look, I'm beginning to get irritated. I want to know about those glasses ...

ARMSTRONG: There's nothing I can tell you about them, absolutely nothing, other than the fact that ...

TEMPLE: Go on ...

A moment.

ARMSTRONG: The first time I met Marquand was six weeks ago – in Cairo. He told me that a friend of his – a man called Richard Sullivan – had lost a pair of horn-rimmed spectacles and that he, Marquand, was prepared to pay four thousand pounds for them. At first I thought the man was crazy and the whole business was a sort of practical joke. Later, however, he paid me

	two thousand pounds in advance and commissioned me to find the glasses.
TEMPLE:	Did you ever meet this friend of Marquand's, this Richard Sullivan?
ARMSTRONG:	(*After a moment*) No.
TEMPLE:	What were you doing in Bournemouth?
ARMSTRONG:	I went to Bournemouth to interview Joyce Raymond.
TEMPLE:	Did you? That's very interesting. When I interviewed Miss Raymond – or rather when she interviewed me – it was in London. Then for some reason or other she took it into her head to dash down to Bournemouth. Why, I wonder? (*Pause*) Incidentally, who told you about Joyce Raymond in the first place?
ARMSTRONG:	Marquand did. He said she might have information about the spectacles.
TEMPLE:	Did you see Miss Raymond in Bournemouth? … Well, did you?
ARMSTRONG:	No.
TEMPLE:	(*Watching ARMSTRONG*) You know what happened to her.
ARMSTRONG:	(*Worried*) Yes, I read about it … It was … most unfortunate.
TEMPLE:	(*Quietly*) Most unfortunate …
ARMSTRONG:	Why are you looking at me like that?
TEMPLE:	(*Slowly*) Did you murder Joyce Raymond?
ARMSTRONG:	No! No! I swear I didn't!
A pause.	
TEMPLE:	That place that Constantine mentioned. The El Passaro. What is it?
ARMSTRONG:	It's a café.
TEMPLE:	Where?

ARMSTRONG:	(*After a moment*) In Syracuse.

MARQUAND stirs and groans.

ARMSTRONG:	He's coming round …
MARQUAND:	Gee, I … I … Gosh, my head! What happened? What hit me?
TEMPLE:	He's all yours, Mr Armstrong. Give the gentleman a glass of port.

FADE UP of music.

FADE DOWN of music.

SCENE 3:	The Villa Negara Drive.
STEVE:	Paul! Paul!
TEMPLE:	(*Off*) Where are you, Steve?
STEVE:	I'm over here – near the tree!
TEMPLE:	(*Seeing her*) Oh!

TEMPLE joins STEVE.

STEVE:	Are you all right, darling?
TEMPLE:	Yes.
STEVE:	I was beginning to get worried. What happened?
TEMPLE:	I'll tell you later, Steve. Have you got the glasses?
STEVE:	Why yes!
TEMPLE:	Give them to me.
STEVE:	It's all right, Paul, I can take care of them.
TEMPLE:	Give them to me.

STEVE passes the glasses over.

TEMPLE:	Thanks. Now what happened, after I left you?
STEVE:	Well, that rather bad-tempered little man servant …
TEMPLE:	Yes?
STEVE:	He carried the other man – the man that was shot – down that path.

TEMPLE: Which path?

STEVE: That one – the one over there.

TEMPLE: (*Nodding*) Go on.

STEVE: I followed him part of the way. The path leads down to a private beach: there's a boat house at the bottom. I stood watching him for a little while. It was getting dark though and I couldn't see very well.

TEMPLE: What was he doing?

STEVE: I think he was trying to put the man that was shot into a boat. After a little while I felt frightened and ran back to the gate.

TEMPLE: How far down is the boat house?

STEVE: Oh, about three hundred yards.

TEMPLE: I've got to report this business, Steve, but the trouble is if I don't produce the body nobody's likely to believe my story.

STEVE: All right, let's go down to the beach and have a look round.

TEMPLE: (*Intimately*) Good girl.

STEVE: You can tell me what happened in the house on the way down.

SCENE 4: On the path down to the boathouse.

We hear the sea getting nearer as TEMPLE and STEVE walk down the path.

TEMPLE: … of course, it's pretty obvious from his telephone call what Constantine's trying to do. He's obviously going to try and sell Marquand another pair of spectacles.

STEVE: Yes. I wonder if Marquand knows the real spectacles when he sees them? You know, there must be something pretty big behind all this, darling. After all, Constantine offered you

	£10,000 for them and he must think that Marquand's prepared to bid even higher.
TEMPLE:	Yes.
STEVE:	Did you ask him about the glasses?
TEMPLE:	No. As soon as he started to come round I made a dash for it. Frankly he's not exactly the sort of man you want to take a chance on.
STEVE:	He looked a pretty tough customer.
TEMPLE:	He's tough all right.
STEVE:	How does Armstrong fit into it all?
TEMPLE:	Armstrong says he knew nothing about the glasses but simply followed out Marquand's instructions. Frankly, I think he's telling the truth. I've got a hunch that Thompson, the fellow that was murdered, was in more or less the same position. (*Thoughtfully*) You know, something frightened Thompson. Something I said to him over the telephone when he was preparing to be Richard Sullivan. I'm pretty sure that's how the row started and why Marquand went for him.
STEVE:	Well, you hinted that something had happened to Joyce Raymond. If he didn't know that Joyce had been murdered ...
TEMPLE:	Then he might have jumped to conclusions about the murder and picked a row with Armstrong? Yes. Yes, that's quite possible, Steve.
STEVE:	Be careful here, darling – there's a turning ...

They walk a few steps further, then stop.

| STEVE: | There's the beach, down there ... |

The sea is quite close now.

| TEMPLE: | Where's the boat house? Oh, I see it ... (*Peering ahead*) It looks rather a tricky sort of path ... Give me your hand ... |

They start to move down the path.

TEMPLE: … Do you think you can manage it all right?

STEVE: Yes … Yes … I think so.

TEMPLE: Watch your step!

STEVE: It's … all right …

TEMPLE: Be careful, darling …

TEMPLE and STEVE continue down the path towards the beach.

STEVE: It's not so bad here.

TEMPLE: No … Keep hold of my hand … Steady!

A few more steps, then STEVE stops.

Down on the beach, EMILE the Italian servant can be heard. He is dazed, partly unconscious. He is just coming round after having been knocked out.

STEVE: (*Very quietly*) Paul …

TEMPLE: What is it?

STEVE: Listen …

A moment as TEMPLE listens.

TEMPLE: … That's coming from the beach. There must be someone down there … Yes! There's someone at the bottom of the path! Look, Steve!

STEVE: Who is it?

TEMPLE: Come on – we'll soon see!

TEMPLE and STEVE hurry down the path.

SCENE 5:   The Beach

On the beach at the end of the path, EMILE is lying groaning as the TEMPLES approach.

TEMPLE: Hold the torch!

STEVE: Who is it?

TEMPLE: It's that Italian fellow, the servant. The man that brought Thompson down here.

STEVE: But what's happened to him?

TEMPLE: He's been knocked out by someone! Hold the torch up.

STEVE: Look at his head …

TEMPLE: He's only been stunned. He'll be alright in an hour or so.

STEVE: Paul, what do you think happened?

TEMPLE: I don't know … He must have been on his way back to the house … Someone must have crept up behind him and taken him by surprise … Anyway, let's have a look at the boathouse.

STEVE: If he was on his way back to the villa, Paul, then he must have already disposed of the body – of Thompson, I mean.

TEMPLE: (*Thoughtfully*) Yes, unless of course … Let's have a look round, darling.

STEVE: But Paul, ought we to leave this man like this?

TEMPLE: There's nothing we can do for him. He'll be all right. Come on, Steve, give me your hand.

FADE UP of music.

FADE DOWN of music.

SCENE 6: Outside the Boathouse

TEMPLE: It's rather a luxurious sort of boathouse … Where's the door?

STEVE: There it is.

TEMPLE: Oh, yes … Don't make any more noise than you can help.

STEVE: Yes, all right …

TEMPLE and STEVE ascend the wooden steps to the door of the boathouse. TEMPLE tries the door.

TEMPLE: The door's locked.

STEVE: Are you sure?

TEMPLE tries the door again.

TEMPLE: Yes.

STEVE: Is there a keyhole?

TEMPLE: (*A little laugh*) Of course there's a keyhole, darling … The door is locked!
STEVE: Yes, I know! But can you see through it?
TEMPLE: (*After a moment*) No, it's far too dark. Wait a minute, though … I've got some keys here somewhere … (*He takes keys from his pocket*) … Ah, here we are … (*He tries a key*) Mm, that's not much good, I'm afraid. Wait a minute though, I think I've got one here that … (*He tries a second key*) That's it!

The lock turns.

TEMPLE: Yes …

TEMPLE opens the door.

TEMPLE: … Keep behind me darling, just in case.
STEVE: (*Soft whisper*) Here's the torch.
TEMPLE: Thanks.

TEMPLE and STEVE enter the boathouse.

STEVE: The place seems deserted, there isn't – Paul! There's Thompson! Look – in the corner!
TEMPLE: (*Moving to the body*) Yes, I see him.
STEVE: That man must have just brought him down here and dumped … Paul, what is it?
TEMPLE: This isn't Thompson. It's Mr Constantine. Don't come too near, darling …
STEVE: What's happened to him?
TEMPLE: He's been stabbed. Hold the torch.
STEVE: Is he … dead?
TEMPLE: (*A moment*) Yes.
STEVE: … How long has he been dead, do you know?
TEMPLE: It's difficult to tell. But he's certainly been dead an hour or so, perhaps even longer.
STEVE: But he can't have been, Paul!
TEMPLE: Why, what are you thinking of? That telephone call to Marquand?

STEVE: Yes.

TEMPLE: (*Shaking his head*) That can't have been
            Constantine. It can't possibly have been
            Constantine!

STEVE: Then who was it?

TEMPLE: I wish I knew.

STEVE: Paul, what are we going to do? You'll have to
            contact the police.

TEMPLE: (*Thoughtfully: determined manner*) Whoever
            made that telephone call is at the Passaro café
            waiting for Marquand.

STEVE: Where is this place – in Augusta?

TEMPLE: No, it's in Syracuse, about twelve miles away.
            (*Suddenly*) We'll go back to the hotel and I'll
            phone the police from there … (*He hesitates*)

STEVE: Then what?

TEMPLE: Then we'll go to the El Passaro. I'm rather
            anxious to take a look at this gentleman who
            claims to be Mr Constantine.

FADE UP of music.

FADE DOWN of music.

SCENE 7:   The Lobby of the TEMPLES' Hotel

Guests come and go in the background.

TEMPLE: (*An urgent manner*) You wait here, Steve – I'll
            go up to the room and telephone.

STEVE: Yes, all right.

TEMPLE: Oh, you might try and find out how far this El
            Passaro place really is. If it's very far, do your
            best to get hold of a car – or a buggy. (*Going*) I
            shan't be long …

STEVE: All right, darling.

TEMPLE: (*Almost bumping into MISS FRASER*) Oh, hello,
            Miss Fraser!

85

FRASER: (*Pleasantly*) Hello, Mr Temple! You appear to be
            in rather a hurry!

TEMPLE: Yes, I'm afraid I am!

FRASER: Well, you know what they say, more hurry less –
            (*She loses her grip on her handbag*) – Oh!

STEVE: Your bag, Miss Fraser!

The handbag falls to the ground, the contents scatter.
TEMPLE moves to pick them up.

FRASER: T't – I don't know why it is but I always seem to
            be dropping my bag these days! I just can't …
            Oh, don't bother, Mr Temple! Really, it's quite
            all right …

TEMPLE: Oh, that's all right, Miss Fraser. Here's your
            handkerchief … and your comb …

FRASER: Oh, thank you …

TEMPLE: And your powder compact.

FRASER: Oh, thank you, I … Oh, please, Mrs Temple!
            Please! Please, don't bother …

STEVE: (*Laughing*) Here's your purse.

FRASER: Really, it makes me feel quite helpless! You'll
            hardly believe it, but do you know that's the third
            time I've dropped my bag in the last twenty-four
            hours. If it happens again I swear I'll throw the
            blessed –

TEMPLE: Look out!

FRASER: (*Clutching her handbag*) Oh! Oh! God bless my
            soul, I nearly dropped the blessed thing again!
            Whatever's the matter with you, woman! You're
            a bag of nerves!

TEMPLE and STEVE laugh.

TEMPLE: Are you just going to have dinner, Miss Fraser?

FRASER: Me? No. No, I'm just going upstairs to change.
            Believe it or not, I've got a date!

STEVE: (*Laughing*) A date? That's quick work!

FRASER: Yes … There's life in the old girl yet!
TEMPLE: (*Amused*) See you later, Steve!
STEVE: Yes. All right!
FRASER: Goodnight, Mrs Temple!
STEVE: Goodnight, Miss Fraser.

SCENE 8:   In the Street Outside the Hotel
A horse and buggy draws up. The DRIVER is French and droll.
STEVE: Are you engaged?
DRIVER: Where do you want to go?
STEVE: We want to go to the El Passaro.
DRIVER: We?
STEVE: My husband and I. He'll be out in a moment.
DRIVER: El Passaro? (*He shrugs*) It's a long way. Cost a lot of money.
STEVE: Well, how much money?
DRIVER: Don't know. (*He shrugs again*) Just cost a lot of money.
STEVE: Well, how much?
DRIVER: (*Blandly*) How much you got?
STEVE: Now listen to me, Gordon Richards …
DRIVER: No, Pascall … Georges Pascall.
STEVE: Well, listen to me, Mr Pascall …
DRIVER: Count Pascall, if you please!
STEVE: (*Nonplussed*) <u>Count</u> Pascall … Are you really a Count?
DRIVER: (*Whispering back at STEVE*) Yes.
STEVE: Well, I'm a Duchess. Drive us to the El Passaro!
FADE UP of music.

FADE DOWN of music.

SCENE 9:   In the Horse and Buggy, trotting along.

STEVE: We seem to have been travelling for hours, Paul.

TEMPLE: Yes, I'll have a word with the driver. (*Raising his voice*) I say!

DRIVER: (*Turning*) Monsieur?

TEMPLE: How much further have we got to go?

DRIVER: To the top of the hill, monsieur, then you will see the El Passaro.

STEVE: What sort of a place is it?

DRIVER: Pardon, mademoiselle?

STEVE: (*To TEMPLE: aside*) I say, I like that mademoiselle touch.

TEMPLE: My wife says, what sort of a place is it?

DRIVER: You have not been there before? It is very nice. Everybody goes to the El Passaro at this time of the year.

TEMPLE: Who runs the place, do you know?

DRIVER: (*Puzzled*) Runs the … Oh, the owner! It is a man called Schreider. He is a very clever young man. He has a café in Naples, a café in Palermo, a café in Brindisi, cafés all over the place!

TEMPLE: He sounds a very clever young man.

The buggy trots on.

STEVE: You haven't told me what the police said.

TEMPLE: I was rather lucky, I got hold of a man called Rossetti. Apart from speaking pretty good English he seemed a very sensible sort of fellow. He apparently met Sir Graham about two or three years ago, so that was a great help.

STEVE: Did you tell him about the glasses?

TEMPLE:	I told him part of the story. The local people have apparently had their eye on Marquand for some time.
STEVE:	Well, what's happening? Are you meeting this man Rossetti?
TEMPLE:	Yes, I've arranged to see him at the El Passaro.
DRIVER:	Pardon, monsieur!
TEMPLE:	(*Raising his voice*) Yes, what is it?
DRIVER:	There is El Passaro, monsieur – at the top of the hill.
STEVE:	Oh, yes! It looks rather nice.
DRIVER:	We shall be there in a few moments, mademoiselle.

SCENE 10: The El Passaro Café

A band plays for a very gay crowd of people.

WAITER 1:	Buena sera, Signore … Signora.
TEMPLE:	We'd like a table for two, if you please.
WAITER 1:	You have reserved a table, signor?
TEMPLE:	No, I'm afraid we haven't.

The music finishes: it is followed by applause and laughter.

WAITER 1:	Tt – Tt – I hate to disappoint you, signor – but we are very full, you can see for yourself.

SCHREIDER approaches. He is Swiss, about thirty-five.

SCHREIDER:	(*Pleasantly*) What seems to be the trouble, Charles?
WAITER 1:	The gentleman wishes a table for two, Herr Schreider. It is impossible.
SCHREIDER:	Nothing is impossible at the El Passaro – I have told you that before. (*To TEMPLE*) If you will wait a few moments, sir, I will see what I can do.
TEMPLE:	Thank you. That's very kind of you.

The band starts to play again.

STEVE: There is someone waving at us. That man over there.

TEMPLE: Where?

STEVE: It's Mr Darwin.

TEMPLE: So it is!

STEVE: He's coming over.

DARWIN arrives.

DARWIN: (*Pleasantly*) Well, hello! Fancy bumping into you two again!

TEMPLE: Hello, Darwin!

DARWIN: What are you doing – waiting for a table?

TEMPLE: Yes, as a matter of fact we are.

DARWIN: Well, join me – I'd be delighted.

TEMPLE: Are you alone?

DARWIN: At the moment, yes. I am expecting a guest – but that's all right.

TEMPLE: It's awfully nice of you.

DARWIN: Don't be silly, old boy! Delighted. Come along, Mrs Temple.

They move over to DARWIN's table.

DARWIN: Bring another chair, waiter.

WAITER 2: Si, signore.

DARWIN pulls out a chair for STEVE.

DARWIN: Mrs Temple.

STEVE: (*Sitting*) Thank you.

DARWIN and TEMPLE sit.

DARWIN: Well, this is a pleasant surprise!

STEVE: I hope we haven't butted in on a party or anything?

DARWIN: Nonsense! Of course you haven't!

TEMPLE: Cigarette?

DARWIN: Oh, thanks, old boy. (*He takes one and lights it*) Have you been here before?

TEMPLE: To Syracuse?

DARWIN: No, I mean here … to the El Passaro?

TEMPLE: No, I'm afraid I haven't.

DARWIN: A chap told me about it in Paris, oh, ages ago. Smashing place, he said. Absolutely smashing. By George. He's right!

STEVE: (*Laughing*) It's certainly very gay!

DARWIN: He's a very bright lad, you know – this fellow Schreider, I mean. He's got cafés dotted all over the place.

TEMPLE: So I believe.

A moment.

DARWIN: (*Casually*) What time is it?

TEMPLE: It's just a quarter past nine.

DARWIN: Oh …

TEMPLE: Is your … friend late?

DARWIN: Yes, I'm rather afraid … Ah! Here we are! At last!

MISS FRASER arrives.

FRASER: I'm so sorry I'm late, Mr Darwin … Why, good evening, Mrs Temple! Mr Temple. This is a pleasant surprise!

TEMPLE and STEVE are slightly taken aback.

STEVE: Good evening.

TEMPLE: Good evening, Miss Fraser. So … this is your date …

FADE UP of music.

END OF EPISODE THREE

EPISODE FOUR

CAIRO

ANNOUNCER: Just before leaving for Egypt, Paul Temple receives a visit from a Miss Joyce Raymond who asks Temple to deliver a pair of spectacles to a friend of hers in Cairo called Richard Sullivan. Two days later Temple and Steve arrive at Poole, and – together with Harold Darwin, an acquaintance of theirs – proceed out to the B.O.A.C. flying boat. On board they meet a Scots lady, Miss Fraser. Shortly before arriving at Augusta – which is the overnight stopping place – a passenger introduces himself to Temple as Mr Constantine. Constantine offers Temple £10,000 for the spectacles. Temple treats the offer as a joke. When he arrives at Augusta, he receives a phone call from a man claiming to be Richard Sullivan. The man is an imposter. Later the same night, Temple and Steve visit the El Passaro, a famous café owned by a man called Olaf Schreider. Harold Darwin is at the café and invites Temple and Steve to his table.

SCENE 1: The Café El Passaro
As in the final scene of Episode 3:
A band plays to a very gay crowd of people.

DARWIN: Well, this is a pleasant surprise!
STEVE: I hope we haven't butted in on a party or anything?
DARWIN: Nonsense! Of course you haven't!
TEMPLE: Cigarette?
DARWIN: Oh, thanks, old boy. (*He takes one and lights it*) Have you been here before?
TEMPLE: To Syracuse?

DARWIN: No, I mean here … to the El Passaro?
TEMPLE: No, I'm afraid I haven't.
DARWIN: A chap told me about it in Paris, oh, ages ago.
             Smashing place, he said. Absolutely
             smashing. By George. He's right!
STEVE: (*Laughing*) It's certainly very gay!
DARWIN: He's a very bright lad, you know – this fellow
             Schreider, I mean. He's got cafés dotted all
             over the place.
TEMPLE: So I believe.
A moment.
DARWIN: (*Casually*) What time is it?
TEMPLE: It's just a quarter past nine.
DARWIN: Oh …
TEMPLE: Is your … friend late?
DARWIN: Yes, I'm rather afraid … Ah! Here we are! At
             last!
MISS FRASER arrives.
FRASER: I'm so sorry I'm late, Mr Darwin … Why,
             good evening, Mrs Temple! Mr Temple. This
             is a pleasant surprise!
TEMPLE and STEVE are slightly taken aback.
STEVE: Good evening.
TEMPLE: Good evening, Miss Fraser. So … this is your
             date …
FRASER: Yes.
STEVE: How do you feel after the journey?
FRASER: Oh, I feel fine! I wouldn't have missed it for
             the world!
DARWIN: Do sit down here …
FRASER: (*Sitting*) Thank you. I'm quite looking
             forward to tomorrow morning you know and
             the rest of the trip. Now where did I put my

	handbag, I'm always losing it … Oh, here it is.
DARWIN:	Miss Fraser and I have discovered that we have a great deal in common. Haven't we, Miss Fraser?
FRASER:	I should say so! Mr Darwin's a great friend of my brother's. They've met several times, isn't that so?
DARWIN:	Yes, rather! Several times. Awfully nice chap. (*To TEMPLE*) We do a lot of work for the T.E.O.C. people you know. I think I mentioned it to you.
TEMPLE:	Oh, yes.
DARWIN:	(*Significantly*) Miss Fraser's brother has a very important position with the T.E.O.C.
TEMPLE:	Really?
DARWIN:	(*A little laugh*) Yes … (*Quickly*) Well, what would you like, Miss Fraser?
WAITER:	The menu, signore.
FRASER:	Oh, thank you. Have you ordered?
DARWIN:	No, as a matter of fact we haven't. What do you feel like? Mrs Temple?
WAITER:	(*To TEMPLE*) Excuse me, sir?
TEMPLE:	Yes?
WAITER:	Herr Schreider would like to see you if you can spare a few moments.
TEMPLE:	(*A moment's hesitation*) Yes, certainly! (*He rises*) Excuse me.
DARWIN:	Well, to start with, I think it would be an awfully good idea if we ordered a bottle or two of …

Mix to another part of the café.

| TEMPLE: | Herr Schreider? |

SCHREIDER: (*Politely*) Yes? Oh, of course, you are Mr
             Temple?
TEMPLE: Yes.
SCHREIDER: There's a gentleman to see you from the
             police – Signore Rossetti. He is in my office.
             Would you come this way, please?
TEMPLE: (*Quietly, detaining SCHREIDER*) Herr
             Schreider ...
SCHREIDER: Yes?
TEMPLE: Do you happen to know a gentleman – I think
             a patron of yours – by the name of
             Constantine?
SCHREIDER: Constantine? No, I can't say I do.
TEMPLE: I believe he's here – in the café – this evening
             ... Could you contact him for me?
SCHREIDER: If he is here, but of course. Certainly.
TEMPLE: Thank you.
SCHREIDER: This way, please ...

SCENE 2:   SCHREIDER's Office
The door opens and SCHREIDER shows TEMPLE in.
ROSSETTI is a brisk, dapper little man.
SCHREIDER: Mr Temple ...
ROSSETTI: (*Nodding: briskly*) Thank you, signore. Now,
             if you will be so kind as to leave us for a
             moment ... Thank you.
SCHREIDER leaves and closes the door.
ROSSETTI: Mr Temple?
TEMPLE: Yes.
ROSSETTI: My name is Rossetti, we spoke over the
             telephone about an hour ago. Would you sit
             down, please?
TEMPLE sits.

98

ROSSETTI: (*Pleasantly*) It is an honour to make your acquaintance, signore. By sheer coincidence I have only just finished reading one of your novels, Crime à La Villa Espana. (*Amused*) It was most engrossing, if a little … far-fetched.

TEMPLE and ROSSETTI laugh.

ROSSETTI: However, let us get to business. (*In an official manner*) After you telephoned, my men visited the Villa Negara. There was no trace of the man Thompson. We did however, as you said, find the body of a Mr Constantine in the cabin.

TEMPLE: And Colonel Marquand?

ROSSETTI: There was, I regret to say, no sign of Colonel Marquand or his colleague Mr Armstrong. But, please. First, let me hear your side of the story.

TEMPLE: A young woman called Joyce Raymond asked me to deliver a pair of spectacles to a friend of hers in Cairo called Richard Sullivan. Shortly after she gave me the spectacles Miss Raymond was murdered. This morning, coming out here on the plane, a man called Constantine offered me £10,000 for the spectacles. I refused, but when I arrived at Augusta I received a phone call from a man claiming to be Richard Sullivan – he said he was staying with a Colonel Marquand. When my wife and I turned up at the Villa Negara, this man – who incidentally was called Thompson – was attempting to escape from the villa. He did escape but was unfortunately shot. I went back to the house with Colonel Marquand and he tried to pass off his friend

99

Armstrong as Richard Sullivan. When he realised the game was up he got tough with me and was about to get really nasty when he received a phone called from Mr Constantine. Mr Constantine said he had the glasses and would be willing to do a deal with Marquand if he would meet him here – tonight – at the El Passaro.

ROSSETTI: (*Surprised*) But it could not have been Constantine because …

TEMPLE: Because Constantine was already dead – exactly!

ROSSETTI: M'm. We've been watching this fellow Marquand for some little time. Frankly, we don't know what he's up to. He took a short lease on the Villa Negara just before Christmas of last year. The other man – Armstrong – what is he like?

TEMPLE: He's about medium height. Well dressed. Sandy coloured hair. I noticed he was wearing a signet ring on the little finger of his left hand.

ROSSETTI: M'm.

There is a knock and the door opens.

SCHREIDER: I beg your pardon, Signore Rossetti, but …

ROSSETTI: Please! Please! Come in, Schreider …

SCHREIDER: I have made enquiries about the gentleman you asked me about, Mr Temple – Mr Constantine.

TEMPLE: Well?

SCHREIDER: He is not in the café, sir.

TEMPLE: You're sure?

SCHREIDER: Quite sure, sir. (*A shrug*) Whether he has been here earlier this evening I do not know.

100

ROSSETTI: Is this Mr Constantine an habitué of the El Passaro?

SCHREIDER: The name is quite unknown to me, signore. Quite unknown.

ROSSETTI: M'm. Herr Schreider, tell me: is it not true that you are a friend of Colonel Marquand?

SCHREIDER: Well, hardly a friend, signore. An acquaintance, perhaps.

ROSSETTI: But you have, on occasion, visited the Villa Negara?

SCHREIDER: On two occasions, signore – that is all.

ROSSETTI: Well, perhaps you will be kind enough to bear in mind, Herr Schreider, that Colonel Marquand is wanted by the poliziotto.

SCHREIDER: By the poliziotto?

ROSSETTI: For questioning – that is all. Should he visit the El Passaro, however …

SCHREIDER: You will be informed instantly, signore!

ROSSETTI: (*Dismissing SCHREIDER*) Thank you, Herr Schreider.

SCHREIDER: Thank you, signore.

SCHREIDER leaves and closes the door.

TEMPLE: I gather he's quite a shrewd young man?

ROSSETTI: (*A moment*) Herr Schreider?

TEMPLE: Yes.

ROSSETTI: They tell me he's very shrewd. (*A complete change of conversation*) When are you leaving us, Mr Temple?

TEMPLE: Tomorrow morning.

ROSSETTI: For Cairo?

TEMPLE: Yes.

ROSSETTI: And are you staying in Cairo for very long?

TEMPLE: It's difficult to say. A fortnight, three weeks, perhaps even longer.

ROSSETTI: Where are you staying?

TEMPLE: You can get in touch with me at the Hotel Continental.

ROSSETTI: Thank you, signore. Oh – one little point …

TEMPLE: Yes?

ROSSETTI: (*Smiling*) Just out of curiosity, signore – Have you got the glasses on you – could I, perhaps, examine them?

A tiny pause.

TEMPLE: Yes, certainly.

TEMPLE takes out the glasses and passes them over to ROSSETTI.

ROSSETTI: Thank you.

A pause.

TEMPLE: Well?

ROSSETTI: (*Simply, yet perplexed*) They appear to be a perfectly ordinary pair of spectacles. It is most odd. (*Returning the glasses*) Here you are, signore.

TEMPLE: Thank you.

ROSSETTI: I hope that you will have a very pleasant journey tomorrow.

TEMPLE: Thank you. (*An afterthought*) I hope so too.

FADE UP of music.

FADE DOWN of music.

SCENE 3: The Flying Boat Cabin

The aircraft is at cruising height.

FRASER: (*Quite excited*) Look, Mrs Temple! Look! We're just passing over the coast!

STEVE: Oh, yes …

TEMPLE: How far are we from Cairo now, Darwin?

DARWIN: About forty-five, fifty minutes, that's all.

FRASER: I suppose we're not very far from El Alamein?

DARWIN: No … there's the road … you can see it.

TEMPLE: Is that the famous road – the one they took the supplies along?

DARWIN: Yes, that's it.

FRASER: (*Casually: aside*) Would you care for a peppermint, Mrs Temple?

STEVE: No, thank you.

DARWIN: It's pretty dull for the next fifteen minutes or so, I'm afraid. Would you like a cigarette?

TEMPLE: Oh, thanks.

FADE UP noise of the aircraft engines.

Time passes.

Then hold the engines under again.

STEVE: What are those small squares … down there, darling?

TEMPLE: (*Yawning*) I don't know …

DARWIN: It's just farmland, Mrs Temple. You know, strips that have been cultivated.

STEVE: I don't see the Nile …

TEMPLE: (*Sleepily*) What's that?

STEVE: I said: I don't see the Nile …

TEMPLE: I don't see it either …

STEVE: You're not looking, you silly chump!

They all laugh.

DARWIN: As a matter of fact, it's awfully difficult to pick it out.

FRASER: (*Peering*) You can see the villages very clearly, it's extraordinary how they stand out!

DARWIN: Yes.

Pause.

TEMPLE: (*Taking more interest*) That road we passed over … the long, straight macadam road … was that the road from Alexandria?

DARWIN: Yes. You probably noticed the aerodromes; relics of the war.

TEMPLE: No, I'm afraid I didn't.

DARWIN: One of them was Cairo West or ... Now what was it?

FRASER: L.G. 224.

DARWIN: (*Surprised*) Yes, that's right, Miss Fraser ... L.G. 224. Used to be pretty well known to Transport Command passengers.

A pause.

FRASER: It's getting a wee bit bumpy!

TEMPLE: Yes, we're not quite so high.

Bring up the noise of the aircraft engines.

More time passes.

Hold the engines under again.

STEVE: I'm beginning to feel quite excited!

TEMPLE: We can't be far from Cairo, now –

FRASER: (*Interrupting*) Look! There's a light over the door ... the panel's lit up ... What does it say?

DARWIN: Oh – no smoking ... Fasten your safety belts.

General conversation from other passengers.

STEWARD: (*Off*) Fasten your safety belts, please! Let me help you, madam ... (*Coming nearer*) Fasten your belts, please. Fasten your safety belts, please. (*Raising his voice*) Ladies and gentlemen, I have been informed by the captain that we are a few minutes ahead of schedule and that he is making a wide approach to Cairo. If you look out from the port side you'll see the pyramids. Fasten your safety belt, please, sir ...

FRASER: I don't see any signs of the pyramids, steward.

DARWIN:	There they are, Miss Fraser … Look!
STEVE:	I see them!
FRASER:	Oh! Good gracious me, yes!
STEVE:	Is that the Sphinx?
TEMPLE:	Where?
DARWIN:	Yes, that's it … It looks very small I'm afraid, from here.

The aircraft has descended to a much lower altitude: bumps can now be felt.

TEMPLE:	There's Cairo!
DARWIN:	There's the Nile, Mrs Temple!
STEVE:	Are we going to land on that?
DARWIN:	I'm afraid we are!
TEMPLE:	Look, darling, it runs right through the city …

The aircraft is rapidly descending: flaps coming out from the wings.

STEVE:	Paul, look! Look! What is that place? It looks exactly like a palace!
DARWIN:	(*Laughing*) It is a palace!

General background of conversation.

PASSENGER 1:	There's the golf course, dear – do you see it?
PASSENGER 2:	That's a little island – see the swimming pool?
PASSENGER 3:	Don't the buildings seem tall …
PASSENGER 4:	It's not a bit like I expected, not a bit …
STEVE:	What's that place, Mr Darwin?
DARWIN:	It's a mosque.
STEVE:	Oh.
TEMPLE:	See the race course …

The aircraft is descending rapidly towards the river.

STEVE:	Look at that bridge, Paul!
DARWIN:	We'll be on the water in a minute!

FRASER: I should say so, we're almost level with the
             banks of the river now.
The aircraft lands on the water.
TEMPLE: There we are …
DARWIN: We're on the water …
TEMPLE: Well, here we are, darling … at last.
STEVE: Cairo …
FADE UP of music.

FADE DOWN of music.
SCENE 4:   Cairo: The Temples' Sitting Room in the
             Hotel Continental
TEMPLE is on the telephone.
TEMPLE: Hello? Who is that, please?
OPERATOR: (*On the other end of the line*) This is Cairo
             78926 – Trans Eurasian Oil Company.
TEMPLE: Could I speak to Mr Sullivan, please?
OPERATOR: Who is calling?
TEMPLE: My name is Temple.
OPERATOR: Hold the line please …
A moment.
STEVE: What's happening?
TEMPLE: I think she's putting me through.
OPERATOR: Hello? (*Puzzled*) Who are you calling?
TEMPLE: Mr Sullivan. Mr Richard Sullivan.
OPERATOR: One moment …
*The line is switched through to an extension. We hear the
receiver lifted and a man's voice, away from the phone
saying:*
SULLIVAN: If the Detroit people get difficult I shall turn
             the whole thing over to MacFarlane.
*Faintly irritated, SULLIVAN now gives his attention to the
phone.*
SULLIVAN: Hello?

106

TEMPLE:	Mr Sullivan?
SULLIVAN:	Yes.
TEMPLE:	Is that Mr Sullivan speaking personally?
SULLIVAN:	Yes.
TEMPLE:	(*A note of relief*) Well, this is Temple here, Paul Temple … I've got your glasses.
SULLIVAN:	(*Astonished*) My what?
TEMPLE:	Your glasses … your spectacles.
SULLIVAN:	Don't be ridiculous – I'm wearing them.
TEMPLE:	(*A moment*) That is Mr Sullivan?
SULLIVAN:	Yes, this is Sullivan.
TEMPLE:	(*A little laugh*) Well, I've got your glasses, the pair that Miss Raymond gave me.
SULLIVAN:	Miss Raymond? Who's Miss Raymond? Is this some kind of joke, old boy?
TEMPLE:	Look here, are you or are you not Richard Sullivan?
SULLIVAN:	(*Exasperated*) This is Clarence Sullivan. Extension 72. Export Department.
TEMPLE:	Oh, that explains it. I'm sorry, I'm afraid they've put me through to the wrong office.
SULLIVAN:	Well, who is it you want? I'll get you transferred.
TEMPLE:	I want Mr Richard Sullivan.
SULLIVAN:	Richard Sullivan?
TEMPLE:	Yes.
SULLIVAN:	I suppose you know that this is the Trans Eurasian Oil Company – Cairo 78926?
TEMPLE:	Yes, I know that. I want Mr Richard Sullivan.
SULLIVAN:	Well, I'm the only Sullivan here, old boy. There isn't another Sullivan, not with the T.E.O.C.
TEMPLE:	Are you sure?
SULLIVAN:	Absolutely sure.

TEMPLE:	(*A moment*) I see. (*Thoughtfully*) Well, I'm sorry you've been troubled.
SULLIVAN:	That's all right. It's made a nice break.

TEMPLE replaces the receiver.

STEVE:	Well?
TEMPLE:	There isn't a Richard Sullivan. Not with the T.E.O.C.
STEVE:	(*Quietly*) Oh. I'm not surprised.
TEMPLE:	No, neither am I.
STEVE:	I had the feeling that this would happen when he didn't meet the plane.
TEMPLE:	Yes. (*Almost to himself*) And yet, Miss Raymond said he was with the T.E.O.C. Why should she say that I wonder, unless ... (*He stops*)
STEVE:	Unless what?
TEMPLE:	... Nothing. I was just thinking. (*Suddenly*) I expect you're pretty hungry?
STEVE:	Hungry and curious, darling. I'm dying to see Cairo.
TEMPLE:	All right, let's go down and have a drink and then we'll go for a stroll.
STEVE:	Yes, all right. (*A moment*) Paul ... Are you worried about this business; about the glasses, I mean?
TEMPLE:	I think we've got to be careful.
STEVE:	(*Laughing*) In view of what's happened, that's a delightful understatement! (*Seriously*) What are you going to do with them?
TEMPLE:	I suppose the most sensible thing would be to hand them over to the police. And yet ... I'd really like to get to the bottom of this, Steve, and find out what it's all about.
STEVE:	Yes, I think I would too, darling.

TEMPLE: Let's go down and have that drink.

SCENE 5:   The Hotel Cocktail Bar.
A dance orchestra plays. People are laughing and chatting: it is a large, cosmopolitan crowd of people speaking many languages.

TEMPLE: Here's a stool, dear.
STEVE: Thanks.
BARMAN: What can I get you, sir?
TEMPLE: What would you like, Steve?
STEVE: Well, I don't know … What does one usually drink out here?
TEMPLE: You drink what you feel like. Dry Martini?
STEVE: Er – yes. I'll have a dry Martini.
TEMPLE: Dry Martini and a whisky and soda.
BARMAN: Thank you, sir.
QUINN: Could I trouble you for a light, sir?

PATRICK QUINN is an Irishman: about fifty-five. He is, as always, faintly inebriated.

TEMPLE: Certainly.

TEMPLE takes out his lighter, flicks it.

TEMPLE: Here you are …
QUINN: Ah, thank you … (*He lights his cigar*) That's very kind of you now, very kind. You know I don't think there's anything I enjoy quite so much as a good cigar … (*He puffs away*) Be'dad, I think it's going to be troublesome. Could I encroach on your kindness once again?
TEMPLE: Yes, of course.

TEMPLE flicks his lighter again.

QUINN: Thank you. (*He re-lights his cigar*) Ah, that's better … Much more satisfactory. I'm indebted to you, sir.
TEMPLE: (*Pleasantly*) That's all right.

109

The BARMAN returns.

BARMAN: Dry Martini … Whisky and soda.

TEMPLE: Thank you … keep the change.

BARMAN: (*To QUINN*) Can I get you anything, sir?

QUINN: Yes. I'd like a brandy and soda … large.

BARMAN: Yes, sir.

STEVE suddenly coughs.

QUINN: Oh, I beg your pardon, ma'am! Did the smoke from my cigar …

STEVE: No, that's quite all right.

QUINN: How very careless of me.

STEVE: It's quite all right, really.

QUINN: No, t'was careless, ma'am, and I apologise. Have you just arrived in Cairo, sir?

TEMPLE: Yes – this afternoon.

QUINN: Your first visit, ma'am?

STEVE: Yes.

QUINN: And yours, sir?

TEMPLE: No, I've been here before.

QUINN: You know it well?

TEMPLE: I wouldn't say I know it well.

QUINN: No. No, of course not! A stupid question, sir!

The BARMAN returns.

BARMAN: Brandy, sir.

QUINN: Thank you. Thank you, boy. (*Helping himself to soda*) How I envy you. How I envy you, ma'am, seeing this ancient, illustrious city for the first time.

STEVE: I must confess I'm looking forward to it.

QUINN: Show her everything, sir. The pyramids, the sphinx, the mosque at El-Hakim, the exquisite Maristan … Don't neglect your duty, show her everything. Remember, "He who hath not seen Cairo hath not seen the world: its soil is gold; its

110

Nile is a wonder; its women are like the black-eyed Virgins of Paradise". (*Raising his glass*) Your very good health, sir, and yours too, ma'am.

STEVE: Thank you.

TEMPLE: Cheers.

QUINN: Should you wish to return to the land of austerity with a small choice memento of your brief sojourn in this historic capital, may I respectfully draw your attention to the House of Bahri. From which flowery phraseology you will gather that I am nothing more nor less than a glorified tout. However, permit me to introduce myself, sir. The name is Quinn. Patrick Norman Quinn.

TEMPLE: (*Amused*) Glad to meet you, Mr Quinn. My name is Temple.

QUINN: Temple? Temple, did you say? Now that's a name that strikes a familiar note. Temple … (*Shaking his head*) It escapes me. Just for the moment the significance of the name escapes me.

TEMPLE: Who was that man you mentioned – Bahri?

QUINN: Zoltan Bahri? He's a Turk. He has a curio shop in the Avenue Shulamar. You should go there, ma'am. I'll give you the address … (*He feels in his pocket*) I have a card somewhere with the … ah! Here we are! Take it!

STEVE: (*Taking the card*) Thank you.

QUINN: Mention my name. Don't forget to mention my name. Quinn, sir. Patrick Norman Quinn.

TEMPLE: We shan't forget.

QUINN: 'Tis the commission I'm concerned with, of course – that you'll readily understand.

TEMPLE: Would you like another brandy and soda, Mr Quinn?

111

QUINN: No. No, I'll be making a move. I'm showing a party of distinguished ladies and gentlemen round the city this evening so … (*A sudden thought*) You wouldn't care to join the party, I suppose?

TEMPLE: Do you recommend it?

QUINN: Professionally, I can't speak too highly of the project. But speaking to you as a friend – privately, as you might say – I should give it a miss. It'll be as dull as dishwater and as boring as blazes.

STEVE: (*Laughing*) That's frank enough.

QUINN: You'll find me dishonest, ma'am, but strictly frank. If I can be of any service to you at any time – night or day – just speak to the concierge. He'll know where to find me.

TEMPLE: We'll bear that in mind, Mr Quinn.

QUINN: You would be well advised to, sir. (*As he leaves*) Goodnight ma'am! Goodnight, sir!

TEMPLE laughs.

STEVE: He's quite a character!

TEMPLE: Yes, but a little goes a very long way. Well, how about that stroll, darling?

STEVE: I'm ready! (*Suddenly*) Oh!

TEMPLE: What is it?

STEVE: My ring … My diamond ring … (*Annoyed with herself*) I must have left it in the bathroom!

TEMPLE: That wasn't very bright! I'll run up and get it.

STEVE: (*Quickly*) No, I'll go. I can also powder my nose. See you in the hall.

TEMPLE: Yes, all right. Have you got the key?

STEVE: Yes.

TEMPLE: Don't be long!

SCENE 6:   Hotel Corridor

STEVE, singing softly to herself, arrives at their bedroom door. She takes the key from her handbag, inserts it in the lock, turns it and opens the door. The balcony windows are open, and we hear Cairo street sounds in the background.

STEVE: ... Now where's the switch, I ... (*She stops*) Who is that? Who is it?

ARMSTRONG: (*Quickly: tensely*) Don't touch that switch. D'you hear me? Don't touch it!

STEVE: Who are you? What do you want?

ARMSTRONG: (*Drawing nearer to STEVE*) If you touch that switch, I'll ...

STEVE: Don't come near me! Do you hear what I say?! Don't you dare come near me! (*Suddenly screaming*) Help!

ARMSTRONG: (*Springing at STEVE*) Why you little – I'll ...

STEVE: (*Struggling*) Leave me alone! Take your hands off me ... Help!

ARMSTRONG: Keep your mouth shut you little fool!

STEVE: Leave me alone! Take your hands ... off ... my face ... Help! Help!

ARMSTRONG: You little vixen – I'll teach you to open your mouth and ...

STEVE: Paul! Help!

ARMSTRONG: Do you hear what I say? Keep your mouth closed or I'll ... (*A cry of pain*) Ow! My hand! You've bitten it – you little –

STEVE: (*Almost exhausted*) Help!!!

The door is thrown open. SIDNEY JEANS is a faintly masculine, but pleasant AMERICAN woman of about thirty-eight.

SIDNEY: For Pete's sake, what on earth is going on ...

113

SIDNEY stops: she switches the light on. ARMSTRONG dashes through the open windows and over the balcony and disappears. STEVE is utterly exhausted.

SIDNEY: Are you all right?

STEVE: (*Gasping for breath*) Has he gone? Has ... he ...

SIDNEY: Yes, he's gone all right ... He went through the window and over the balcony ...

STEVE: He must have come in that way ...

SIDNEY: Yes ... the four-flushing Romeo!

STEVE: Would you ... be good enough ... to ...

SIDNEY: Now just a minute! Relax! Take it easy ... Lie on the bed!

STEVE drops onto the bed. She is gradually getting her breath back.

STEVE: It's ... a good job ... you heard me ...

SIDNEY: It's a mighty good job I heard you! That wolf was just about getting into his stride!

A pause.

STEVE: I feel better now ...

SIDNEY: Good.

STEVE: Would you mind getting my husband ... He's waiting for me downstairs, near the reception desk ... the name's Temple.

SIDNEY: O.K. Will you be all right?

STEVE: Yes, I think so.

SIDNEY: I'll close the window ... (*She crosses the room and closes the window*) You know, it's a peculiar thing that nothing like this ever happens to me.

STEVE laughs.

SIDNEY: You can laugh, sister, but it's pretty serious ... (*She goes to the door*) I'll fetch that husband of yours. Oh, by the way, the name's Jeans. Sidney Jeans.

STEVE: Well, I'm very grateful to you, Miss Jeans.

SIDNEY: That's all right. You can do the same for me
            sometime – I hope.

SCENE 7:   The Same, a few minutes later
TEMPLE: Are you really all right, dear?
STEVE: Yes, quite all right, darling.
SIDNEY: If there's anything I can do just let me know.
TEMPLE: You've been awfully kind, Miss Jeans, we're
            very grateful.
SIDNEY: Think nothing of it. It was just the old routine so
            far as I was concerned. Although, come to think
            of it, I don't think I've scared 'em away quite so
            fast before!

They laugh.

TEMPLE: We're going for a stroll, and then we shall have a
            spot of dinner. Would you like to join us?
SIDNEY: That's very sweet of you: but actually I've got a
            date.
STEVE: Secretly, I bet you just string 'em along!
SIDNEY: The female Rasputin, that's me. After all, what's
            Barbara Stanwyck got that I haven't got? And
            don't say Robert Taylor! I'm right next door if
            you want me any time. Don't knock, just walk
            straight in.
TEMPLE: O.K.
SIDNEY: See you later!

The door opens and closes as SIDNEY leaves.

TEMPLE: Here's your ring. It was in the bathroom.
STEVE: Oh, thanks.
TEMPLE: Do you feel like going out or …
STEVE: Yes, I'm all right now.
TEMPLE: Sure?
STEVE: Sure …

A slight pause.

115

TEMPLE: (*Quietly, as if not wishing to speak of the matter*)
           What happened?
STEVE: He was searching the room. I disturbed him …
TEMPLE: (*A moment*) Did you recognise him?
STEVE: Yes. It was the man we saw in Bournemouth.
           The man you met at Augusta with Colonel
           Marquand.
TEMPLE: (*Faintly surprised*) Armstrong?
STEVE: Yes.
TEMPLE: Are you sure?
STEVE: Yes, Paul.

TEMPLE crosses the room to the window and opens it.

TEMPLE: Well, this is how he got in … He wouldn't have
           much difficulty with this balcony. I'll speak to
           the manager tomorrow morning – we'll change
           the room.
STEVE: (*Joining TEMPLE at the window*) It's a pity. It's
           a lovely view, darling.
TEMPLE: Yes.
STEVE: What's that place?
TEMPLE: Where?
STEVE: Over there.
TEMPLE: It's the University.

Pause.

STEVE: (*Hesitatingly*) I suppose there's no doubt about
           what he wanted!
TEMPLE: What do you think? He was after the glasses all
           right … Well, are you ready?
STEVE: Yes, I'm ready, darling.

TEMPLE closes the window.

MIX TO:

*Music – Egyptian in mood: mingled with the music is a
background of crowded streets and many voices. The music*

116

rises to a crescendo and then, together with the street noises, stops dead.

SCENE 8:   The Main Hall of the Hotel Continental
There is a background of quiet voices.

TEMPLE: Well, did you enjoy it?

STEVE: Enormously!

TEMPLE: You haven't seen anything yet!

STEVE: I don't know about that, I feel as if I've been walking for hours! My feet!

TEMPLE: Have you got the key?

STEVE: Yes.

The CLERK approaches. He is an Egyptian, about thirty.

CLERK: Excuse me, sir.

TEMPLE: Yes.

CLERK: Mr Temple?

TEMPLE: Yes.

CLERK: There is a gentleman to see you, sir. He has been waiting for some little time.

TEMPLE: To see me?

CLERK: Yes, sir. It is the Commandant from the Governorate.

TEMPLE: Where is he?

CLERK: He's in my office, sir. Will you come this way, please?

TEMPLE: Yes, certainly. (*To STEVE, as he goes*) I shan't be a moment, darling. I'll see you in the lounge.

STEVE: Yes, all right.

SCENE 9:   An Office
The door closes. HAKIM is an Egyptian: brisk and very sure of himself.

HAKIM: Mr Temple?

TEMPLE: Yes?

HAKIM: My name is Hakim. Commandant-Lewa Hakim
            from the Governorate.

TEMPLE: (*Pleasantly*) What can I do for you,
            Commandant?

HAKIM: I am making investigations concerning a man
            called Quinn – Patrick Norman Quinn. Correct
            me if I am mistaken, but he is, I believe, a friend
            of yours?

TEMPLE: I'm afraid you're very much mistaken, sir.

HAKIM: (*Annoyed*) Does that mean that he is not a friend
            of yours?

TEMPLE: It most certainly does.

HAKIM: I think perhaps that I ought to warn you that you
            were seen together, earlier this evening, drinking
            in the cocktail bar.

TEMPLE: Did you see us?

HAKIM: No. One of my men saw you.

TEMPLE: Did he? Now that's very interesting …

HAKIM: (*Sharply*) How long have you known this man?

TEMPLE: Which man?

HAKIM: (*Angrily*) Quinn! The man we're talking about.

TEMPLE: The man you're talking about, Commandant.
            However, to satisfy your curiosity, Mr Quinn
            introduced himself to me for the first time this
            evening at about a quarter to seven.

HAKIM: And he left you – ?

TEMPLE: He left us – that is, my wife and me – at about
            six or seven minutes to.

HAKIM: You have not seen him since?

TEMPLE: No. Now, why may I ask, are you asking these
            questions?

HAKIM: Don't you know why?

TEMPLE: Well, if I knew I shouldn't ask you, should I?

A moment.

118

HAKIM: Quinn was murdered.

TEMPLE: Murdered?

HAKIM: Yes.

TEMPLE: When?

HAKIM: Shortly after leaving you this evening.

TEMPLE: How … was he murdered?

HAKIM: (*Slowly: watching TEMPLE*) He was shot between the eyes … at very close quarters. It was most unfortunate – for Mr Quinn.

A pause.

TEMPLE: (*Quietly: thoughtfully*) I'm sorry. I rather liked the old boy. Still, I'm afraid there's nothing I can tell you, Commandant. Nothing you don't already know.

HAKIM: (*A moment*) Very well … Oh, I should like to see your passport.

TEMPLE takes out his passport and hands it over to HAKIM.

TEMPLE: Well – here it is.

A pause.

HAKIM: Thank you. You may go.

SCENE 10: The Main Hall of the Hotel Continental

STEVE: (*Calling*) Over here, darling!

TEMPLE: Oh, hello.

STEVE: I've ordered some coffee.

TEMPLE: (*His thoughts elsewhere*) Oh, good.

STEVE: Paul, is anything the matter?

TEMPLE: (*Quietly*) Yes. You remember that fellow we met in the cocktail bar?

STEVE: Quinn? Yes …

A pause.

TEMPLE: He's been murdered.

STEVE: Murdered? When?

TEMPLE: Shortly after he left us. Apparently he was shot …

STEVE: Oh dear – poor man. He was rather nice.

Another pause.

TEMPLE: Steve, he gave you a card, didn't he – with an address on it?

STEVE: Yes, that's right. The man with the curio shop: Avenue Shulamar. (*She opens her handbag*) Here it is …

TEMPLE: (*Reading*) "Zoltan Bahri. Art Dealer. Curios a speciality. 227, Avenue Shulamar. English Visitors Welcome."

STEVE: What are you thinking?

TEMPLE: (*Slowly*) I was just wondering if by any chance Mr Quinn – (*He stops dead*)

STEVE: What is it?

TEMPLE: Have you seen the other side of this card? Have you seen what he's drawn on the other side?

STEVE: No …

TEMPLE: Well, look!

STEVE: (*Staggered*) Why – it's a pair of spectacles!

FADE UP of music.

END OF EPISODE FOUR

EPISODE FIVE

THE HOUSE OF BAHRI

SCENE 1:   The Main Hall of the Hotel Continental.

As in Episode 4, Scene 10.

TEMPLE: (*Quietly*) Yes. You remember that fellow we met in the cocktail bar?

STEVE: Quinn? Yes …

A pause.

TEMPLE: He's been murdered.

STEVE: Murdered? When?

TEMPLE: Shortly after he left us. Apparently he was shot …

STEVE: Oh dear – poor man. He was rather nice.

Another pause.

TEMPLE: Steve, he gave you a card, didn't he – with an address on it?

STEVE: Yes, that's right. The man with the curio shop: Avenue Shulamar. (*She opens her handbag*) Here it is …

TEMPLE: (*Reading*) "Zoltan Bahri. Art Dealer. Curios a speciality. 227, Avenue Shulamar. English Visitors Welcome."

STEVE: What are you thinking?

TEMPLE: (*Slowly*) I was just wondering if by any chance Mr Quinn – (*He stops dead*)

STEVE: What is it?

TEMPLE: Have you seen the other side of this card? Have you seen what he's drawn on the other side?

STEVE: No …

TEMPLE: Well, look!

STEVE: (*Staggered*) Why – it's a pair of spectacles!

TEMPLE: Yes.

STEVE: (*Thoughtfully*) Patrick Quinn told us to take this card to Mr Bahri, didn't he?

TEMPLE: Well?

123

STEVE: (*Still in a thoughtful mood*) I've got a hunch that Mr Quinn was waiting for us. He knew that we were staying in the hotel and that sooner or later we'd drift into the cocktail bar. I think that if you present this card to Zoltan Bahri he'll make you an offer for the spectacles.

TEMPLE: Well, I've already had one offer. Constantine offered me £10,000 for them.

STEVE: (*After a moment: quietly*) What are you going to do about the spectacles, Paul? Obviously we can't just carry them about with us …

TEMPLE: No, you're right – I'm not taking any more chances. I'm taking them down to the bank first thing tomorrow morning. They'll stay there until the real Mr Sullivan puts in an appearance.

STEVE: If there is a real Mr Sullivan.

TEMPLE: Hello? Have you changed your mind? I thought you were under the impression that Harold Darwin was Richard Sullivan?

STEVE: I don't know … sometimes I think that Richard Sullivan might be just a name. Possibly I was wrong about Darwin, and Joyce Raymond intended that we should deliver the spectacles to – well – to someone else.

TEMPLE: Someone that ought to have met us the moment we stepped off the plane?

STEVE: Yes.

TEMPLE: Yes, but what's the mystery behind these glasses? Why was Constantine willing to pay £10,000 for them – that's what I'd like to know!

STEVE: I don't care what the police say, they can't be just an ordinary pair of spectacles.

TEMPLE: Darling, they are an ordinary pair of spectacles, that's the extraordinary part about it!

124

STEVE: Well, in the first place … (*She stops*) Here's
            Miss Jeans.

SIDNEY JEANS arrives.

SIDNEY: Hello, there!

STEVE: Hello!

SIDNEY: Are you feeling any better?

STEVE: Yes, I'm all right thanks.

SIDNEY: Good.

TEMPLE: We've just ordered some coffee – would you
            care to join us?

SIDNEY: Well now, that's very sweet of you! May I?

STEVE: Yes, of course!

TEMPLE: We'd be delighted.

SIDNEY: (*Taking a seat*) Gosh, I'm tired! My feet! Holy
            smoke, are they giving me what for!

STEVE laughs.

SIDNEY: I don't know whether you find it so, but I think
            this place is pretty tiring.

STEVE: We only arrived this afternoon, so it's early
            days!

SIDNEY: Mind you, I like the place, but – gee, my dogs!

They laugh.

SIDNEY: How long are you staying?

TEMPLE: In Cairo? Oh – a fortnight or three weeks. It
            rather depends.

SIDNEY: I should think you've got a pretty awful
            impression of the place, Mrs Temple, after what
            happened this evening.

STEVE: Oh, I don't know. I suppose that sort of thing
            could happen almost anywhere.

SIDNEY: Yeah, it could, but the fact remains it happened
            here! Still I'm glad you've got over it. Have you
            changed your room yet?

125

TEMPLE: Not yet. I'll probably speak to the manager tomorrow morning.

SIDNEY: Yes, do. This place fascinated me. I came for two weeks and I've already stayed here five. The way things are going I shall probably spend the rest of my life in this crazy town.

TEMPLE: You must know Cairo pretty well, Miss Jeans. Tell me: where exactly is the Avenue Shulamar?

SIDNEY: (*After a moment: the name obviously strikes a note*) Avenue Shulamar?

TEMPLE: (*Casually*) Yes.

SIDNEY: It's – er – in the old part of the town, about three or four hundred yards from the East Wall.

TEMPLE: Oh … I think I know where you mean.

SIDNEY: Are you thinking of going there?

TEMPLE: Yes, someone recommended a shop to us. A curio shop. The House of Bahri – you've probably heard of it?

SIDNEY: No, I can't say I have. Of course, you've got to be careful around here, you know – otherwise you'll find yourself loaded down with a lot of junk that comes from good old Birmingham – and I don't mean Birmingham Alabama!

They laugh.

SIDNEY: Curios are a dime a hundredweight!

TEMPLE: Well, this place – the House of Bahri, I mean – was recommended to me by a man called Quinn. He seemed a decent sort of chap. He introduced himself to us in the cocktail bar.

SIDNEY: (*Laughing*) Yeah, well that's just the sort of thing you've got to be careful of! Quinn's all right but –

TEMPLE: (*Interrupting SIDNEY*) You know him?

SIDNEY: I've seen him around. He's an Irishman, isn't he?

126

TEMPLE: Yes.

SIDNEY: Yeah, I know the fellow you mean. Frankly, I wouldn't have too much to do with him.

TEMPLE: Well, there's no fear of that!

SIDNEY: What do you mean?

TEMPLE: Mr Quinn's dead.

SIDNEY: What do you mean?

TEMPLE: He was murdered.

A moment.

SIDNEY: (*Softly; tensely*) When?

TEMPLE: (*Watching SIDNEY*) Some time this evening.

SIDNEY: (*Quickly*) Are you sure about this? Who told you?

TEMPLE: The police.

SIDNEY: The police? What happened?

TEMPLE: (*Still watching SIDNEY*) Apparently he was shot.

SIDNEY: I can hardly believe it! I saw him earlier this evening … he was sitting at the bar … the poor little guy didn't look as if he'd got a care in the world. Shot, you say? Who did it? Do they know?

TEMPLE: (*Slowly*) No, I don't think they do.

SIDNEY: But … Gee, I can hardly believe it! Who'd want to do a thing like that, anyway? Pat Quinn of all the people!

STEVE: Here's the waiter, darling.

TEMPLE: What would you like, Miss Jeans?

SIDNEY: Can I have some coffee?

TEMPLE: Yes, of course. Bring some more coffee and another cup, waiter.

WAITER: Yes, sir.

The WAITER puts down a tray and STEVE starts to pour coffee.

TEMPLE: (*After a moment*) Miss Jeans …

127

SIDNEY: Yes?

TEMPLE: Did you recognise the man in our room?

SIDNEY: Recognise him? – Why, no!

TEMPLE: Would you know him if you saw him again?

SIDNEY: (*Thoughtfully*) No, I don't think I would. I saw him, of course – quite clearly – but it's very doubtful whether I should recognise him again. What about you, Mrs Temple?

STEVE: Yes, I think I would.

SIDNEY: (*Trying to change the mood*) Well, that's something! If you see the skunk when I'm around just holler – I'll be right there! And, lady, I'll tan the hide off that guy!

They laugh.

TEMPLE: Will you have a cigarette?

SIDNEY: Oh, thanks.

TEMPLE: Steve?

STEVE: No, thanks.

SIDNEY lights her cigarette.

SIDNEY: You know, I can't get over what you've told me. Quinn of all people! (*Almost to herself*) Now why should anyone want to murder him?

TEMPLE: (*Lightly*) Well, your guess is as good as mine, Miss Jeans. (*With a laugh*) It might even be better …

There is a moment's hesitation then SIDNEY starts to laugh. But she is not sure of the joke.

FADE UP of music.

FADE DOWN of music.

SCENE 2:   The TEMPLES' Hotel Bedroom.

TEMPLE and STEVE are in bed. TEMPLE is snoring, very lightly. He stops and turns over. STEVE gives a sigh; she is obviously wide awake. A moment. STEVE sighs again.

TEMPLE: What's the matter, Steve?

STEVE: I can't get to sleep. It's so hot …

TEMPLE: Shall I open the windows?

STEVE: They are wide open already.

TEMPLE: (*Yawning*) What time is it?

STEVE: I don't know. We seem to have been in bed for hours.

TEMPLE: I'll switch the light on. (*He does so*)

STEVE: It's a quarter to four.

TEMPLE: I thought it was later than that.

STEVE: (*Getting out of bed*) I'm going out on to the balcony, I simply must get a breath of air.

TEMPLE: Yes, all right. Pass me my cigarette case.

STEVE: Oh, darling, you're not going to smoke – not now!

TEMPLE: (*Resigned*) All right.

STEVE crosses to the window.

STEVE: It's a heavenly night …

TEMPLE: I thought you said it was too hot.

STEVE: (*From the balcony*) Not out here it isn't.

TEMPLE: I'm going to sleep …

A pause.

STEVE: (*Quietly*) Paul …

TEMPLE: M'm? What is it?

STEVE: There's someone next door – talking to Miss Jeans. I can hear them.

TEMPLE: So what?

STEVE: Well, darling, it is a quarter to four!

TEMPLE: You're probably imagining things. Come on – get into bed and try to sleep.

A moment.

STEVE: (*Tensely*) Paul! (*Returning into the room*) Come over here – to the balcony.

TEMPLE: No, I'm too comfy where I am.

129

STEVE:	(*A tense whisper*) Paul, please!
TEMPLE:	(*Puzzled by STEVE's tone of voice*) What is it?
STEVE:	You know that man – in Augusta – the American?
TEMPLE:	Colonel Marquand? Yes?
STEVE:	He's next door – he's talking to Miss Jeans …
TEMPLE:	Don't be silly!
STEVE:	Paul, I'm certain it's Marquand! Absolutely certain! I heard his voice that night at the gate of the Villa Negara.
TEMPLE:	Wait a minute! (*He gets out of bed*) Where's my dressing gown? … Oh, here it is.

TEMPLE joins STEVE.

STEVE:	Listen!

A pause.

TEMPLE:	I can't hear a darn thing!
STEVE:	Listen!

A second pause.

From the room next door we hear the voices of SIDNEY JEANS and COLONEL MARQUAND. The voices are very faint and can hardly be recognised.

TEMPLE:	What makes you think that's Marquand? I'm not even sure it's Miss Jeans.
STEVE:	Go out on the balcony.
TEMPLE:	(*After a moment*) All right …

FADE UP the voices of SIDNEY JEANS and MARQUAND. It is now just possible to hear what they are saying and to recognise their voices.

MARQUAND:	(*Annoyed*) Don't argue the point, Sidney! How could I possibly tell you beforehand?
SIDNEY:	You told Armstrong!

MARQUAND:	I did not tell Armstrong!
STEVE:	(*Quietly, tensely*) Now do you believe me?
TEMPLE:	Yes … Yes, it's Marquand all right … Sh!
SIDNEY:	If you want my frank opinion this Sullivan business is beginning to get on my nerves. I don't like it.
MARQUAND:	You're not expected to like it! Now listen to me, Sidney. Don't start jumping the rails; play the whole thing the way I told you to play it and we'll be sitting pretty.
SIDNEY:	I don't know. I don't like it, Arthur. Things are far trickier than I expected. Look at this Quinn business for instance.
MARQUAND:	For Pete's sake forget Quinn! (*Gently*) I've told you, there's nothing to worry about. Once we've got the glasses the rest should be child's play.
SIDNEY:	But we haven't got the glasses!
MARQUAND:	It's a pity Armstrong was disturbed.
SIDNEY:	If Temple's got the glasses he carries them about with him – or she does. At any rate they're not in the room.
MARQUAND:	(*Faintly surprised*) How do you know?
SIDNEY:	I searched it.
TEMPLE:	(*To STEVE*) Did she, by Jove!
MARQUAND:	When?
SIDNEY:	They went out for a walk: they were gone about three quarters of an hour. I went over the room with a tooth-comb; believe me, the glasses aren't in the room.
MARQUAND:	(*Grimly*) We've got to get those glasses, Sidney. I don't give too hoots how we get them, but we've got to get them.
SIDNEY:	(*Thoughtfully*) Arthur …

131

MARQUAND: Yes?

SIDNEY: Supposing I told Temple that Sullivan was a friend of mine – that he'd gone out of town for two or three days – and that he'd asked me to pick up the glasses.

MARQUAND: He wouldn't fall for that! In any case he'd want to know why you hadn't mentioned it before.

SIDNEY: (*Irritated*) Then why not find someone to impersonate Sullivan?

MARQUAND: For Heaven's sake! Don't you think I've thought of that! I tried it with Armstrong.

SIDNEY: Armstrong's a blundering fool! It's time you got rid of him!

MARQUAND: He may be a fool, but at least I can trust him!

SIDNEY: What do you mean? What do you mean by that?

A moment.

MARQUAND: (*Calming SIDNEY down*) O.K. O.K. We'll skip it! I'll ring you tomorrow about 10.30.

SIDNEY: (*A moment: quietly*) Yes, all right.

MARQUAND: Now remember what I told you. Keep on friendly terms with them and don't let them out of your sight.

SIDNEY: O.K.

TEMPLE: (*A whisper: taking STEVE by the arm*) Come on, Steve – let's get back into the room.

TEMPLE and STEVE leave the balcony.

TEMPLE: I'm going to close the window for a minute.

STEVE: Yes, all right.

132

TEMPLE closes the window.

TEMPLE: Well, we live and learn …

STEVE: (*Very puzzled*) Paul, there's one thing I don't understand. If she's in league with Marquand and that other man Armstrong, then why did she dash in here when I was shouting for help?

TEMPLE: The answer to that is simple my sweet. In fact, I ought to have thought of it before. Things were getting pretty hot and she dashed in here to warn Armstrong that you were making yourself heard. Also, don't forget it served a very useful purpose: Miss Jeans made your acquaintance under – so far as she was concerned – very favourable circumstances.

STEVE: (*Thoughtfully*) Yes. (*Faintly worried*) Paul, what are we going to do?

TEMPLE: We're going to keep on nice friendly terms with Miss Jeans, just as if we trusted her implicitly.

STEVE: And the glasses?

TEMPLE: I've told you what I'm going to do with the glasses, darling. I'm putting them in a safe deposit first thing tomorrow morning.

STEVE: Yes. I wonder how Mr Quinn fitted into all this?

TEMPLE: Well, obviously he was in the same boat as Constantine.

STEVE: What do you mean?

TEMPLE: Quinn was also after the glasses but operated – or worked if you like – independently.

STEVE: You mean independent of Marquand?

TEMPLE: Of both Marquand and Constantine – yes.

STEVE: (*Shaking her head*) I'm not so sure of that …

TEMPLE: Why?

STEVE: I don't think Quinn was after the glasses, darling. If you want my opinion, I think he was just a contact man.

TEMPLE: A contact man?

STEVE: Yes.

TEMPLE: Well, if he was he must have been working for someone? Who? It certainly wasn't Marquand.

STEVE: No. Quinn was probably working for the man who owns the curio shop – Zoltan Bahri. I don't think that Quinn knew anything at all about the glasses, he was just told to get in touch with us and deliver that card.

TEMPLE: (*Pondering*) Yes, you might be right …

STEVE: Miss Jeans knew about Quinn and to my way of thinking she knows something about the House of Bahri. You saw how she reacted when you mentioned the Avenue Shulamar.

TEMPLE: Yes …

STEVE: (*A moment*) Paul, do you think anyone else is after the glasses: Miss Fraser, for instance?

TEMPLE: I don't know about Miss Fraser. Darwin … I'm a little doubtful about. For one thing, he's just a shade too friendly for my liking. Also, his appearance at Sandbanks when that launch capsized us seemed to me to be rather too much of a coincidence.

STEVE: Yes. (*Suddenly*) Darling, supposing someone turns up and claims to be Richard Sullivan, someone that seems perfectly genuine; then what are you going to do?

TEMPLE: Well, once I'm absolutely sure that he is the real Richard Sullivan … I'm going to ask him what the heck it's all about!

STEVE: (*Laughing*) Yes, but will you give him the glasses?

TEMPLE: Of course! (*Suddenly*) You know, Steve, you seem to be taking a great interest in this affair.

STEVE: (*Smiling*) Do you think so?

TEMPLE: I do.

STEVE: Any objection?

TEMPLE: (*Laughing at STEVE*) No, of course not, but in the ordinary course of events you'd be begging me to drop this business like a hot potato!

STEVE: I know, darling. But somehow … we've got to get to the bottom of this, Paul. No matter what happens we've got to get to the bottom of it!

TEMPLE: If you insist, Mrs Temple. If you insist.

STEVE laughs.

FADE UP of music.

FADE DOWN of music.

SCENE 3: The Main Hall of the Hotel Continental.

TEMPLE: Have you any stamps please?

CLERK: Yes, sir. Shall I post the letter for you?

TEMPLE: Oh, thank you.

SCHREIDER: Excuse me, are there any letters for me – Room 132?

CLERK: Your name, sir?

SCHREIDER: Schreider.

A moment.

CLERK: No, I'm sorry. There's nothing for you, Herr Schreider.

SCHREIDER: Thank you.

TEMPLE: (*Pleasantly surprised*) Good morning, Mr Schreider! I didn't expect to find you in Cairo.

SCHREIDER: (*Coldly*) I'm sorry, I'm afraid I don't recognise …

TEMPLE: Temple.

SCHREIDER: Temple? Oh, yes, of course! I remember … You were at my café the night before last with Signor Rossetti.

TEMPLE: Yes.

SCHREIDER: (*A concealed note of sarcasm*) Did you find your friend?

TEMPLE: My friend?

SCHREIDER: Yes – you made enquiries, if I remember correctly, about a man called Constantine. (*Faintly amused*) For some reason or other you thought he was at my café.

TEMPLE: (*Quietly: watching SCHREIDER*) Oh, yes. Yes, I found him, thank you.

SCHREIDER: I'm so glad. (*Going*) Well, if you'll excuse me.

TEMPLE: Yes, of course.

STEVE walks up.

STEVE: Who was that, Paul?

TEMPLE: Didn't you recognise him?

STEVE: No.

TEMPLE: (*Thoughtfully*) It's Olaf Schreider, the man who owns the El Passaro.

STEVE: You mean the café at Syracuse?

TEMPLE: Yes.

STEVE: Is he staying here?

TEMPLE: Yes, apparently he's just arrived. (*Suddenly*) Well, I'm off to the bank. You can either come with me or I'll call back for you.

136

STEVE:	I want to do some shopping. I'll meet you back here in about forty-five minutes.
TEMPLE:	(*After a momentary hesitation*) Yes, all right. Take care of yourself.
STEVE:	I will.
TEMPLE:	(*Quietly*) And if you bump into Miss Jeans, don't forget, Steve …
STEVE:	I'll be as nice as pie!
TEMPLE:	Yes; we don't want her to jump to any conclusions about last night.
STEVE:	No, of course not.
TEMPLE:	See you later!
STEVE:	Bye.

FADE UP of music.

CROSS FADE the music into a Cairo busy street. In the distant background the priest can be heard, from the minaret, summoning the people to prayer.

FADE UP and away, the sound of a car.

FADE UP and away the noise of a flock of geese and a babble of many voices which takes us to:

SCENE 4:	A Street Market Stall
STEVE:	(*Firmly*) One hundred and twenty-five piastres, not one more – nor one less!
SALESMAN:	Dear lady, I swear to you – I swear to you that if they are worth one hundred and seventy-five piastres they are worth –
STEVE:	One hundred and twenty-five.
SALESMAN:	One hundred and twenty-five! (*Laughing*) You are not serious – you are joking.
STEVE:	One hundred and twenty-five, take it or leave it!
SALESMAN:	(*Scoffing*) One hundred and twenty-five! But I cannot accept one hundred and twenty-five

	piastres for such an exquisite pair of gloves, why –
STEVE:	Very well, then don't accept.
SALESMAN:	No! – No! – No! Wait! – Wait! Please! One moment – don't go away. Look at them! Examine them! Touch with your fingers … you see the lace, you see what beautiful soft lace –
STEVE:	One hundred and twenty-five piastres!
SALESMAN:	(*A moment: then nodding*) A hundred and twenty-five.

SIDNEY JEANS approaches.

SIDNEY:	(*Laughing*) Good for you, Mrs Temple!
STEVE:	(*Turning: laughing*) Oh, hello, Miss Jeans.
SALESMAN:	(*To SIDNEY*) You like some nice gloves, dear lady? (*Taking the gloves from the stall*) One hundred and ninety piastres a pair. Very nice – very lovely …
SIDNEY:	No, thank you.
SALESMAN:	One hundred and seventy piastres a pair … one hundred and fifty piastres.
SIDNEY:	(*Laughing*) And one hundred and twenty-five piastres! No, thank you, brother!

STEVE laughs.

SHE and SIDNEY move away from the stall. The SALESMAN concentrates on a new arrival.

SIDNEY:	(*Amused*) You seem to have been making a morning of it!
STEVE:	(*Laughing*) I've just bought one or two odds and ends.
SIDNEY:	And where are you off to now?
STEVE:	I'm on my way back to the hotel. What are you doing – just strolling around?

SIDNEY: Yeah – I have been – and gosh my feet are killing me! I'm just going to have some coffee. Why don't you join me?

STEVE: Well I promised to meet my husband at half past eleven, so …

SIDNEY: Well, what of it? He surely won't panic over half an hour! And what are husbands for, anyway?

STEVE: (*A moment's hesitation*) Yes, all right.

SIDNEY: Swell. I'll take you to Flambert's and I'll bet you it's the quaintest little place you've ever been in.

STEVE: I've been in some pretty quaint places. Is it far from here?

SIDNEY: No, it's just on the corner. Here, let me carry some of those parcels! Gosh, these are nice shoes! Where d'you get these? (*Enviously*) Can you wear heels like this?

STEVE: (*Amused*) Yes …

SIDNEY: (*With a sigh*) Ah, gee …

STEVE laughs and they move away into the crowd.

SCENE 5: The Outer Hall of FLAMBERT's Café

The door opens with the soft tinkle of a bell, and STEVE and SIDNEY enter from the street.

The door closes and they pass through a beaded curtain.

They open a second door and move into the courtyard. A fountain plays gently.

Somewhere in the background, there is a suggestion of music. Several of the tables are occupied.

STEVE: (*Surprised*) Why, it's a courtyard!

SIDNEY: Do you like it?

STEVE: It's heavenly! And just look at that fountain!

SIDNEY: You might be miles from anywhere! It's extraordinary! You can hardly hear the street noises.

STEVE:	It's most attractive.
SIDNEY:	I thought you'd like it. It's quite a haunt of mine. Ah, here's Flambert!

FLAMBERT is a Frenchman of about fifty.

FLAMBERT:	(*Pleasantly*) Good morning, madamoiselle! Nice to see you again! (*To STEVE*) Good morning.
SIDNEY:	Good morning!
STEVE:	Good morning.
FLAMBERT:	Voici votre place habituelle, madamoiselle!
SIDNEY:	Thank you, Mr Flambert.
FLAMBERT:	Coffee and a few pastries?
SIDNEY:	(*To STEVE*) O.K.?
STEVE:	Yes.
SIDNEY:	That'll do fine.
FLAMBERT:	Merci.
SIDNEY:	(*To STEVE*) Will you excuse me a moment?
STEVE:	Yes, of course.
SIDNEY:	(*To FLAMBERT: softly*) Where's Armstrong?
FLAMBERT:	(*Faintly nervous*) In my office. I'll take you to him.

SCENE 6:	FLAMBERT's Office

The door opens, SIDNEY and FLAMBERT enter. Door shuts.

ARMSTRONG:	Is she here?
SIDNEY:	Yes. (*Business-like*) You've got the car?
ARMSTRONG:	Yes, of course!
SIDNEY:	Where is it?
ARMSTRONG:	It's where we arranged it would be – facing the corner.

SIDNEY:	Right. (*To FLAMBERT*) You know what to do, Flambert?
FLAMBERT:	Yes, but I am a little worried. I do not like the thought of the young lady being taken ill in my café.
SIDNEY:	Don't worry, there'll be no trouble. (*To ARMSTRONG*) It'll take about four or five minutes for the drug to work. Go back to the car and wait.
ARMSTRONG:	Yes, all right.
SIDNEY:	Keep the car ticking over.
ARMSTRONG:	Yes.
SIDNEY:	And drive carefully. Remember it's a bad road.
ARMSTRONG:	I'll be careful.
SIDNEY:	(*Briskly, to FLAMBERT*) Give me two or three minutes, and then serve the coffee.
FLAMBERT:	I trust that there will be no noise or disturbance. It would be most unfortunate if ...
SIDNEY:	Don't worry. Everything will be done quickly and quietly, she won't even know what's happening. I'll be most discreet.
FLAMBERT:	Very well.
ARMSTRONG:	(*Opening the door*) I'm going back to the car; is there anything else you want to say?
SIDNEY:	No. Only don't forget what I've told you. Keep the engine ticking over and drive carefully.
ARMSTRONG:	(*Curtly: nodding*) I shan't forget.

The door closes.

SCENE 7:   The Street Outside The Café

Nearby is ARMSTRONG's car, the engine ticking over. STEVE and SIDNEY approach. STEVE is weak, dazed and rather confused.

STEVE: I don't know what happened … One minute I was feeling perfectly all right, the next I … I …

SIDNEY: Have you ever felt like this before?

STEVE: No, never … it's most extraordinary … it's just as if … my legs … Everything seems so heavy and …

SIDNEY: Do you think it's the heat?

STEVE: No … No, I don't think so; I've never felt like this before, I …. I'm so dizzy, I … I …

SIDNEY: There's a car over here. Maybe he'll drive us back to the hotel.

STEVE: I ought to walk … perhaps if I walk I … I … should … (*Desperately trying to pull herself together*)

SIDNEY: Lean on my shoulder.

STEVE: (*A little frightened*) I don't know what's happening to me … (*Weakly: fainting*) Oh …

ARMSTRONG arrives.

ARMSTRONG: (*Tensely*) Can you manage all right?

SIDNEY: (*Supporting STEVE*) Yes, yes, it's o.k., I've got her … Get the door open!

ARMSTRONG opens the car rear door, and SIDNEY starts to half lift STEVE into the back of the car.

ARMSTRONG: Where are you going to sit?

SIDNEY: I'll sit with her in the back, just in case she comes round.

142

ARMSTRONG:	Yes, all right. Did you have much trouble with her in the café?
SIDNEY:	No, it was easy.
ARMSTRONG:	Can you manage?
SIDNEY:	Yes …

SIDNEY props STEVE up in the car.

ARMSTRONG:	All set?
SIDNEY:	Yeah … o.k.

ARMSTRONG shuts the rear door, climbs in behind the wheel, shuts his own door, engages gear and the car moves away.

SCENE 8:	The Car interior, speeding along
ARMSTRONG:	Is she all right?
SIDNEY:	Yes. I think she's coming round.
ARMSTRONG:	Well, watch her! If she gets suspicious she might start shouting.
SIDNEY:	Don't worry, I'll take care of her. You just watch what you're doing.
STEVE:	(*Weakly*) What happened? Did I faint?
SIDNEY:	(*Pleasantly*) Feeling better?
STEVE:	Yes, but what happened? (*Faintly alarmed*) Where am I? Where are we going?
SIDNEY:	(*Laughing*) It's o.k.! We're going back to the hotel; isn't that where you want to go?
STEVE:	Yes, but – Oh, gosh, my head! It's absolutely splitting.
SIDNEY:	If I were you I should sit back and take it easy. Just relax!
STEVE:	But what happened to me? I shouldn't have fainted like that. Oh! Gosh, my head! I feel as if …

143

From the road ahead, a sudden angry blast from the motor horn of an approaching car is heard.

ARMSTRONG: Why the fool!

SIDNEY: Look out, or you'll hit him!

ARMSTRONG: He came out of that street without the slightest …

SIDNEY: Look out! Look out, or you'll hit him!

STEVE gives a quick little gasp.

ARMSTRONG's car hits the second car and the collision – which is quite slight – is followed by the noise of a burst tyre. The car stops.

SIDNEY: (*Intensely angry*) You fool! You could have missed him if you'd –

ARMSTRONG: How the blazes could I have missed him! He came out of that street without –

SIDNEY: Was that our tyre that burst?

ARMSTRONG: Yes.

SIDNEY: (*Almost under her breath*) You blundering fool.

We move out into the busy street.

DARWIN is approaching from the second car.

DARWIN: What's the big idea? Are you trying to make this barouche of mine look worse than it is?

ARMSTRONG: Why on earth don't you look where you're going?

DARWIN: (*Quite pleasantly, although apparently annoyed*) Why don't you look where you're going! You're on the wrong side of the road anyway!

ARMSTRONG: Listen to me! If you'd put your blasted brakes on instead of –

SIDNEY: (*To ARMSTRONG; tensely*) Shut up.

DARWIN: (*Astonished*) Why, hello, Mrs Temple! I say, you look off-colour!

SIDNEY: I was just taking her back to her hotel – she hasn't been very well.

DARWIN: She certainly doesn't look very well!

STEVE: I passed out a few moments ago.

DARWIN: I'm not surprised, with this fellow driving you around.

SIDNEY laughs.

SIDNEY: Do you think you could give us a lift? I'm afraid we're in rather a spot right now!

DARWIN: Yes, of course!

STEVE: (*Weakly*) Oh, this is Miss Jeans – Mr Darwin.

DARWIN: How do you do, Miss Jeans?

SIDNEY: Glad to know you, Mr Darwin!

The car door opens.

DARWIN: Come along, Mrs Temple – give me your hand! (*Suddenly: obviously weighing up the situation*) I say, you certainly do look off-colour.

SCENE 9: The Main Hall of the Hotel Continental

TEMPLE: (*Obviously worried*) I beg your pardon, but are you sure there isn't a message for me?

CLERK: Quite sure, sir. But I'll make quite certain. One moment, if you please! (*He lifts the telephone receiver*) Has there been a message for Mr Temple – Room 187? … No? … Thank you. (*He replaces the receiver*) I'm sorry, sir.

TEMPLE: (*Turning away*) Thank you.

FRASER: (*Brightly*) Hello! What's the trouble? You're looking very despondent this morning, Mr Temple!

TEMPLE: Oh, hello, Miss Fraser. It's nice to see you again. How are you?

FRASER:	I'm fine! But you don't appear to be so pleased with life, not just at the moment.
TEMPLE:	It's that dear little wife of mine! She promised to meet me at 11.30 and here it's nearly a quarter past one.
FRASER:	Good gracious me, aren't you used to that sort of thing by now?
TEMPLE:	(*Laughing*) And what time was <u>your</u> appointment?
FRASER:	Half past twelve.
TEMPLE:	It seems to me you women are all alike!
FRASER:	I expect if the truth were known she's still shopping. There are some fascinating shops in Cairo, you know.
TEMPLE:	Yes.
FRASER:	(*With a little laugh*) She's probably browsing away in some old curio shop or other …
TEMPLE:	(*Quietly: a sudden thought*) Y-e-s, I hadn't thought of that.
FRASER:	(*Suddenly*) Well, I must be getting along.
TEMPLE:	Yes, of course.
FRASER:	When you do see Mrs Temple – don't forget now – give her my very kind regards.
TEMPLE:	Yes, I will certainly.
FRASER:	Goodbye!
TEMPLE:	Goodbye, Miss Fraser. (*To the CLERK*) Get me a cab, will you, please.
CLERK:	Yes, sir.

Bring up the hotel background as TEMPLE crosses the reception hall. He passes through the main door and out of the hotel into:

SCENE 10:	The Crowded Street Outside the Hotel
SCHREIDER:	Mr Temple.

TEMPLE: (*Surprised*) Oh, hello, Schreider.

SCHREIDER: So you got my message?

TEMPLE: Your message?

SCHREIDER: Yes, I left a message for you with the concierge.

TEMPLE: I'm afraid I didn't get it. Well, what can I do for you, Schreider?

SCHREIDER: I saw you talking to Miss Fraser just now – the Scots lady – and I was wondering if …

TEMPLE: Yes?

SCHREIDER: I was wondering if – by any chance she was a friend of yours?

TEMPLE: Miss Fraser's an acquaintance – we met on the flying boat.

SCHREIDER: An acquaintance? But you dined together at my café – El Passaro?

TEMPLE: We dined with Mr Darwin and Miss Fraser happened to be his guest.

SCHREIDER: (*Dubiously*) I see.

TEMPLE: I wonder if you do see, Mr Schreider.

SCHREIDER: What do you mean?

TEMPLE: You sound rather doubtful about it all. Why are you interested in Miss Fraser?

SCHREIDER: Early this morning Miss Fraser had an interview with a man called Hakim – Commandant Hakim. Shortly afterwards I was compelled to …

TEMPLE: Compelled to what, Schreider?

SCHREIDER: I was compelled to answer a number of quite unnecessary questions.

Pause.

TEMPLE: What sort of questions?

SCHREIDER: They wanted information about a man called Quinn – Patrick Norman Quinn.

TEMPLE: Was he a friend of yours?

SCHREIDER: No. I'd never heard of him, but I'm quite sure that Miss Fraser told the Commandant that he <u>was</u> a friend of mine.

In the background, a taxi cab draws up.

TEMPLE: But why should she do that?

SCHREIDER: I don't know … any more than I know why she searched my room.

TEMPLE: She searched your room?

SCHREIDER: Yes.

TEMPLE: You're sure it was Miss Fraser?

SCHREIDER: Quite sure.

TEMPLE: Mr Schreider, did Commandant Hakim ask you anything else?

SCHREIDER: I've told you what he asked me. He simply wanted to know whether Quinn was a friend of mine.

TEMPLE: You know of course that Quinn was murdered last night?

SCHREIDER: Yes, Hakim told me. Apparently there was a warrant out for his arrest.

TEMPLE: For Quinn's arrest?

SCHREIDER: Yes.

TEMPLE: I didn't know that.

SCHREIDER: Well, apparently there was. He was wanted on an embezzlement charge.

CLERK: Excuse me, sir. Your cab is waiting, sir.

TEMPLE: Oh, thank you. I'll probably see you later, Schreider. I shouldn't worry too much about Miss Fraser if I were you.

DRIVER: (*An Egyptian*) Where do you wish to go, sir?

TEMPLE: (*Briskly*) I want you to take me to the House of Bahri.

TEMPLE opens the cab door.

148

DRIVER: The House of Bahri?
TEMPLE: Yes. 227. Avenue Shulamar.
FADE UP of music.

FADE DOWN of music.
SCENE 11:   The House of Bahri.
It is a small shop. In the background two men are discussing a possible purchase: they speak quietly and politely to each other in Egyptian.

The door opens with a soft musical chime and TEMPLE enters.

After a moment the men stop talking. ZOLTAN BAHRI turns his attention to TEMPLE. BAHRI is a Turk: he speaks excellent English.

BAHRI: Are you looking for anything in particular, sir?
TEMPLE: (*Pleasantly*) Well, as a matter of fact, I'm looking for my wife.
BAHRI: (*Amused*) Your wife?
TEMPLE: Yes, we seem to have missed each other. I think she called on you this morning. I was wondering if you could tell me what time she left?
BAHRI: Madam is English?
TEMPLE: Yes.
BAHRI: (*Shaking his head*) We have had no English visitors this morning, sir.
TEMPLE: Oh, that puts rather a different complexion on it. This is the House of Bahri, of course?
BAHRI: Of course.
TEMPLE: Well, I feel sure my wife intended to call here. As a matter of fact your house was recommended to us by a man called Quinn. Patrick Quinn. (*He feels in his pockets*) He gave us a card – I do believe I've got it here somewhere …

BAHRI: (*Quietly: watching TEMPLE: not smiling*) When did Mr Quinn recommend The House of Bahri?

TEMPLE: (*Still searching for the card*) Last night. We met him in a cocktail bar at the Continental.

BAHRI: (*A moment*) Have you got the card?

TEMPLE: Well, I did have … Oh, here it is.

TEMPLE passes the card over to BAHRI.

BAHRI: Thank you. (*A pause; softly; politely*) Your name is Temple?

TEMPLE: Yes.

BAHRI: (*Moving towards a door*) Will you come this way, please?

BAHRI opens a door, and he and TEMPLE move into a corridor.

BAHRI: The ceiling is very low in here – please, mind your head. Through here, Mr Temple.

BAHRI opens a second door and they enter a small room.

TEMPLE: Thank you.

QUINN: So here you are, at last! Why, man, you've been a devil of a time coming! I'd almost given you up as a bad job!

TEMPLE: (*Completely taken aback*) Well I'll be – Mr Quinn!

FADE UP of music.

END OF EPISODE FIVE

EPISODE SIX

A MESSAGE FROM SIR GRAHAM

OPEN TO:

SCENE 1: The Back Room at the House of Bahri

As in Episode 5, Scene 11

BAHRI: (*Shaking his head*) We have had no English visitors this morning, sir.

TEMPLE: Oh, that puts rather a different complexion on it. This is the House of Bahri, of course?

BAHRI: Of course.

TEMPLE: Well, I feel sure my wife intended to call here. As a matter of fact your house was recommended to us by a man called Quinn. Patrick Quinn. (*He feels in his pockets*) He gave us a card – I do believe I've got it here somewhere …

BAHRI: (*Quietly: watching TEMPLE: not smiling*) When did Mr Quinn recommend The House of Bahri?

TEMPLE: (*Still searching for the card*) Last night. We met him in a cocktail bar at the Continental.

BAHRI: (*A moment*) Have you got the card?

TEMPLE: Well, I did have … Oh, here it is.

TEMPLE passes the card over to BAHRI.

BAHRI: Thank you. (*A pause; softly; politely*) Your name is Temple?

TEMPLE: Yes.

BAHRI: (*Moving towards a door*) Will you come this way, please?

BAHRI opens a door, and he and TEMPLE move into a corridor.

BAHRI: The ceiling is very low in here – please, mind your head. Through here, Mr Temple.

BAHRI opens a second door and they enter a small room.

TEMPLE: Thank you.

QUINN: So here you are, at last! Why, man, you've been a devil of a time coming! I'd almost given you up as a bad job!

153

TEMPLE: (*Completely taken aback*) Well I'll be – Mr Quinn!

QUINN: Why sure it's Mr Quinn! Come in! Don't stand in the doorway!

BAHRI and TEMPLE enter. BAHRI closes the door.

QUINN: Man, you look as if you've seen a ghost.

TEMPLE: I feel as if I've seen a ghost. I thought you were dead.

QUINN: Now that's a nice thing to say. And whatever gave you that idea?

TEMPLE: A gentleman by the name of Hakim told me that you'd been shot. He seemed quite convinced of it in fact.

QUINN: Did he, now? Well that's very gratifying, I must say. Do you hear that, Bhari? Get the gentleman a chair.

BAHRI produces a chair and TEMPLE sits down.

QUINN: That's better! Now, Mr Temple, in a manner o' speaking I feel that I owe you both an apology and an explanation.

TEMPLE: Well, supposing we have the explanation first.

QUINN: You would prefer it that way? Very well. (*A moment: watching TEMPLE*) You have a pair of glasses, Mr Temple – a pair of spectacles – belonging to a man called Richard Sullivan. (*A moment – quite simply*) I want those spectacles.

TEMPLE: Why?

QUINN: (*Slightly taken aback*) I beg your pardon?

TEMPLE: I said, why? Why do you want the spectacles?

QUINN: (*A moment's hesitation, then suddenly laughing*) Why the devil do you think I want them? I want to hand them over to Mr Sullivan.

154

TEMPLE: Why doesn't Mr Sullivan come and get them himself? He knows where I am – or at any rate he could very easily find out.

QUINN: Ah, that's an interesting point! Now you've hit the nail on the head as you might say.

TEMPLE: I'm delighted to hear it.

QUINN: You see, Mr Temple, Mr Sullivan, as you know – (*Changing his mind*) Well, I suppose I'd better begin at the beginning. Sullivan paid a visit to London but unfortunately lost his glasses. They were found by a friend of his – Miss Raymond. She gave them to you and asked you to deliver them to Mr Sullivan when you arrived in Cairo. Correct?

TEMPLE: Correct.

QUINN: Well, have you ever wondered why Mr Sullivan hasn't got in touch with you? Why he didn't, in fact, meet the plane?

TEMPLE: I've thought quite a lot about Mr Sullivan during the past two or three days. Quite a lot!

BAHRI: You thought what, for instance, Mr Temple?

TEMPLE: Well, for instance, this man that was shot, the man that our friend Hakim mistook for Mr Quinn. (*He is watching QUINN and BAHRI: slowly*) I don't suppose he could have been Sullivan, by any chance?

A moment.

QUINN: He could have been – but he wasn't. Now don't let your imagination run riot, Mr Temple. The explanation about Sullivan is really quite simple. Sullivan is a friend of mine, a very close friend; unfortunately his movements are, to say the least, restricted. You see there's a warrant out for his arrest.

155

TEMPLE: (*Surprised*) A warrant for his arrest? What for?

QUINN: I don't think we'll go into that. The point is this: Sullivan needs his glasses, the poor chap can't even read a newspaper without them. He daren't go into an opticians and order a new pair for the simple reason that the police are after him; don't you understand, the man's in hiding!

TEMPLE: M'm.

QUINN: Don't you believe my story?

TEMPLE: You produce Mr Sullivan. Prove to me – without any shadow of doubt – that he is Mr Sullivan and I'll produce the glasses.

QUINN: Well, now – that's fair enough.

BAHRI: Mr Temple, have you got the spectacles with you – at the moment?

TEMPLE: No I haven't, Mr Bahri. I don't make a habit of carrying spectacles about with me – not when they're worth £10,000.

QUINN: (*Astonished*) What the devil d'you mean - £10,000?

TEMPLE: (*Politely: calmly*) Oh, didn't I tell you? A gentleman by the name of Constantine offered me £10,000 for them.

QUINN: (*Quickly*) When?

TEMPLE: Two days ago.

QUINN: (*Tensely: quickly*) Did you – ?

TEMPLE: (*Interrupting QUINN*) No, I didn't! You know, Mr Quinn, you appear to be almost as concerned about Mr Sullivan's spectacles as Colonel Marquand.

QUINN: (*Quietly*) And who might he be?

TEMPLE: Don't you know? I was beginning to think he might be a friend of yours.

QUINN: I've never heard of him.

TEMPLE: Or Mr Armstrong?

QUINN: Or Mr Armstrong.

TEMPLE: (*Watching QUINN*) But you'd heard of Mr Constantine, I take it?

A moment.

BAHRI: Constantine was an acquaintance of mine. He frequently visited the House of Bahri. (*Slowly*) He was a collector of curios.

TEMPLE: Well, he won't visit the House of Bahri any more, my friend.

BAHRI: What do you mean?

TEMPLE: He 'collected' a knife – between the shoulder blades.

A moment.

BAHRI: (*Quietly*) Where did this happen?

TEMPLE: In Augusta.

BAHRI: When?

TEMPLE: Two days ago.

BAHRI: (*Interested: quietly watching TEMPLE*) You suspect that this Colonel Marquand had something to do with it?

TEMPLE: (*After a pause*) It's a possibility. Colonel Marquand was, still is, interested in the spectacles: so was Mr Constantine.

QUINN: (*With a little laugh*) Well, so am I, but that doesn't mean I murdered Constantine.

BAHRI: (*Quickly*) We seem to be getting away from the point, Mr Quinn. Mr Temple has got the spectacles, therefore it is essential that we introduce him, as soon as possible, to the real Mr Sullivan.

QUINN: (*After a moment*) Can you meet me tonight?

TEMPLE: Where?

QUINN: Now let's see … There's a man called Durant, he runs one or two river excursions, you know the sort of thing I mean.

TEMPLE: Tom Durant?

QUINN: That's the fellow.

TEMPLE: I've noticed several of his boats. Well?

QUINN: Durant has a place on the Nile, it's about two hundred yards from the Anglo-Egyptian Club. D'you know it?

TEMPLE: No, but I could easily find it.

BAHRI: All right – find it. Ask for Tom Durant and mention my name … Bahri.

TEMPLE: Tonight?

BAHRI: Yes.

QUINN: Tonight at half past six.

TEMPLE: Right.

QUINN: Oh – and Mr Temple …

TEMPLE: Yes?

QUINN: I trust you'll treat this interview as confidential. I should hate our friend Hakim to be disillusioned.

TEMPLE: What do you mean?

QUINN: Commandant Hakim – and a great many other people in Cairo – are labouring under the impression that I've passed away. I should prefer that they continue to think along those lines.

TEMPLE: Mr Quinn, so far as I'm concerned you're a dead duck. Produce Mr Sullivan and I'll produce his spectacles.

QUINN: (*Chuckling*) You're a man after my own heart!

FADE UP of music.

FADE DOWN of music.

158

SCENE 2:	The Main Hall of the Hotel Continental
TEMPLE:	(*Briskly*) Has my wife returned yet?
CLERK:	Mrs Temple? Yes, I think you'll find she's in her room, sir.
TEMPLE:	Thank you.
FRASER:	(*Pleasantly*) Hello, Mr Temple!
TEMPLE:	Oh, hello, Miss Fraser!
FRASER:	Mrs Temple came in shortly after you left – you only just missed her.
TEMPLE:	Oh, what a pity!
FRASER:	Mr Darwin was with her and a young lady called Miss Jeans.
TEMPLE:	Miss Jeans?
FRASER:	Yes. I hope you don't mind my mentioning it, Mr Temple, but frankly I didn't think your wife looked too well. (*Faintly puzzled*) Apparently she'd fainted or something.
TEMPLE:	Fainted?
FRASER:	Yes.
TEMPLE:	Who told you that?
FRASER:	Mr Darwin told me.
TEMPLE:	Well – what happened, do you know?
FRASER:	I believe she went into some café or other with this Miss Jeans and – well – just turned queer.
TEMPLE:	Oh … Well, if you'll excuse me …
FRASER:	Yes, of course. If there's anything I can do, please let me know. Cairo 8-792 will always find me.
TEMPLE:	(*As he leaves*) That's very kind of you, Miss Fraser.
FRASER:	Not at all.

Mix over to near the lifts.

The lift arrives, the gates open and several other people step out into the hall.

TEMPLE: (*Off, calling*) Darwin!

DARWIN: (*Turning*) Oh, here you are, old boy! I was just coming down to look for you.

TEMPLE: How's my wife?

DARWIN: Oh, she's all right now. She had a nasty turn, but she'll be all right.

TEMPLE: Yes, I've just seen Miss Fraser, she told me Steve fainted or something.

DARWIN: Yes. (*With a little laugh: but puzzled*) Frankly, I can't quite figure out what happened. It all seems a little mysterious. Anyhow, she's all right now, that's the main thing. Oh, by the way, I've invited you both to have dinner with me tonight.

TEMPLE: That's very nice of you.

DARWIN: Not at all. Delighted. Pick you up at eight o'clock.

TEMPLE: Well, could you make it a little later – say, half past?

DARWIN: Yes, of course! And don't worry about Mrs Temple, old boy. She'll be all right. Goodbye!

TEMPLE: Good … (*Suddenly, stopping DARWIN*) Oh, Darwin!

DARWIN: Yes?

TEMPLE: What exactly happened? Were you in the café when Steve fainted?

DARWIN: No, I bumped into them in my car just as … Well, look here – I'm sure Mrs Temple will want to tell you all about it herself.

TEMPLE: Yes, all right.

DARWIN: (*A sudden thought*) Oh, by the way – is this … Miss Jeans an old friend of yours or …

TEMPLE: No, just an acquaintance. As a matter of fact we met her for the first time last night.

DARWIN: (*Non-committally*) Oh.

160

TEMPLE: Why do you ask?

DARWIN: (*Vaguely*) Nothing. I wondered, that's all. (*With a shrug*) … Well, see you tonight!

TEMPLE: Yes.

DARWIN: Cheers!

TEMPLE: Goodbye, Darwin!

SCENE 3: The TEMPLES' Hotel Bedroom.

TEMPLE and STEVE are talking quietly and confidentially.

TEMPLE: Well, we seem to have had quite a morning, darling. What with your experience at Flambert's, and me at the House of Bahri.

STEVE: (*A little laugh*) Yes.

TEMPLE: (*Curious*) Steve, tell me: did Miss Jeans realise that you'd spotted Armstrong as the driver of the car?

STEVE: I don't know. If she did she certainly carried it off pretty well. As a matter of fact I wasn't quite so far gone as she thought I was. I had a hunch the coffee had been tampered with and I didn't drink it all.

TEMPLE: It was certainly a lucky coincidence bumping into Darwin.

STEVE: Yes. He was awfully sweet. (*Puzzled*) I wonder if he really is mixed up in this business, Paul?

TEMPLE: I've got a jolly good mind to ask him.

STEVE: (*Laughing*) It might be quite an idea. (*Seriously*) You don't think he's working for Sir Graham by any chance?

TEMPLE: What on earth do you mean?

STEVE: Attached to Scotland Yard?

TEMPLE: (*Laughing*) I hardly think so, darling. (*Seriously*) Steve, I want you to forget what I told you about

161

	Miss Jeans. From now on give her a pretty wide berth – she's dynamite.
STEVE:	I suppose they meant to hold me as a sort of hostage until you handed over the spectacles.
TEMPLE:	Yes.
STEVE:	Mr Quinn – are you going to keep that appointment with him?
TEMPLE:	(*A moment*) I might.
STEVE:	Why? Do you think he was telling the truth: do you think he really knows Richard Sullivan?
TEMPLE:	(*Shaking his head*) I'm pretty sure he doesn't. As a matter of fact, Steve, I'm slowly coming round to the idea that Mr Constantine might possibly have been right after all, and that there is no Richard Sullivan! After I deposited the spectacles in the bank this morning I went round to police headquarters and had a chat with Hakim. He checked on the Trans-Eurasian Oil Company for me: they'd never even heard of Richard Sullivan.
STEVE:	Had Hakim heard of Sullivan?
TEMPLE:	No.
STEVE:	Well surely that proves that Quinn was lying. Hakim must have heard of Sullivan if there's a warrant out for him.
TEMPLE:	Exactly. You know, Steve, this business intrigues me and I'm determined to get to the bottom of it. Why is there all this fuss over a perfectly ordinary pair of spectacles?
STEVE:	If you intend to keep your appointment with Mr Quinn, what are you going to do about the spectacles?
TEMPLE:	I'll produce the spectacles after Mr Quinn produces Mr Sullivan. I'm taking no chances.

STEVE: It seems to me we're taking a pretty big chance by keeping the appointment.

TEMPLE: What do you mean – <u>we</u>? …

There's a knock on the door.

A moment.

TEMPLE: Come in!

The door opens.

SIDNEY: Sorry to disturb you, but this cable was pushed under my door a few moments ago. It's marked Room 186 but it's got your name on it, Mr Temple.

SIDNEY passes the cable to TEMPLE.

TEMPLE: Oh, thank you, Miss Jeans.

SIDNEY: That's all right. (*To STEVE*) Are you feeling o.k. now?

STEVE: Yes, I'm all right, thanks.

SIDNEY: (*To TEMPLE*) You know, we had quite a morning! Your wife passed out and on top of that a crazy cab driver drove us bang slap into a friend of yours.

TEMPLE: Yes! So my wife's just been telling me.

SIDNEY: Well, I'm glad you're feeling better anyway.

STEVE: I'll be all right.

SIDNEY: (*Moving to the door*) If there's anything I can do, just ask. You know where to find me.

STEVE: Thanks.

SIDNEY: Bye!

The door closes.

A moment.

STEVE: Who's the cable from?

TEMPLE: I don't know. I haven't opened it yet.

TEMPLE rips the cable open.

A slight pause.

STEVE: Well?

163

| TEMPLE: | Speak of the devil. Listen to this, Steve! "Arriving in Cairo today. Will contact you Hotel Continental. Regards. Forbes." |
| STEVE: | (*Staggered*) Sir Graham! |

SCENE 4: A Quay on the Nile

TOM DURANT is working on a rowing boat tied to the quay. He's an Englishman: about forty: his manner is rather unfriendly, but he isn't at all surly or petulant. He is singing to himself. Suddenly he has noticed TEMPLE and STEVE.

TEMPLE:	(*Politely*) Mr Durant?
DURANT:	Yes?
TEMPLE:	My name is Temple.
DURANT:	Well?
TEMPLE:	Mr Bahri told me to get in touch with you.
DURANT:	Oh. (*Slowly: studying TEMPLE*) You're the party that wants to go out to the houseboat?
TEMPLE:	Well, he didn't say anything about a houseboat, but –
DURANT:	(*Interrupting TEMPLE*) That's all right. Jump in … Hello! Who's this?
TEMPLE:	This is my wife.
DURANT:	Is she coming with you?
TEMPLE:	If you've no objection.
DURANT:	Makes no difference to me, only Bahri didn't say anything about a lady.
STEVE:	(*With a little laugh*) You're not going to come between husband and wife, are you, Mr Durant?
DURANT:	(*After a moment: nodding*) Get in.
TEMPLE:	I'll get in first, Steve.

TEMPLE steps into the boat.

| STEVE: | Hold my hand … |
| TEMPLE: | Steady …! |

STEVE climbs into the boat.

TEMPLE: … that's it …

DURANT: Do you mind moving out to the right a little …
           (*Taking the oars*) … that's better.

TEMPLE: How far are you taking us?

DURANT: (*Faintly surprised*) Don't you know?

TEMPLE: No.

DURANT: I've been told to take you to that houseboat. The
           one with the blue shutters – do you see it?

A moment.

TEMPLE: Yes. Whose is it?

DURANT: (*Getting the oars into position*) I don't know. It's
           been there about a week, that's all I know.

TEMPLE: (*Quietly*) Did Mr Bahri tell you to wait for me?

DURANT: No; he simply asked me to take you over to the
           houseboat. (*A moment*) Do you want me to wait?

TEMPLE: Yes.

DURANT: How long are you likely to be?

TEMPLE: Oh, I don't know. Not very long. In any case, I'll
           make it worth your while.

DURANT: (*Nodding*) All right, I'll wait.

DURANT starts to row.

Mix to:

SCENE 5:   The Nile, midstream.

DURANT is rowing along.

TEMPLE: Have you brought anyone else out here?

DURANT: Tonight?

TEMPLE: Yes.

DURANT: No.

STEVE: Not even Mr Bahri?

DURANT: No. (*A moment: still rowing*) I did bring a man
           out here two or three days ago: a little Irish
           fellow. Name of Quinn.

TEMPLE: Oh, yes.

165

STEVE: (*Watching DURANT*) I seem to remember reading something about a man named Quinn. Wasn't he murdered?

DURANT: (*Dryly*) He was. He was shot … Poor devil.

A pause.

TEMPLE: Is Bahri a friend of yours?

DURANT: Bahri? (*He laughs*) It's easy to tell you haven't lived in Cairo for very long. Mr Zoltan Bahri is a millionaire: he chooses his friends almost as carefully as his curios, and some of them are just as priceless.

TEMPLE: Why did Mr Quinn come out here – to the houseboat?

DURANT: I don't know. I suppose he had an appointment with someone. It never entered my head to ask him.

A pause.

DURANT continues to row.

STEVE: (*Quietly*) We're nearly there, Paul.

TEMPLE: Yes.

DURANT: There's a rope ladder on the other side … sit still … I'll row you round there …

Another pause.

TEMPLE: Was Quinn a friend of yours?

DURANT: No.

TEMPLE: Did you wait for him?

DURANT: No, I left him on the boat.

TEMPLE: Did you see anyone?

DURANT: What do you mean?

TEMPLE: Did you see anyone on the houseboat?

DURANT: I never bothered to look. Providing I'm paid for what I do – and it's on the level – I'm not exactly curious.

STEVE: There's the ladder.

166

DURANT: Yes … wait a minute …

DURANT takes one oar out of the water.

The boat draws nearer to the houseboat.

TEMPLE: (*Calling*) Hello there! (*A moment*) Hello, there!

STEVE: There doesn't seem to be anyone about.

TEMPLE: No … Shall I go first? Then I can give you a hand?

STEVE: Yes, all right.

DURANT: Watch yourself … I'll try and keep the boat as steady as I can.

TEMPLE: I'll be all right.

TEMPLE climbs onto the rope ladder.

STEVE: Steady, Paul!

TEMPLE: (*Climbing*) It's all right, Steve … it's quite easy …

A pause.

DURANT: (*Looking up at TEMPLE*) Are you all right?

TEMPLE climbs the last rungs and jumps down onto the deck of the houseboat.

TEMPLE: Yes.

DURANT: (*To STEVE*) Now watch that rung at the bottom.

STEVE steps onto the rope ladder and climbs.

DURANT: That's it …

TEMPLE: Steady …

STEVE reaches the side of the deck.

TEMPLE: Now jump! (*As STEVE jumps*) That's a good girl!

STEVE joins TEMPLE on the deck of the houseboat.

STEVE: I don't see any sign of Mr Quinn.

TEMPLE: (*Looking about him*) No …

DURANT: (*From the boat below*) Are you all right?

TEMPLE: (*Leaning over the side*) Yes … I don't expect we shall be very long!

DURANT: (*Nodding*) I'll hang on!

167

TEMPLE and STEVE begin to explore the houseboat.

STEVE: (*Quietly*) I don't think there's anyone here …

TEMPLE: No … neither do I …

STEVE: Did Quinn mention any special time for you to come?

TEMPLE: He said 6.30, but it's after that now.

STEVE: Yes.

TEMPLE: There's a cabin over there.

TEMPLE and STEVE cross towards the cabin.

STEVE: If there's anyone on board surely they'd have heard us.

TEMPLE: I wonder what the idea is?

STEVE: (*After a moment*) Was it Quinn's suggestion that you should meet him or Mr Bahri's?

TEMPLE: Bahri's.

STEVE: Yes, well there's no sign of either Bahri or Quinn – to say nothing of the elusive Mr Sullivan!

TEMPLE: Let's try the cabin …

TEMPLE pushes open the door and they enter.

TEMPLE: (*Staggered*) Good Lord!

STEVE: What's happened? What's been going on here?

TEMPLE: Just look at the place! It's been absolutely ransacked!

STEVE: Look at the chairs and table … Paul, what has been happening?

TEMPLE: (*Quietly: taking stock*) There's been a fight … a struggle I should think … look at that desk, it's been completely turned over … Someone's put up a pretty good show! (*Faint laugh*) By George, just look at the place!

A moment.

STEVE: (*Quietly*) Paul, what's this?

PAUL: Let me have a look …

STEVE passes the item over.

168

STEVE: What is it?

TEMPLE: Where did you find it?

STEVE: It was on the back of this chair. I felt it touch my hand. What is it?

TEMPLE: (*After a moment – dismissing the matter*) It's a piece of cord, that's all – someone must have dropped it. There's another cabin over here. Let's have a look …

TEMPLE moves and opens a second door.

STEVE: Is that all right?

TEMPLE: Yes. This doesn't seem to have been disturbed. (*Thoughtfully*) I wonder if Quinn did come here … was followed by someone and then … (*He stops*)

STEVE: (*Quietly*) Paul – have you noticed these, they're nearly all maps …

TEMPLE: (*Interested*) Maps?

STEVE: Yes … Look, they're all over the place … Maps of Cairo, Alexandria, Haifa … the Suez Canal.

TEMPLE: So they are … you're right. There's a compass over here too … (*Quietly intrigued*) Now that's interesting …

STEVE: What?

TEMPLE: I'm just looking at this map of Cairo … someone's been working on it … Do you see those red dots?

STEVE: Yes.

TEMPLE: I wonder what they've been trying to do?

STEVE: That's the hotel, isn't it?

TEMPLE: Where? Oh, yes, that's right …

STEVE: And isn't that the Avenue Shulamar – the line with the red dot on it?

TEMPLE: Yes … (*Thoughtfully*) I should think that red dot marks the House of Bahri.

169

STEVE: Then what are the others?

TEMPLE: (*His thoughts elsewhere*) I don't know …
            (*Suddenly*) I'm taking this map back to the hotel
            with me.

STEVE: Aren't you going to wait for Quinn?

TEMPLE: I don't think there's any point, dear. It's my bet
            that Quinn's already been here.

STEVE: Then why didn't he wait?

TEMPLE: (*With a laugh*) Quite obviously the gentleman
            was disturbed.

STEVE: Paul, I've got a hunch that something's happened
            to Quinn.

TEMPLE: Well, judging by the look of this place,
            something's certainly happened to someone!

STEVE: Supposing Quinn told you the truth this morning
            and Sullivan was here – the real Richard
            Sullivan? Supposing Quinn came here tonight –
            or this afternoon for that matter – saw Sullivan,
            told him what had happened between you and …

TEMPLE: And Sullivan didn't care for it, fell out with
            Quinn and had a first class row?

STEVE: Yes.

TEMPLE: But if Sullivan was here and really needed the
            glasses as badly as Quinn said he did, then why
            should he fall out with Quinn?

STEVE: Er, yes … well … you answer that one darling!

TEMPLE: (*After a moment: quietly*) Your hunch might be
            right, Steve. I must confess I've had an odd sort
            of feeling about Quinn ever since the first night
            we met him. We'll probably find the poor little
            devil with his throat cut, or floating down the
            river.

STEVE: Darling, don't!

TEMPLE: Anyway, there's obviously no point in staying here. Let's go back to the boat.

SCENE 6:   DURANT's Rowing Boat

STEVE is climbing aboard.

TEMPLE: Watch yourself, Steve … that's it!

STEVE takes her place in the boat.

TEMPLE: (*To DURANT*) Can you manage all right, Durant?

DURANT is manipulating the oars, pushing the boat away from the houseboat. During the following the boat moves away.

DURANT: Yes ... you weren't very long …

TEMPLE: No. Durant, tell me: what did Bahri say to you, when he gave you your instructions?

DURANT: Instructions?

TEMPLE: To take me out to the houseboat.

DURANT: Instructions is hardly the right word. He paid me a thousand piastres and asked me to be on the look-out for you.

TEMPLE: But he did tell you to take me out to the houseboat?

DURANT: Yes.

TEMPLE: I'm rather interested in what you told me about that Irish fellow – Quinn. Was that the first time you'd seen him?

DURANT: No.

TEMPLE: You'd seen him before?

DURANT: Yes.

TEMPLE: Where?

DURANT: (*A little laugh*) You seem to be a pretty inquisitive sort of fellow. Do you always go round asking these questions?

TEMPLE: I make quite a point of it.

171

DURANT: I'll bet you do!

A pause as DURANT continues to row.

TEMPLE: Was Quinn a friend of yours?

DURANT: No, he wasn't. I've already told you that. (*A moment*) I'd seen him around – in pubs and places – you know how it is.

TEMPLE: Yes.

A pause, then a grunt from DURANT as his oar catches something in the water.

STEVE: (*Alarmed*) Paul, there's something in the water!

DURANT: Be careful! Don't rock the boat!

STEVE: Paul!

TEMPLE: Don't move, Steve! (*To DURANT*) What is it, Durant?

DURANT: (*Leaning over the side*) I don't know. I felt one of the oars strike something and … she's right! Look!

TEMPLE: What is it?

DURANT: There's someone in the water!

TEMPLE: Steve, keep still – you'll turn us over …

DURANT: Wait a minute – (*Moving an oar*) – I'll get this oar … over the other side … That's it! Now give me a hand!

TEMPLE: Don't move, Steve!

TEMPLE and DURANT lean out of the boat.

DURANT: You keep hold of me … That's it …

TEMPLE: (*Straining*) Have you got it?

DURANT: Yes. Now pull … pull …

DURANT is straining. Endeavouring to pull the body out of the water.

STEVE: Be careful!

TEMPLE: Watch it! Watch it for goodness sake, or you'll have us over …

172

DURANT: I've got it, but I can't quite … Hold on! Now, pull, pull!

The boat is rocking dangerously, near to overturning.

STEVE: Look … the body … it's turned over … it's … Do you see who it is? (*Desperately*) Paul, do you see who it is?

TEMPLE: (*Softly; staggered*) Good Lord – it's Miss Jeans!

FADE UP of music.

FADE DOWN of music.

SCENE 7: The TEMPLES' Hotel Bedroom

STEVE is getting ready for the evening.

A door opens, and TEMPLE enters.

TEMPLE: It's gone half past eight, darling. Are you nearly ready?

STEVE: Yes, I shan't be long. I've just got to fasten this clip. There!

TEMPLE: There's a message through from Darwin, he wants us to meet him at the Karamet.

STEVE: The Karamet?

TEMPLE: It's a hotel.

STEVE: Is it far from here?

TEMPLE: Yes, it's almost on the fringe of the desert. By the way, Steve, where did you put that map I gave you?

STEVE: It's in the dressing case by the side of the bed.

TEMPLE: Have you locked it?

STEVE: Yes. (*Turning*) All right, dear, I'm ready.

TEMPLE: Are you sure you feel up to this, Steve, because if you don't I can easily telephone Darwin.

STEVE: No, I'm all right. It was an awful shock, finding Miss Jeans like that, but I'm really all right now.

The telephone rings. STEVE lifts the receiver.

STEVE: Hello?

FORBES:	(*On the other end of the line*) Hello? Who is that?
STEVE:	This is Mrs Temple speaking – Room 187.
FORBES:	Hello, Steve!
STEVE:	Sir Graham! I didn't recognise you! Where are you speaking from? (*Aside to TEMPLE*) It's Sir Graham!
FORBES:	I'm in Cairo. I landed just over an hour ago. Is that husband of yours around?
STEVE:	Yes, of course! Here he is.
TEMPLE:	(*Taking the phone*) Hello. Sir Graham!
FORBES:	(*A serious note in his voice*) Hello, Temple. How are you?
TEMPLE:	Oh, I'm all right, I suppose.
FORBES:	Did you get my cable?
TEMPLE:	Yes. When did you arrive?
FORBES:	About an hour ago.
TEMPLE:	Where are you speaking from – you're not in the hotel?
FORBES:	(*A little laugh*) No, as a matter of fact, I'm with a friend of yours.
TEMPLE:	Oh? Who's that?
FORBES:	Commandant Hakim.
TEMPLE:	(*Laughing*) Hakim! That bumptious little owl.
FORBES:	I thought you'd say that! His bark's much worse than his bite.
TEMPLE:	Yes, well frankly I don't care for either.
FORBES:	I'd like to see you, Temple – when can we get together?
TEMPLE:	Well, that's up to you. Steve and I have a dinner engagement but we should be back by eleven at the latest.
FORBES:	All right. If it's not too late let's say your hotel – eleven thirty.

TEMPLE:	Fine. Look forward to seeing you. Oh, the room's 187 – come straight up.
FORBES:	Yes, all right.
TEMPLE:	(*Suddenly: an afterthought*) Oh, Sir Graham …
FORBES:	Yes?
TEMPLE:	(*With a little laugh*) What are you doing here? What has brought you out to Cairo anyway?

A moment.

FORBES:	(*Quite serious*) A pair of spectacles.

FADE UP of music.

FADE DOWN of music.

SCENE 8:   The Karamet Hotel Dining Room

A dance band plays: the music is soft in tone and not the conventional dance music. There is a faint background of chatter.

ZILLA, the head waiter at the Karamet, speaks softly and with an accent.

SCHREIDER:	Good evening, Zilla.
ZILLA:	Good evening, Herr Schreider. It is nice to see you again.
SCHREIDER:	Thank you. I'm expecting a guest, a Mr Whiteman.
ZILLA:	Mr Whiteman has already arrived, sir. He is on the terrace having a cocktail.
SCHREIDER:	(*Quietly*) Oh.
ZILLA:	Shall I send for him, sir?
SCHREIDER:	(*Making to move away*) No, it's all right, Zilla. I'll join him later.
ZILLA:	Thank you, sir.
SCHREIDER:	Oh – I gave my order to Angelo, I hope everything will be all right.
ZILLA:	Everything is exactly as you ordered it, sir.

SCHREIDER: (*Going*) Thank you.

ZILLA: Thank you, Herr Schreider.

Pause.

The orchestra continues.

The TEMPLES arrive.

TEMPLE: Good evening.

ZILLA: Good evening, sir. Good evening, madam.

TEMPLE: I think you have a table reserved for a Mr Darwin?

ZILLA: Mr Darwin? One moment, if you please. (*Consulting his list*) Mr … That is quite correct – Mr Darwin. But he has not arrived yet, sir.

TEMPLE: Oh.

ZILLA: If you would like to go to the table – or perhaps a cocktail on the terrace?

TEMPLE: It looks awfully nice on the terrace, darling.

ZILLA: It is a very fine terrace, madam. Perhaps the finest in the East. When it is clear – like this evening – you can see for miles, right across the desert.

STEVE: It sounds heavenly! Come along, darling!

ZILLA: (*Bowing*) Thank you, madam.

MIX to the terrace.

The orchestra is FADED DOWN to the distant background.

STEVE: He was certainly right, Paul! It's a magnificent view.

TEMPLE: Yes.

STEVE: Just look at those lights, and the desert … Darling, it's terribly romantic.

TEMPLE: Now don't start going all Ethel M Dell!

STEVE: (*Laughing*) I shall read The Way of An Eagle all over again! No, but seriously, you know Miss Fraser was right about this place – about

176

	Cairo, I mean – she said that in spite of all the – (*She stops*) What are you staring at?
TEMPLE:	The man with the moustache; the old boy with the walking stick. I've seen him before, darling … (*Softly*) By Timothy! Steve, it's Marquand! (*Suddenly*) Stay here, Steve …

STEVE makes to go with TEMPLE.

TEMPLE:	No, no, I shan't be a minute. Stay here, darling!

TEMPLE crosses the terrace to where MARQUAND is sitting.

TEMPLE:	(*Pleasantly*) Good evening, Colonel Marquand.
MARQUAND:	(*Looking up*) I beg your pardon?
TEMPLE:	I said, good evening, Colonel Marquand.
MARQUAND:	(*With a slight Southern accent*) You have the advantage of me, sir. My name is Whiteman.
TEMPLE:	Since when?
MARQUAND:	(*With dignity*) What do you mean, sir?
TEMPLE:	You called yourself Marquand in Augusta, so …
MARQUAND:	(*Angrily*) I tell you my name is Whiteman, sir. Oliver J. Whiteman of Charleston, South Carolina.

A pause.

TEMPLE:	(*With a polite little bow*) I beg your pardon. Obviously I've made a mistake. (*With a little laugh*) It's a pity you're not Colonel Marquand because I've got something which I think belongs to him.
MARQUAND:	(*Intrigued: his normal voice*) What?
TEMPLE:	But of course if your name is Whiteman, sir, then …

177

MARQUAND: (*With authority: the old note of menace*) What have you got that belongs to Colonel Marquand?

A moment.

TEMPLE: (*Quietly*) This …

A moment.

MARQUAND: (*Puzzled*) What is it?

TEMPLE: (*Watching MARQUAND*) What does it look like?

MARQUAND: Well, it looks like a piece of cord …

FADE UP of music.

END OF EPISODE SIX

EPISODE SEVEN

MR DARWIN ENTERTAINS

OPEN TO:

The Terrace of the Hotel Karamet.
As in Episode 6, Scene 8.

MARQUAND: (*Angrily*) I tell you my name is Whiteman, sir. Oliver J. Whiteman of Charleston, South Carolina.

A pause.

TEMPLE: (*With a polite little bow*) I beg your pardon. Obviously I've made a mistake. (*With a little laugh*) It's a pity you're not Colonel Marquand because I've got something which I think belongs to him.

MARQUAND: (*Intrigued: his normal voice*) What?

TEMPLE: But of course if your name is Whiteman, sir, then …

MARQUAND: (*With authority: the old note of menace*) What have you got that belongs to Colonel Marquand?

A moment.

TEMPLE: (*Quietly*) This …

A moment.

MARQUAND: (*Puzzled*) What is it?

TEMPLE: (*Watching MARQUAND*) What does it look like?

MARQUAND: Well, it looks like a piece of cord …

TEMPLE: For your information – it is a cord. Probably part of a Venetian blind. It was used for a very horrible purpose.

MARQUAND: What do you mean?

TEMPLE: A girl was strangled with it.

MARQUAND: What girl?

TEMPLE: A certain Miss Jeans. She was strangled and her body was thrown into the Nile.

MARQUAND: (*Continuing to bluff*) Yes, well all this is mighty interesting, sir, but confusing, you see. My name is Whiteman, sir – Oliver J. Whiteman and believe me I've never even heard of your friend Colonel …?

TEMPLE: Marquand.

MARQUAND: Colonel Marquand.

TEMPLE: (*A note of sarcasm, as he leaves*) I'm sorry to have disturbed you, Mr Whiteman.

MARQUAND: Not at all, sir.

TEMPLE crosses the terrace and returns to STEVE.

STEVE: What did he say?

TEMPLE: He says his name's Whiteman, and he's got an accent as phoney as his moustache!

STEVE: I saw you take something out of your pocket just now and show it to him. What was it, darling?

TEMPLE: It was this.

STEVE: (*A little surprised*) Why, that's the piece of cord you found on the houseboat.

TEMPLE: Yes. (*A moment*) Steve, did you take a good look at Miss Jeans when she was in the water?

STEVE: Yes.

TEMPLE: She'd been strangled; did you realise that?

STEVE: (*Softly*) Yes. I saw the red mark across her throat. I thought something like that had happened. (*Puzzled*) Paul, was she murdered on the houseboat and then thrown into the river?

TEMPLE: Yes.

STEVE: (*Bewildered*) But what was she doing on the boat in the first place?

TEMPLE: Someone must have sent for her. Unless of course …

STEVE: Unless what, darling?

TEMPLE: (*Thoughtfully*) Well, Miss Jeans was working with Marquand, we know that because of the conversation we overheard in the bedroom … Now if Marquand deliberately – (*He stops speaking*)

STEVE: (*Softly*) Who's this?

TEMPLE: Good evening, Herr Schreider!

SCHREIDER: (*Taken by surprise*) Mr Temple, this is a surprise!

TEMPLE: I don't think you know my wife?

SCHREIDER: No, I have not had that pleasure. How do you do?

TEMPLE: (*To STEVE*) Mr Schreider owns the El Passaro, dear – in Augusta – do you remember?

STEVE: Oh, yes! A delightful restaurant.

SCHREIDER: You are very kind, madam, I'm so glad you liked it.

TEMPLE: Will you join us in a cocktail?

SCHREIDER: Well, that's very kind of you, but I am supposed to be dining with a business friend and – well – I am already a little on the late side. (*Smiling*) So – if you will excuse me?

TEMPLE: Yes, of course.

SCHREIDER: Delighted to have made your acquaintance, Mrs Temple. (*Going*) I hope we shall meet again.

STEVE: I hope so too.

TEMPLE: Oh, Mr Schreider!

SCHREIDER: (*Turning*) Yes?

TEMPLE:	This friend of yours wouldn't by any chance be Colonel Marquand?
SCHREIDER:	(*Apparently amazed*) Colonel Marquand? But of course not! (*A note of confidence*) There is a warrant out for his arrest, didn't you know that?
TEMPLE:	I did hear a rumour.
SCHREIDER:	Mr Temple, I wonder if you will forgive me if I ask you a rather personal question?
TEMPLE:	(*Smiling*) That depends what it is.
SCHREIDER:	What are you <u>doing</u> here – in Cairo?
TEMPLE:	Well, I came originally to get data for a new book I'm writing, but …
SCHREIDER:	But you've had other fish to cook?
They laugh.	
TEMPLE:	That's one way of putting it!
SCHREIDER:	After you left my café that night I talked to Signore Rossetti. You remember Signore Rossetti?
TEMPLE:	Yes.
SCHREIDER:	He told me that you had been asked to deliver a pair of spectacles to a man in Cairo by the name of Richard Sullivan. Is that correct?
TEMPLE:	What else did he say?
SCHREIDER:	(*Smiling*) He told me that you had been offered £10,000 for the spectacles. (*Highly amused*) That seems an awful lot of money, for just a perfectly ordinary pair of spectacles, don't you agree?
TEMPLE:	An awful lot of money, Mr Schreider.
SCHREIDER:	But of course, it was just a joke.
TEMPLE:	I don't think so.
SCHREIDER:	But who would make such an offer – seriously, I mean?

TEMPLE: A Mr Constantine.

SCHREIDER: Mr Constantine? But he was the man you were looking for, the man you expected to find at my café.

TEMPLE: Yes.

SCHREIDER: (*Seriously*) Why did he want those glasses, do you know?

TEMPLE: Well, presumably for the same reason that Colonel Marquand wants them.

SCHREIDER: (*Surprised*) Did Colonel Marquand offer you £10,000 for them?

TEMPLE: Not exactly.

SCHREIDER: (*A little laugh*) Well, it's all very odd, but most intriguing; don't you agree, Mrs Temple?

STEVE: Most intriguing. (*Lightly*) How long have you been interested in them, Mr Schreider?

SCHREIDER: Oh, I'm just curious, that's all. Ever since Signore Rossetti told me about the spectacles I have been rather intrigued.

TEMPLE: (*Laughing*) Then I take it you're not going to fall into line and make me an offer for them?

SCHREIDER: My offer is 12/6d, take it or leave it!

They all laugh.

SCHREIDER: Now, if you'll excuse me? Goodnight, Mrs Temple.

STEVE: (*Still amused*) Goodnight, Mr Schreider.

SCHREIDER: (*To   TEMPLE,   as   he   leaves*) Auf Wiedersehen!

TEMPLE: Goodbye, Schreider!

A pause.

STEVE: Well, what do you make of that, darling?

TEMPLE: What do you make of it?

STEVE: Obviously Schreider doesn't know why Constantine offered you such a ridiculous sum for the glasses and he was trying to find out if you knew.

TEMPLE: That's one way of looking at it.

STEVE: What's the other way?

TEMPLE: (*Quietly: serious*) Schreider knows what's behind the glasses all right and he knows why Constantine offered me £10,000 for them.

STEVE: Then why should he so obviously go out of his way to pump you about them?

TEMPLE: Because he's not sure, in his own mind, just exactly how much I know about this business – and he'd like to find out.

STEVE: How much do you know, darling?

TEMPLE: (*Smiling at STEVE*) You'd be surprised … Ah, here's Darwin!

DARWIN arrives at the table.

DARWIN: I do apologise! I'm terribly sorry, Temple! It's really quite unforgivable of me to keep you both waiting like this! So sorry, Mrs Temple.

STEVE: (*Pleasantly*) That's all right. You sit here.

DARWIN: Thanks. (*He sits*) Well, how are you, Mrs Temple? Are you feeling any better? You certainly look much better. You certainly look much better than you did this morning!

STEVE: I'm much better thanks. I certainly felt awful this morning.

DARWIN: Good. You know that was a peculiar business. I don't understand even now what really happened.

STEVE: Well, I think I fainted.

DARWIN: Yes, but what made you faint?

STEVE: I really don't know. I suppose it must have been the heat.

DARWIN: Well, it didn't look like the heat to me.

STEVE: What did it look like?

DARWIN: It looked to me as if you'd been drugged or something.

STEVE: Drugged?

DARWIN: Yes.

TEMPLE: Why should anyone want to drug my wife?

DARWIN: Supposing you answer that question, Temple?

TEMPLE: What do you mean?

DARWIN: Do you remember when we first met – the three of us? It was the night when we discovered the body of Joyce Raymond.

TEMPLE: Yes, I remember.

DARWIN: Do you remember our second meeting? At Sandbanks, when your boat had somewhat mysteriously overturned and I pulled you out of the water.

TEMPLE: Well?

DARWIN: Well, by nature, I'm not a particularly inquisitive sort of person, Temple, but – quite frankly … What the devil's it all about?

TEMPLE: (*A moment: then quietly*) Let's have a cocktail and then I'll tell you what it's all about.

DARWIN: Right! Shall we go inside or stay out here on the terrace? They've got rather a cute little bar here, Mrs Temple, if you haven't seen it.

STEVE: Is this the place I've read about – the bar's in the middle of a sort of illuminated aquarium?

DARWIN: That's it. (*Laughing*) Even the fish are lit up!

STEVE: Sounds fascinating!

DARWIN: (*Taking STEVE by the arm*) Come along, Mrs Temple.

187

SCENE 2: The Bar

There is a low background of conversation.

DARWIN: … But this is an incredible story – I can hardly believe it!

TEMPLE: (*Pleasantly*) Whether you believe it or not, Darwin, it's true.

DARWIN: (*Still astonished*) But this girl – Sidney Jeans – was <u>she</u> after the glasses?

TEMPLE: Yes.

DARWIN: But it really is incredible, why should she go to such lengths to get hold of a perfectly … You know, quite honestly, I still can't believe it. Oh, please, don't misunderstand me; I don't doubt your word for a moment, but it really is quite a story!

STEVE: I couldn't agree with you more, Mr Darwin!

DARWIN: Is it your opinion then that these people are all working together or …

TEMPLE: Miss Jeans was working with Marquand, so is the other man I mentioned – Armstrong. But Quinn, the Irish fellow –

DARWIN: The man that's supposed to be dead?

TEMPLE: Yes. He's obviously hand in glove with Bahri.

DARWIN: And what about the other man – the man you met on the flying boat – Constantine?

TEMPLE: Well, he was obviously working alone – or with someone else we haven't yet met.

DARWIN: In other words it's your opinion that there are three or four separate groups of people all trying to get hold of the spectacles.

TEMPLE: Yes.

DARWIN: Well, it really is quite incredible! What are they like, anyway – these spectacles?

TEMPLE: They're just a pair of spectacles.

DARWIN: Have you got them on you?

TEMPLE: No.

STEVE: Why, would you like to buy them, Mr Darwin?

DARWIN: Buy them! After what your husband's told me I'd give the best of five hundred pounds to get rid of the things.

They all laugh.

DARWIN: No, but seriously, I would rather like to see them.

TEMPLE: All right, pop into the hotel one morning and we'll – (*He sees the waiter approaching*) Yes, waiter, what is it?

GUSTAV: I beg your pardon, sir – Mr Temple?

TEMPLE: Yes?

GUSTAV: I was asked to deliver this note to you, sir.

TEMPLE: Oh – thank you. Wait a moment!

TEMPLE takes the note: opens it and reads it.

TEMPLE: (*Quietly*) Who gave you this?

GUSTAV: A gentleman on the terrace, sir.

TEMPLE: Which gentleman?

GUSTAV: He gave no name, sir.

TEMPLE: Well, what did he look like?

GUSTAV: Well he was an oddly dressed little man, sir. his hair was – what do you call it? – a reddish colour – auburn. He spoke English with a strange accent.

TEMPLE: A foreign accent?

GUSTAV: Not exactly foreign, sir.

STEVE: (*Softly: surprised*) It's Quinn, darling!

TEMPLE: Yes. All right, waiter. Thank you.

GUSTAV: (*Going*) Thank you, sir.

DARWIN: (*Curious*) What is it?

STEVE: What does the note say?

189

TEMPLE: It doesn't say anything: at least nothing that makes sense. (*Handing over the note*) Here we are, read it for yourselves.

DARWIN: (*Slowly: reading*) X K D 88.

STEVE: X K D 88 … What does that mean?

DARWIN: Well, it doesn't mean anything to me.

STEVE: Well, it must mean something, otherwise. What do you think, Paul?

A moment.

TEMPLE: (*Quietly: to DARWIN*) Have you got your car here?

DARWIN: Why yes, of course, I came in it.

TEMPLE: What's the number?

DARWIN: D L K 94 … Look here, do you think this refers to a car, then? Do you think it's a registration number?

TEMPLE: Well, if it isn't – what else is it?

DARWIN: (*A little laugh*) I don't know; but I fail to see why Quinn should … (*He stops*) I say, just a minute! I'm beginning to catch on! This looks to me as if Quinn wants to see you and he's sent you the number of his car in the hope that …

STEVE: Where's the car park here?

DARWIN: Yes, of course; it's over on the other side of the hotel.

TEMPLE: Come on, Darwin – show me where it is!

SCENE 3: The Hotel Car Park

Cars are drawing up, we hear their brakes and car doors opening and closing. We also hear one or two voices of people passing into the hotel.

STEVE: Well, this is certainly the car park but I don't see any sign of X K D 88.

DARWIN: No, neither do I.

190

TEMPLE: (*Away from the others: calling across*) What's that red car … the coupé …?
DARWIN: The one with the GB plate?
TEMPLE: Yes.
DARWIN: (*A moment, as he looks*) No, I don't think …
STEVE: No, it's K Y … something or other …
TEMPLE: (*Joining DARWIN and STEVE*) Well, it doesn't seem to be here …
DARWIN: No, I'm afraid it doesn't.
STEVE: I noticed one or two cars parked over on the other side, did you?
TEMPLE: Where?
STEVE: Near the terrace.
DARWIN: (*Shaking his head*) No …
TEMPLE: Let's have a stroll round there.
DARWIN: You know, maybe you were wrong about this, Temple. Perhaps it isn't a car number after all …
In the background there is the sound of a revolver shot.
DARWIN: … in which case we're on the wrong track.
STEVE: Did you hear that?
TEMPLE: Yes!
DARWIN: What was it?
TEMPLE: (*Doubtfully*) Well, it might have been a car backfiring, but …
STEVE: It didn't sound like a car to me!
TEMPLE: No, it didn't to me either!
DARWIN: Well whatever it was, it was over on the other side where Mrs Temple said the cars were parked.
TEMPLE: Yes. Come on, let's go round there!

SCENE 4: In the Hotel Ground near the terrace
About four or five rather excited people are crowding round a stationary car.

TEMPLE arrives.

TEMPLE: What's happened here?

MAN: Some crazy guy's blown his brains out! Didn't you hear the shot?

TEMPLE: Yes.

DARWIN and STEVE arrive.

DARWIN: What is it? What happened?

STEVE: What's happened, darling?

TEMPLE: I don't know, Steve. (*Starting to elbow his way through the group*) Will you excuse me please, I …

DARWIN: (*Suddenly: quietly*) Temple!

TEMPLE: (*Turning*) Yes? What is it?

DARWIN: (*Quickly*) Look at the car! Look at the number!

STEVE: This is the one, Paul! Look – X K D 88.

TEMPLE: (*Forcing his way through the group*) Excuse me … Excuse me, please … Do you mind, please … Thank you …

A definite pause.

TEMPLE surveys the scene at the car.

Then he returns to STEVE and DARWIN.

TEMPLE: Excuse me … Thank you.

DARWIN: Who is it? Is it Quinn?

TEMPLE: Yes, he's apparently shot himself: he's still got the revolver in his hand.

DARWIN: (*Non-plussed*) Suicide!

STEVE: But why should Quinn commit suicide?

TEMPLE: (*Thoughtfully: he hasn't heard what STEVE has said*) Let's go back into the hotel.

FADE UP of music.

FADE DOWN of music.

SCENE 5:   The Hotel Restaurant

The orchestra is playing.

TEMPLE, STEVE and DARWIN are at a table.

DARWIN: You know, Temple, the thing I can't understand is why Quinn sent you this note. If he wanted you to meet him why did he commit suicide?

STEVE: If it was suicide.

TEMPLE: Well, from what I can gather the police seem pretty convinced.

DARWIN: What do you think?

TEMPLE: (*Thoughtfully*) Well, it looked like suicide – on the other hand I must confess I'm not exactly happy about that note.

DARWIN: Did you tell the Inspector – or Commandant – or whatever he calls himself – about the note?

TEMPLE: Yes.

STEVE: What did he say?

TEMPLE: He doesn't seem to attach a great deal of importance to it, he seems pretty set on the suicide theory.

DARWIN: M'm.

GUSTAV is approaching.

STEVE: Here's the waiter – it's the one that brought you the note, Paul.

TEMPLE: Yes.

GUSTAV: May I take your order, sir?

DARWIN: Yes, by all means … I think to start with we'll have some of these flowers off the table!

TEMPLE: (*Laughing*) It is rather like the botanical gardens!

STEVE: Oh, not the pink ones! They're lovely!

DARWIN: Leave the pink ones, Gustav.

GUSTAV: Very good, sir.

DARWIN: Now what would you like, Mrs Temple? I can recommend the – (*He stops: to GUSTAV*) Those are the pink flowers! Leave those and take the others!

GUSTAV: Oh I'm so sorry, sir.

DARWIN: (*Amused*) The poor blighter seems to be in quite a dither!

TEMPLE: Yes. I think the police had a word with him about the note.

DARWIN: That accounts for it. Now, Mrs Temple, as I was saying, I can recommend …

STEVE: You can recommend what you like, Mr Darwin! I know what I'm having! I'm having a large steak and chips.

DARWIN: (*Amused*) This isn't the sort of place that specialises in steak and chips, Mrs Temple, but I can recommend the Gebna Beida Bel –

STEVE: (*Interrupting DARWIN politely*) No.

DARWIN: No?

STEVE: Ever since we left England, I've been looking forward to a square meal. So where is the sort of place that specialises in steak and chips?

They all laugh.

SCENE 6:   The Car Park

DARWIN opens the door of his car for STEVE.

DARWIN: Jump in, Mrs Temple.

STEVE: Are you sure this isn't taking you out of your way?

DARWIN: Of course it isn't … I can drop you at the hotel as easy as pie. (*He notices TEMPLE*) What's the matter, old boy?

TEMPLE: (*Searching his pockets*) I seem to have lost my confounded cigarette case, I'm sure I had it …

STEVE: You had it at the table, darling.

TEMPLE: (*Still searching*) Yes, I know I did …

DARWIN: Is it in your inside pocket?

TEMPLE: No … No, I'm afraid it isn't. I must have put it down somewhere.

DARWIN: I hope you haven't lost it!

TEMPLE: I'll pop back to the table. Will you excuse me a moment?

DARWIN: Yes, of course.

TEMPLE: I shan't be long, Steve.

SCENE 7: The Hotel Restaurant

The orchestra finishes a number. There is slight applause.

TEMPLE: (*Quietly*) Waiter …

WAITER: Sir?

TEMPLE: Would you mind telling that waiter over there I'd rather like to have a word with him.

WAITER: (*Surprised*) Which waiter, sir?

TEMPLE: The dark one, with the black hair, the one they call Gustav. I shall be on the terrace.

WAITER: Very good, sir.

SCENE 8: The Terrace

GUSTAV: You wanted to see me, sir?

TEMPLE: (*Pleasantly*) Ah, yes! I gather the Commandant had a chat to you about that note?

GUSTAV: Yes, he wanted to know who gave it to me.

TEMPLE: What did you tell him?

GUSTAV: (*Surprised*) Why, I told him the truth. It was given to me by the gentleman who committed suicide.

TEMPLE: Mr Quinn?

GUSTAV: Yes. Mr Quinn.

TEMPLE: Did you identify Mr Quinn?

GUSTAV: (*Puzzled*) What do you mean, sir?

TEMPLE: You've seen Quinn, I take it – since he was shot?

GUSTAV: Yes.

TEMPLE: Did you identify him as the man who handed you the note?

GUSTAV: But of course! He was the man who gave me the note.

TEMPLE: Had you ever spoken to him before?

GUSTAV: Why no, sir – I'd never even seen him before.

TEMPLE: Had anyone else spoken to you about him?

GUSTAV: No, sir.

TEMPLE: (*Quietly*) What is your name?

GUSTAV: Gustav Valkerie, sir.

TEMPLE: Well, Valkerie, I wonder if you would do something for me? Just come over here for a moment.

A pause.

TEMPLE: Now … you see that lady over there – at the table near the window?

GUSTAV: Yes, sir?

TEMPLE: Tell me: what sort of a dress is she wearing?

GUSTAV: What sort of a dress is she wearing?

TEMPLE: Yes. What colour is it?

GUSTAV: (*Laughing*) I'm sorry, sir, I can't tell you the colour.

TEMPLE: Oh? Why not?

GUSTAV: Because I'm what you call colour blind, sir.

TEMPLE: Colour blind?

GUSTAV: Yes, sir.

TEMPLE: (*Nodding*) Yes, I rather gathered that when you made the mistake with the flowers. Well, if you're colour blind, Valkerie, would you mind explaining to me how you were able to describe Mr Quinn as an oddly dressed little man with reddish – auburn – hair?

GUSTAV: But … he was an oddly dressed little man with auburn hair!

196

TEMPLE: That's not quite the point: how did you know?

GUSTAV: I could see him.

TEMPLE: You could see the colour of his hair?

GUSTAV: (*Angrily*) Look here, what are you getting at?

TEMPLE: (*Obviously not going to stand any nonsense*) I'll tell you what I'm getting at. I'm getting at the fact that in my opinion Quinn didn't give you that note: someone else gave it to you; and told you to bring it to me.

GUSTAV: That's a lie! I tell you that Quinn …

TEMPLE: Who gave you that note?

GUSTAV: (*Slowly: watching TEMPLE*) Quinn gave it to me: he gave me the note and told me to deliver it to you in the cocktail bar.

TEMPLE: I don't believe you, Valkerie.

GUSTAV: It's a matter of complete indifference to me whether you believe it or not.

TEMPLE: Is it?

GUSTAV: What are you getting at?

TEMPLE: Supposing I told you that the police are under the impression that Quinn was murdered.

GUSTAV: But Quinn committed suicide, he had the revolver in his hand.

TEMPLE: He had a revolver in his hand.

GUSTAV: (*A moment: a little frightened*) What do you mean?

TEMPLE: (*Watching GUSTAV*) I've got a theory about this, Valkerie: about what happened tonight I mean. Before I can prove whether my theory's right or wrong, I've got to know the truth. Who gave you that note?

GUSTAV: I've told you.

TEMPLE: (*With force*) Who gave you that note?

GUSTAV: If you think you're going to bully me into –

197

TEMPLE: (*Softly*) Who gave you that note?

GUSTAV: I've told you Quinn gave it to me …

TEMPLE suddenly grabs GUSTAV's arm.

GUSTAV: My arm! Don't! Please, don't! Don't!

TEMPLE: Are you going to tell me what happened?

GUSTAV: Don't … Please, don't …

TEMPLE: Are you going to tell me what happened, Valkerie?

GUSTAV: I've told you the truth. I swear.

TEMPLE: Are you going to tell me …

GUSTAV: (*Suddenly: desperately*) All right! All right, I'll tell you what happened. I'll tell you the truth … I'll tell you exactly what happened …

TEMPLE: Go on. (*A moment*) Go on, Valkerie …

GUSTAV: (*Hesitantly*) Just before you and Mrs Temple arrived here tonight a man told me to …

SCENE 9:   The Car Park.

TEMPLE arrives a little out of breath.

TEMPLE: Sorry to have been such a long time!

DARWIN: That's all right old boy! Did you find your cigarette case?

TEMPLE: Yes. The waiter had it. I must have left it on the terrace.

DARWIN: (*Laughing*) Well, things certainly seem to happen to you two!

TEMPLE: (*Laughing*) Yes.

STEVE: Your shirt's awfully crumpled, darling.

TEMPLE: M'm?

STEVE: Your shirt.

TEMPLE: Oh, yes … I've been running.

DARWIN: (*Pleasantly*) Well, jump in!

They all get into DARWIN's car, shut their doors and DARWIN starts the engine and drives away.

SCENE 10: The Interior of DARWIN's car, travelling along.

DARWIN: Are you quite comfy, Mrs Temple?

STEVE: Yes, I'm fine thanks.

DARWIN: (*After a pause*) Temple, I've been thinking … about what you've told me, I mean.

TEMPLE: Yes?

DARWIN: Do you think Miss Fraser's mixed up in this business – do you think she's after the spectacles?

TEMPLE: (*With a laugh*) Miss Fraser? Why mention poor Miss Fraser?

DARWIN: Oh, I don't know. Perhaps it's my imagination, but she seems rather an odd sort of person. Also she … (*With a laugh*) Well, she keeps popping up every now and again, doesn't she?

STEVE: What do you mean, Mr Darwin?

DARWIN: Well, she stayed at the hotel in Bournemouth – the one where Joyce Raymond was murdered – she was on the flying-boat, naturally she stayed the night in Augusta, and, well … I've …

TEMPLE: You've what?

DARWIN: I've seen her several times in Cairo.

STEVE: I thought you were quite friendly with her – you invited her to the El Passaro.

DARWIN: (*With a laugh*) Yes, I was rather hoping she'd give me an introduction to her brother.

STEVE: But I thought you knew her brother?

DARWIN: (*Laughing*) No, I've never met him. I'm afraid I was pulling a fast one.

TEMPLE: Yes, well, I don't think we need worry about Miss Fraser.

DARWIN: (*A little surprised*) No?

TEMPLE: No.

199

DARWIN: Well, how do you account for the lozenge – the peppermint?

TEMPLE: (*Innocently*) Which particular peppermint?

DARWIN: (*Faintly bewildered by TEMPLE's attitude*) The one we found by the bedroom door.

TEMPLE: Well, quite obviously, Miss Fraser must have dropped it.

DARWIN: Well, there you are!

TEMPLE: What do you mean, there you are?

STEVE: (*A little surprised by TEMPLE's apparent stupidity*) Mr Darwin means that Miss Fraser must have been in the bedroom otherwise …

TEMPLE: But I know Miss Fraser was in the bedroom!

STEVE: (*Taken aback*) How do you know?

TEMPLE: She told me. Not only that but I enquired at the reception desk. You see Miss Fraser was very late arriving at the hotel. Actually she checked in just as Armstrong was about to leave. They offered her the same room: she took the room and took a dislike to it.

STEVE: Then that accounts for … (*She stops*) Oh, do be careful, Mr Darwin!

TEMPLE: Is anything the matter?

DARWIN: (*After a moment*) I don't know … The steering seemed a bit odd …

TEMPLE: Have you been having trouble with it?

DARWIN: No …

TEMPLE: Well, take it steady, it's rather tricky just here …

DARWIN: I'm dashed if I can understand it.

A pause.

TEMPLE: Is it all right now?

DARWIN: (*A moment: slowly*) Yes, I think so …

STEVE: Do be careful.

DARWIN: Don't worry. Mrs Temple, I won't take any risks … (*Suddenly: alarmed*) It's started again! What the devil is it? Temple, what on earth's the matter with it?

STEVE: (*Alarmed*) Paul!

TEMPLE: Brake! Put your brakes on! Brake!

DARWIN presses on the footbrake: there is a noise as the connecting rod falls to the ground followed by a screeching of brakes.

The car stops.

DARWIN: Well, that's extraordinary! I couldn't control the blessed thing …!

TEMPLE: Are you all right, Steve?

STEVE: Yes, I'm all right, darling.

DARWIN: I'm sorry about this, Mrs Temple.

TEMPLE: Let me feel the steering wheel.

TEMPLE turns the wheel.

DARWIN: Something seemed to snap: I felt it when I put the brake on.

TEMPLE: M'm.

DARWIN: Do you think it's serious?

TEMPLE: Let's get out and have a look. Switch your engine off.

DARWIN switches the engine off.

TEMPLE and DARWIN open their doors and get out of the car. TEMPLE looks under the car.

DARWIN: Can you see anything?

A slight pause.

TEMPLE: (*Straightening himself*) No wonder you couldn't steer very well, Darwin.

DARWIN: Why? What's happened?

TEMPLE: The drag-link's been forced out of its socket. It was only held together by this piece of wire.

DARWIN: (*Seriously*) What do you mean?

TEMPLE: Sooner or later this was bound to give way and the steering go to pieces.

DARWIN: But that's ridiculous! I only had the car overhauled yesterday … Are you trying to tell me that car's been tampered with?

TEMPLE: (*Significantly*) Apparently things happen to you too, Darwin.

FADE UP of music.

FADE DOWN of music.

SCENE 11: The Forecourt of the Hotel Continental

A horse and cart draws up.

DRIVER: (*Egyptian*) Here we are … Hotel Continental.

STEVE: Well, thanks for the buggy ride!

DRIVER: (*Grinning*) Hotel Continental!

DARWIN: I'm terribly sorry about this, Mrs Temple! Do you know I've had that car for five years and that's the first time it's let me down!

TEMPLE: (*Amused*) That's all right, old boy.

DRIVER: (*Still grinning*) Hotel Continental.

STEVE: (*Climbing down*) Gosh, my back!

TEMPLE: (*Climbing down*) Are you coming in to have a drink, Darwin?

DARWIN: No, but I'm coming in to order a car. (*Climbing down*) I've had quite enough of this barouche!

DRIVER: (*Grinning*) Hotel Continental …

STEVE: Darling, what's he keep saying?

DARWIN: He's saying Hotel Continental, but what he really means is how about it! (*Laughing as he hands over money*) Here we are, Ben Hur!

They all laugh.

SCENE 12: The Hotel Reception Desk

DARWIN: Do you think you could get me a private car?

CLERK: Where for, sir?

DARWIN: The Cosmopolitan.

CLERK: Yes, I think so, sir – if you will be kind enough to wait a few moments.

DARWIN: Thank you.

CLERK: Mr Temple?

TEMPLE: Yes?

CLERK: The gentleman you are expecting has arrived, sir: he is in your room.

TEMPLE: Oh – thank you.

CLERK: Thank you, sir.

DARWIN: Well, I'll say goodnight. I'm sorry it turned out to be such a grim evening, Mrs Temple.

STEVE: Oh, that's all right. Goodnight, Mr Darwin.

TEMPLE: Goodnight, Darwin.

DARWIN: Goodnight, Temple. Oh, now don't forget you promised to let me see those glasses.

TEMPLE: Well, I'm afraid I can't show you them tonight, but if you'd care to drop in the hotel tomorrow sometime …

DARWIN: That's a date! (*With a laugh*) You'll never convince me they're just a perfectly ordinary pair of spectacles, not after what you've told me about them.

TEMPLE: Well, if you can find anything … Why, hello, Miss Fraser!

FRASER: (*Pleasantly surprised*) Why good evening, Mr Temple! Mrs Temple! … and Mr Darwin! My word, quite a party!

STEVE: We've just been dining with Mr Darwin at the Karamet and –

FRASER: (*Interrupting STEVE*) At the Karamet? Now isn't that a delightful place! Is it the first time you've been there, Mrs Temple?

STEVE: Yes; it's really lovely.

FRASER: It's one of the nicest places I've ever been to, certainly one of the nicest in Egypt.

CLERK: Your car has arrived, Miss Fraser.

FRASER: Oh, thank you. (*She drops her bag: the contents scatter*) Oh dear! (*Exasperated*) I'm always dropping my handbag! I don't know why it is, but ... T't ... Just look, everything's all over the place!

DARWIN: It's all right, Miss Fraser. (*Picking up the contents of the handbag: laughing*) Here's your glasses ... and your handkerchief.

FRASER: Thank you.

STEVE: And your diary.

FRASER: Thank you ...

TEMPLE: And your purse, Miss Fraser.

FRASER: Oh, thank you! Dear-oh-dear! I certainly am a butterfingers!

TEMPLE: (*Laughing*) I'm rather afraid you've lost one or two peppermints.

FRASER: I shall be losing my head one of these fine days!

STEVE: (*Quietly: seriously*) Is this yours, Miss Fraser?

A moment.

FRASER: (*With a little laugh*) Oh – the revolver! Yes ... yes, that's mine, Mrs Temple. (*Taking it*) Thank you. It's small, but it's a real one you know.

STEVE: Yes, I can – quite believe it.

FRASER: My brother gave it to me a long time ago; it's a sort of curio. Often makes people laugh you know to think of my carrying a thing like that around.

STEVE: (*With a little laugh*) Yes ...

DARWIN: (*Facing MISS FRASER*) Why do you carry it around, Miss Fraser?

FRASER: (*Faintly surprised by the question*) Why? (*Smiling*) Let me show you, Mr Darwin. You hold it in your hand like this. You put your finger on the trigger.

DARWIN: (*Quickly*) Is it loaded?

FRASER: Yes, it's loaded.

DARWIN: Well, would you mind pointing it the other way, just in case.

FRASER: (*Taking no notice of DARWIN*) But it's quite all right, you see you just press the trigger … (*She presses the trigger and DARWIN and STEVE gasp*) … and it springs open and it's (*Smiling*) … loaded with peppermints.

DARWIN: Yes, well … er …

TEMPLE and STEVE laugh. DARWIN sees the funny side of it and starts to laugh.

FRASER: (*To the CLERK*) Did you say my car was ready?

CLERK: Yes, madam.

FRASER: Can I drop you anywhere, Mr Darwin?

DARWIN: Well, I want to get to the Cosmopolitan, but …

FRASER: I'll drop you at the door with pleasure.

DARWIN: That's very kind of you.

FRASER: Not at all. (*Brightly*) Well, we'll say goodnight, Mr … Temple.

DARWIN: (*Pleasantly*) See you tomorrow!

TEMPLE: (*Suddenly*) Look here, why don't you dine with us tomorrow night, Miss Fraser … you too, Darwin?

FRASER: That's very kind of you, Mr Temple – I should be delighted.

TEMPLE: Darwin?

DARWIN: Yes … Yes, splendid, old boy.

TEMPLE: I can show you the glasses then.

DARWIN: Right!

205

TEMPLE: Eight o'clock?

DARWIN: Splendid!

FRASER: (*Going*) Well – till tomorrow night then – au revoir, Mrs Temple!

STEVE: Goodbye, Miss Fraser!

DARWIN: (*Going*) See you tomorrow then!

TEMPLE: Yes.

DARWIN: Cheers!

STEVE: Is Sir Graham upstairs?

TEMPLE: Yes, darling, he's in our room: he's waiting for us.

SCENE 13:   The TEMPLES' Room

TEMPLE: … When I asked you over the telephone, Sir Graham, what you were doing here – in Cairo – you said: I'm here because of the spectacles … What did you mean by that?

FORBES: (*Slowly: seriously*) Have you still got the spectacles, the ones that Miss Raymond gave you?

TEMPLE: Of course I've got them.

FORBES: Well, where are they?

TEMPLE: Well, just at the moment they're in a safe deposit at the Anglo-Egyptian Bank.

FORBES: (*A slow smile*) You obviously don't believe in taking risks, Temple.

TEMPLE: I believe in taking risks, Sir Graham – you know that – but not unnecessary ones.

FORBES: Well, it's darned nice to see you again, both of you: and considering all that's happened you're both looking remarkably fit. By the way, how's the son and heir?

STEVE: Oh, Peter's fine. He's staying down at Bramley Lodge while we're away.

206

FORBES: He must be quite a big boy by now! How old is he, Steve?

STEVE: He's just two, Sir Graham. (*A sigh*) Gosh, I'm longing to see him again!

TEMPLE: In between our gay little escapades Steve is quite the devoted mother, Sir Graham!

FORBES: (*Laughing*) I know that, of course.

TEMPLE: No, but Peter really is an exceptional child – isn't he, darling?

STEVE: Well, I'm – er – a little prejudiced, maybe …

FORBES laughs.

TEMPLE: No, but seriously, Sir Graham. He's terrific! And intelligent! You'd hardly credit it, why only the other morning he –

STEVE: (*Stopping TEMPLE*) Now darling! Remember what we used to say about other people's clever children. We mustn't bore Sir Graham.

TEMPLE: Oh sorry. Er – Yes … (*Changing the subject*) Before we left for Cairo, Sir Graham, I read a report in one of the newspapers that you'd retired: is that true?

FORBES: No, I've been transferred. There's been a sort of general upheaval at the Yard. I'm now in control of what's known as the Central Criminal Investigation Bureau. It means more responsibility but – thank the Lord – I've got a completely free hand.

TEMPLE: Well, that's something!

FORBES: (*With a laugh*) I should say so!

STEVE: (*Smiling*) You still haven't told us what you're doing in Cairo, Sir Graham.

FORBES: Just shortly after you left England, Temple, I received information from the Governorate in Egypt.

STEVE:	What is that?
FORBES:	It's the equivalent of our Scotland Yard … informing me that certain new facts had come to light concerning the Monton robbery. Now the Monton robbery, you may recall actually – (*He stops speaking a moment*) What is that?
TEMPLE:	What?
FORBES:	Didn't you hear it?
TEMPLE:	No.
FORBES:	I could have sworn I …
STEVE:	(*A quick whisper*) Darling!
TEMPLE:	What is it?
STEVE:	Paul, listen!

A moment.

A tapping noise can be heard: someone – softly – tapping the window with a coin.

FORBES:	What is it, Temple?
TEMPLE:	There's someone at the window: someone on the balcony …
FORBES:	I'll draw the curtains …
TEMPLE:	No! No, wait! (*A moment*) Put the light out, Steve.

STEVE switches the light off.

TEMPLE:	Now wait a minute … don't stand too near the window, Steve …

TEMPLE flings back the curtains.

STEVE:	(*Staggered*) Paul!
TEMPLE:	It's Armstrong!

ARMSTRONG is outside the window. He is breathless with a note of desperation in his voice.

ARMSTRONG:	Temple, open the window … Open the window … Be quick!

TEMPLE throws open the window.

TEMPLE: (*Quickly*) What is it? What do you want?

ARMSTRONG: Temple, listen! I want to tell you about Marquand! I want to tell you why he deliberately –

There is a shot from the street below which smashes a pane of glass.

STEVE: Paul!

FORBES: Look out, Temple! There's someone in a car firing from the street ...

A second shot is heard.

STEVE: Be careful, Paul!

ARMSTRONG: (*Desperately*) Temple, Marquand's double-crossed me – he's thrown in his lot with Schreider and decided to –

STEVE: (*With a cry of alarm*) Paul, look out!

ARMSTRONG: It's Marquand! He's trying to stop me ...

FORBES: Get down, Temple! Get down!

STEVE: Get down, Paul!

From the street below a car can be heard driving swiftly past the hotel: there is a volley of shots from a sten gun. The window smashes to pieces and there is a sudden cry of anguish from ARMSTRONG as he falls.

FADE UP of music.

END OF EPISODE SEVEN

EPISODE EIGHT

STILL HAVING A
WONDERFUL TIME

OPEN TO:

SCENE 1:   The TEMPLES' Hotel Sitting Room
As in Episode 7, Scene 13
There is a shot from the street below which smashes a pane of glass.

STEVE: Paul!
FORBES: Look out, Temple! There's someone in a
                    car firing from the street ...

A second shot is heard.

STEVE: Be careful, Paul!
ARMSTRONG: (*Desperately*) Temple. Marquand's double
                    crossed me – he's thrown in his lot with
                    Schreider and decided to –
STEVE: (*With a cry of alarm*) Paul, look out!
ARMSTRONG: It's Marquand! He's trying to stop me ...
FORBES: Get down, Temple! Get down!
STEVE: Get down, Paul!

From the street below a car can be heard driving swiftly past the hotel: there is a volley of shots from a sten gun. The window smashes to pieces and there is a sudden cry of anguish from ARMSTRONG as he falls, slightly wounded in the shoulder. The car in the street below makes a quick getaway.

STEVE: Paul, he's hurt!
FORBES: Who is this man?
TEMPLE: His name's Armstrong. He is – or was – in
                    league with Colonel Marquand.
FORBES: (*Nodding: briskly*) I've heard of
                    Marquand, he's after the spectacles ...
                    Rossetti told me about him.
STEVE: Paul, he's hurt!
ARMSTRONG: (*In pain*) It's my shoulder. I felt something
                    hit me ...

TEMPLE:	Put the light on, Steve. (*To FORBES*) Armstrong was at Bournemouth the night Joyce Raymond was murdered.
ARMSTRONG:	Yes, but I didn't murder Joyce Raymond. I swear I didn't. Temple, I've got to talk to you … agh …
TEMPLE:	Reach me that pillow, Sir Graham, off the bed … That's it! (*Puts the pillow under ARMSTRONG's head*) Is that better?
ARMSTRONG:	Yes … Now, Temple, listen … I was sent to England by Marquand. I was told to get the spectacles! I thought you were playing the same game as Marquand, that's why I followed you down to Sandbanks that afternoon.
TEMPLE:	And provided us with a first class ducking!
FORBES:	Why did Marquand want the spectacles, do you know?

A moment.

TEMPLE:	(*Quietly*) This is Sir Graham Forbes of Scotland Yard.
ARMSTRONG:	I don't know why Marquand wanted the spectacles – he simply told me that if I could get them for him he'd pay me £7000. He warned me that several other people were after them.
FORBES:	Who, for instance?
ARMSTRONG:	Olaf Schreider and a henchman of his called Constantine. Constantine was staying … (*He winces in pain*) … at the hotel in Bournemouth, he searched my room … I know it was Constantine, but I don't think he murdered Joyce Raymond.
TEMPLE:	Who did murder her?

ARMSTRONG:	(*A moment*) I don't know.
TEMPLE:	Armstrong, what happened that night in Augusta, the night I met Colonel Marquand?
ARMSTRONG:	Marquand got hold of a young fellow called Thompson – a friend of Joyce Raymond's. Thompson didn't know what it was all about but Marquand persuaded him to telephone you and pretend to be Richard Sullivan. When you suggested over the phone that something had happened to Joyce Raymond, Thompson jumped to the conclusion that …
TEMPLE:	That <u>you'd</u> murdered her?
ARMSTRONG:	Yes.
STEVE:	Well, who telephoned Marquand – pretending to be Constantine?
ARMSTRONG:	Schreider did. Constantine had already been in touch with Schreider, and Schreider knew that you were at the Villa Negara.
TEMPLE:	How did he know?
ARMSTRONG:	Constantine tailed you from the hotel. Schreider guessed you'd tell Marquand about what happened on the flying-boat, and –
TEMPLE:	And he wanted Marquand to believe that I'd already parted with the spectacles before reaching Augusta?
ARMSTRONG:	Yes.
TEMPLE:	(*Quietly: watching ARMSTRONG*) Why are you telling us all this?
ARMSTRONG:	Because Marquand's double-crossed me: he promised to pay me four thousand

215

	whether I got the glasses or not and now ... (*He winces in pain*) ... he's thrown in his lot with Schreider and refuses to pay.
TEMPLE:	(*Quietly*) Armstrong ...
ARMSTRONG:	Yes?
TEMPLE:	That girl, – the American girl Miss Jeans – was she working for Marquand?
ARMSTRONG:	Yes.
TEMPLE:	But she double-crossed him, didn't she?
ARMSTRONG:	What do you mean?
TEMPLE:	She started to play in with Bahri: Marquand found out, followed her out to the houseboat – which was Bahri's headquarters – and murdered her. That's true, isn't it?
ARMSTRONG:	Yes, it's true.
FORBES:	Why is Bahri – and I presume you mean Zoltan Bahri – after the spectacles?
ARMSTRONG:	Presumably for the same reason as Marquand.
FORBES:	What is the reason?
ARMSTRONG:	I don't know! I've told you, I don't know why Marquand wants the spectacles ... Oh ... Oh, my arm ...
STEVE:	We shall have to get a doctor, Paul.
TEMPLE:	(*Quietly*) In a moment.
FORBES:	There's a warrant out for Marquand: where would you suggest we look for him?
TEMPLE:	You might do worse than the Karamet, Sir Graham. He was there tonight calling himself Oliver J. Whiteman.
FORBES:	(*Surprised*) Marquand was?
TEMPLE:	(*Nodding*) Yes.

ARMSTRONG:	Failing that … you might try Meyerhoff's.
FORBES:	Meyerhoff's? What is that, a shop?
ARMSTRONG:	It's a jewellers: it's about a quarter of a mile past The House of Bahri. And Temple, I warn you, both Schreider and Marquand are pretty dangerous men. Don't underrate them; they're determined to get those spectacles, whatever the cost …
TEMPLE:	I shan't underrate them, Armstrong.

FADE UP of music.

FADE DOWN of music.

SCENE 2:	The TEMPLES' Hotel Room

A door opens.

STEVE:	I'm going out now, darling. I shan't be long.
TEMPLE:	Right. I'll meet you here about twelve o'clock. Oh, I should take a coat, Steve – it's much colder today.
STEVE:	I'll be all right. You look tired, Paul.
TEMPLE:	Yes, I feel it. I didn't get to bed till nearly four o'clock.
STEVE:	You talk about us women nattering but, by George, I thought you and Sir Graham were never going to stop.
TEMPLE:	(*Laughing*) I don't know whether you realise it or not, Steve, but as soon as they took Armstrong away you fell fast asleep.
STEVE:	(*Laughing*) Yes, I know. How is he, by the way? Have you heard this morning?
TEMPLE:	I think he's comfortable. (*Seriously*) Steve, I had a good talk to Sir Graham last night

	about this business and – there's something I think you ought to know.
STEVE:	There's something I'd certainly like to know!
TEMPLE:	What's that?
STEVE:	Why Schreider and Marquand and Zoltan Bahri are after the spectacles. Do you know?

A moment.

TEMPLE:	Yes, darling, I know.
STEVE:	Did Sir Graham tell you?
TEMPLE:	Mrs Temple, please!
STEVE:	You mean, you told Sir Graham?
TEMPLE:	Yes. As a matter of fact I've known for some time. I discovered the secret of them the day … However, that can wait. Steve, now that Marquand and Schreider have joined forces they're obviously going to try something pretty desperate. They know I've got the spectacles and – well – quite honestly, darling, there's a possibility that they may try and pick you up and use you as a sort of hostage.
STEVE:	But Marquand's already tried that and it failed.
TEMPLE:	Yes, thanks to Mr Darwin; but next time he might not be quite so close at hand.
STEVE:	All right, don't worry, Paul – I'll take care.
TEMPLE:	Yes, well do take care, Steve. You know, I'm not so sure whether I should let you go out on your own or not.
STEVE:	I'll be all right, darling!

A knock and the door opens.

FORBES:	May I come in?

218

TEMPLE: Oh, hello, Sir Graham.

STEVE: Come in, Sir Graham.

The door closes.

TEMPLE: How's Armstrong?

FORBES: He'll be all right: he should be out of hospital in a matter of a week or so. We checked on that address, the jewellers he mentioned – there was no sign of Marquand.

TEMPLE: I'm not surprised. They must have known that Armstrong would have mentioned that place. What about Schreider?

FORBES: There was no sign of him either; but of course we've got to go steady as far as Schreider's concerned. We've really got no concrete evidence that he's mixed up in this business.

STEVE: Well, I'll be off, dear. Goodbye, Sir Graham – see you later.

FORBES: Take care of yourself, Steve!

STEVE: (*Laughing, as she opens the door*) Now don't you start! Goodbye.

TEMPLE: Goodbye!

FORBES: Goodbye!

The door closes.

A pause.

TEMPLE: Did you do what I suggested?

FORBES: Yes. I had a word with Hakim. Don't worry. Steve will be watched from the moment she leaves the hotel.

TEMPLE: (*Nodding*) Good.

FADE up of music.

Which mixes to a busy Egyptian street.

Which mixes to:

SCENE 3:   Car Interior / Street

The car is parked in the street with its engine ticking over.

SCHREIDER: (*Quietly*) There she is …

MARQUAND: Where?

SCHREIDER: (*Watching STEVE*) She's just come out of the hotel. Do you see her? Look!

MARQUAND: Oh, yeah … yeah, I see.

SCHREIDER: (*Faintly nervous*) What shall we do?

MARQUAND: (*Quite calmly*) There's no hurry: now just take it easy. Relax.

SCHREIDER: It looks to me as if she's making for the market place.

MARQUAND: That's o.k. Don't worry. We shan't lose her.

SCHREIDER: What shall I do – drive the car further down the road?

MARQUAND: No – just relax. Stay where you are.

SCHREIDER: But if she gets round the corner and into the marketplace it will be almost impossible to find her again.

MARQUAND: Don't worry. Now just keep calm.

A pause.

SCHREIDER: What are you looking at?

MARQUAND: I'm looking at that guy on the corner: he's watching her.

SCHREIDER: You're imagining things.

MARQUAND: Not me, Mr Schreider. I haven't got that type of imagination. He's watching her all right. (*A moment: to himself*) Now what's the idea?

SCHREIDER: He's following her.

MARQUAND: Yeah … It's one of Hakim's men.

SCHREIDER: The police?

MARQUAND: Yeah … They're not taking any chances.

SCHREIDER:	(*Nervously*) What are we going to do? We can't pick her up while he's watching.
MARQUAND:	There's only one thing we can do. Give me back that revolver I gave you – the one with the silencer.
SCHNEIDER:	But what …
MARQUAND:	Give it to me!
SCHREIDER:	(*Handing the revolver to MARQUAND*) What are you going to do?
MARQUAND:	(*Quietly: a note of tenseness*) We'll have to get rid of the man first – it's our only chance!
SCHREIDER:	But you can't possibly …
MARQUAND:	Now listen, Schreider: drop me about thirty or forty yards behind him and then drive slowly …

MIX out to the street: people walking, street chatter.

SCHREIDER is approaching in the car.

MARQUAND:	I beg your pardon, sir …
MAN:	(*Egyptian*) Yes?
MARQUAND:	Could you direct me to the Alexandria Hotel?

The car draws up to the kerb during the next speech.

MAN:	The Alexandria Hotel? You're walking in the wrong direction my friend, you want to turn round and – (*He stops*)
MARQUAND:	(*Quietly; determined*) Get in the car …
MAN:	What do you mean? What …
MARQUAND:	You heard what I said: get in the car!

MARQUAND opens the car door.

MAN:	Look here, what are you trying to do? You can't …
MARQUAND:	Get in that car!

MAN: What is the meaning of this? Why are you
…

MARQUAND: Do as I tell you! Get in the car!

The MAN gets in, MARQUAND follows and slams the door.

SCHREIDER: (*Quickly*) I've seen Mrs Temple, she's …

MAN: Oh, I understand now …

MARQUAND: (*Quickly*) Rev your engine up – Schreider,
rev it up!

SCHREIDER revs the engine, and keeps revving it under the following …

MAN: What are you going to do with that
revolver … No, don't! Don't shoot! Don't
… Don't!

MARQUAND shoots the MAN with the silenced gun.

MAN: Argh …

MARQUAND: O.K.

SCHREIDER stops revving.

SCHREIDER: Is he dead?

MARQUAND: Don't worry about him! Where did you
see Mrs Temple?

SCHREIDER: She's in a dress shop – over on the other
side of the square.

MARQUAND: Are you sure?

SCHREIDER: Yes, I saw her cross over.

MARQUAND: (*Slowly: nodding*) O.K., drive over there
… drive into the kerb … keep your mouth
shut and your eyes open …

FADE UP of music.

FADE DOWN of music.

SCENE 4:   The TEMPLES' Hotel Room

TEMPLE is typing.

The telephone rings, he stops typing and lifts the receiver.

TEMPLE: Hello?

CLERK:	(*On the other end of the line*) Mr Temple?
TEMPLE:	Yes.
CLERK:	Will you hold the line please, there's a call for you.
TEMPLE:	Thank you.

A pause.

TEMPLE whistles to himself and gets faintly impatient.

TEMPLE:	Hello?
CLERK:	Just a moment, please.

Another pause.

MARQUAND:	Hello? Mr Temple?
TEMPLE:	Yes – speaking. Who is that?
MARQUAND:	Don't you recognise me?
TEMPLE:	No, I'm afraid I don't.
MARQUAND:	It's Marquand.
TEMPLE:	(*Surprised*) Marquand!
MARQUAND:	(*Interrupting TEMPLE*) Temple, listen! I've got a friend of yours here: she wants to say a few words to you …
STEVE:	(*A little frightened*) Is that you, Paul?
TEMPLE:	Steve!
STEVE:	(*Quickly*) Marquand picked me up, darling – I was in a dress shop – I'm speaking from a house on –

STEVE is pulled away from the phone.

TEMPLE:	Steve!
MARQUAND:	Did you get that?
TEMPLE:	(*Tensely*) Yes, I got it! Now listen, Marquand; I'm warning you, if anything happens to my wife I'll –
MARQUAND:	Relax, brother! I don't like this corny situation any more than you do. Now listen! I want those glasses. I don't want any alibis. I don't want any ifs or buts or

223

	ands – I just want those glasses – do you get me?
A pause.	
TEMPLE:	I get you, Marquand.
MARQUAND:	Good. Now listen to what I'm saying. I'm sending a car round for you. He'll pick you up at the corner near the newspaper stand. If anyone's tailing you or there's any funny business, then … it'll be just too bad for Mrs Temple. Catch on?
A moment.	
TEMPLE:	(*Quietly*) Marquand …
MARQUAND:	Yeah?
TEMPLE:	I don't think you … quite understand the situation.
MARQUAND:	What do you mean?
TEMPLE:	(*Very quietly*) You harm my wife, you touch so much as one hair of her head and …
MARQUAND:	(*Smiling*) And what?
TEMPLE:	(*Politely*) And do you know what I'll do? I shall drop those glasses on the floor, and smash them to pieces, Colonel Marquand. (*A moment*) Understand?
A pause.	
MARQUAND:	I'm sending the car round straight away. Don't keep it waiting … and don't forget what I've told you.
TEMPLE:	I shan't forget.
FADE UP of music.	

FADE DOWN of music.

SCENE 5:   A Room in MARQUAND's Cairo Apartment

A door is suddenly thrown open and TEMPLE enters, followed by SCHREIDER.

STEVE: (*A cry of relief*) Paul!

TEMPLE: Steve … Steve, darling, are you all right?

MARQUAND: (*With authority*) Stay where you are! Don't move! (*To SCHREIDER*) Were you followed?

SCHREIDER: (*Nervously*) No … No, I don't think so …

MARQUAND: (*Sharply*) What do you mean, you don't think so?

SCHREIDER: No, it's all right … I made a check on it …

MARQUAND: (*Nodding*) O.K., go back to the car, Schreider – turn it round – and wait. (*A moment*) I shan't be long.

SCHREIDER: (*He hesitates: then:*) All right …

SCHREIDER departs closing the door behind him.

MARQUAND: Now, my friend, where are the spectacles?

TEMPLE: Before I hand them over, Colonel Marquand, I should like you to –

MARQUAND: Before you hand them over, Mr Temple, I should like you to get one thing quite clear. (*Quietly*) You see this revolver?

TEMPLE: One could hardly fail to see it.

MARQUAND: If I have any nonsense from you – I shan't hesitate to use it … Now give me the spectacles.

A pause, then TEMPLE moves towards MARQUAND.

TEMPLE: Have I your assurance that once I hand them over –

MARQUAND: Stay where you are! Keep on the other side of the stove … Now, I warn you, Temple, if there's any funny business …

225

TEMPLE: I merely wanted your assurance that once
                 I've …

MARQUAND: Once you've handed over the spectacles
                 you can go back to the hotel.

TEMPLE: Well, in that case, you leave me with very
                 little alternative.

TEMPLE stops speaking. From the street below a motor horn is heard – several angry voices, a sudden, desperate, shout from SCHREIDER. A revolver shot rings out. The horn stops.

STEVE: (*Quickly*) Paul!

MARQUAND: What is it? What the … ?

STEVE: (*Looking down to the street*) It's Sir
                 Graham … and the police … Look! They
                 must have followed you, darling!

TEMPLE: They've picked up Schreider!

MARQUAND: The fool, I warned him to be on the look
                 out.

STEVE: (*Quickly*) Paul!

STEVE screams as MARQUAND fires at TEMPLE and misses. TEMPLE throws himself at MARQUAND.

TEMPLE: Drop the gun. Drop … it …

STEVE: Mind the stove, Paul! Darling, mind the
                 stove or you'll have the place on fire!

TEMPLE: Drop … the … revolver … Do as I …

MARQUAND begins to get the upper hand and lands a blow on TEMPLE.

TEMPLE: Argh! … (*Desperately*) Steve … break the
                 window and …

STEVE smashes the window and shouts down.

STEVE: Sir Graham! Sir Graham!

The struggle continues: chairs are overturned: a table: the stove …

STEVE: Paul, the stove!

MARQUAND: Look out, or you'll have the place on fire!

TEMPLE:	Give me the revolver, Marquand, or I'll … I'll …

The curtains begin to burn.

STEVE:	Paul … the curtains have caught fire! (*Trying to stamp out the fire*) I – I can't stop it …

TEMPLE and MARQUAND are still struggling.

MARQUAND:	Temple … the place is on fire!
TEMPLE:	(*Almost exhausted*) Drop the revolver!
STEVE:	Paul, it's spreading … I can't stop it!

The flames start to roar.

MARQUAND:	Temple, the room's on fire!

Grimly determined, TEMPLE forces MARQUAND's hand back.

TEMPLE:	Give … me … the … revolver … or … I'll …

A sudden revolver shot is heard.

A tense silence follows.

MARQUAND:	Oh … Temple, I … I …

MARQUAND falls.

TEMPLE is almost completely exhausted.

TEMPLE:	Steve, we've … got to get out of here …
STEVE:	(*Coughing*) It's going to be difficult to … reach … the door …
TEMPLE:	Take this handkerchief. Now give me your arm, we've got to make a dash for it … Are you ready?
STEVE:	Yes … Yes, I'm ready.
TEMPLE:	Right, let's go!

TEMPLE and STEVE dash across the room and TEMPLE kicks open the door.

Men are climbing the staircase.

FORBES calls from below.

FORBES:	Temple, are you all right – are you both all right?
TEMPLE:	Yes … Yes, we're all right, Sir Graham!
STEVE:	(*Coughing: weakly*) We're having a wonderful time!
FORBES:	(*Laughing*) Come along, Steve!

FADE UP of music.

FADE DOWN of music.

SCENE 6:	The TEMPLES' Hotel Room
TEMPLE:	Have another drink, Sir Graham.
FORBES:	No, I don't think I will, Temple – thanks all the same. Well, are you feeling any better, Steve?
STEVE:	I'm feeling fine, but you know, Sir Graham, what I don't understand about this business would fill a library.

FORBES laughs.

STEVE:	Now, take that night in Bournemouth for instance. What actually happened that night? Oh, I know Joyce Raymond was murdered and I know –
FORBES:	(*Fairly amused*) Let me begin at the beginning, Steve. (*A moment: seriously*) You remember the Monton robbery?
STEVE:	The Duke and Duchess of Monton? But of course!
FORBES:	About a year ago a collection of jewellery belonging to the Duke and Duchess of Monton, was stolen from Harrington House in Norfolk. It was an extremely valuable – one might almost say unique collection – and the estimated value was somewhere in the region of a million and a quarter. The man mainly

responsible for the job was called Leopold Farrington. Farrington worked with a man called Lewis Carson and believe me they were a couple of pretty smart birds: just how smart we shall never really know. Anyway, to cut a long story short: Farrington got away with the collection and got as far as Cairo. When he reached Cairo however he thought that things were getting a little too hot for him and he decided to bury the collection and make himself scarce. He picked a likely hiding place for the jewellery, made a careful note of its exact whereabouts, and then faded out of the picture. Three months later, Farrington caught typhoid and died.

STEVE: Go on.

FORBES: (*Quietly*) I think you can carry on from here, Temple.

TEMPLE: Before he died, Farrington got friendly with an English girl; as a matter of fact she nursed him during his illness. When he knew that there was very little chance of his making a recovery he told her about the robbery and gave her ...

STEVE: (*Tongue in cheek*) Gave her a secret document explaining the exact whereabouts of the Monton collection!

TEMPLE: Nothing of the sort! He gave her an apparently perfectly ordinary pair of horn-rimmed spectacles and asked her to take them to London and to give them to Lewis Carson.

FORBES: And for your information, Steve, the name of the girl that looked after Farrington – in other

	words the girl that received the glasses – was Lydia Raymond. <u>Lydia</u> Raymond, mind you.
STEVE:	I don't get this. It was Joyce Raymond that came to the flat and asked us to deliver the glasses.
TEMPLE:	Wait a moment, darling! Lydia knew, as soon as she received the glasses from Farrington, that in some mysterious way they were connected with the Monton robbery. As a matter of fact, from that very moment, so far as Lydia was concerned, things begin to happen.
STEVE:	Go on.
TEMPLE:	Zoltan Bahri, Marquand, Schreider and a gentleman by the name of Richard Sullivan all tried to get the spectacles. But Lydia was a pretty determined sort of a girl and she took them to London.
FORBES:	When she arrived in London, she told her sister about them. Now Sullivan had already got in touch with Joyce Raymond and had offered her £5,000 if she would get them for him. Joyce got the glasses from Lydia and brought them to you. She was frightened to take them to Cairo herself because she knew – from what Lydia had told her – that Bahri, Marquand and Schreider were pretty dangerous customers, and would stop at nothing to get hold of them.
STEVE:	Did Joyce murder her sister?
FORBES:	Yes. Lydia found out what Joyce was up to and followed her to Half Moon Street.
STEVE:	But why did Joyce go down to Bournemouth?

230

TEMPLE: For the simple reason that, when she got back to her flat, there was a phone message from Sullivan saying he'd just arrived in England and wanted to see her. She went down to Bournemouth and told him exactly what happened. At first he was annoyed, and then suddenly realised that his best bet was to get rid of Joyce – who by this time knew far too much about things – and simply let us take the risks and carry the spectacles back to Cairo for him!

STEVE: (*Bewildered*) Yes, but – why did Sullivan want the spectacles? Why did Marquand want them? Why did everyone seem to want them?

TEMPLE: Don't you know why?

STEVE: Don't be infuriating, Paul – you know I don't!

TEMPLE: Two days ago, Steve, I took those glasses to an opticians. I told him to make a detailed examination of them and to do something for me. Do you know what that something was?

STEVE: No.

TEMPLE: (*After a moment*) I told him to write down the prescription.

STEVE: The prescription? What do you mean?

TEMPLE: Well you know that every pair of spectacles is made up to a prescription.

STEVE: Yes, of course.

TEMPLE: The number of prescriptions is – well – infinite. There are literally billions of them. When Farrington hid the Monton collection he made a chart showing the exact spot in the desert where the collection was buried. He knew that it was risky to keep the chart, so he converted it into a prescription for a pair of spectacles.

STEVE: So that's it!

TEMPLE: He had the spectacles made up, and then he destroyed both the chart and the prescription. He knew perfectly well of course that whenever he wanted the chart all he had to do was to get an optician to examine the spectacles and write down the prescription for him.

STEVE: I see. In other words, Sullivan, Bahri, Marquand and Schreider wanted the spectacles in order to get the prescription, so that they could find the Monton collection!

TEMPLE: Exactly!

STEVE: Yes, but there's just one point, darling, that you haven't quite explained …

TEMPLE: Oh? And what's that?

STEVE: Who is Richard Sullivan? Is it Darwin?

TEMPLE: Don't you know?

STEVE: Is it Darwin?

TEMPLE: Yes. Why do you think Darwin rescued us that afternoon at Sandbanks? Why do you think he stopped Marquand from holding you as a hostage?

STEVE: I suppose he thought you had the glasses on you and he was frightened of losing them?

FORBES: Yes – and when Miss Jeans picked you up he rescued you because he thought Temple might get cold feet and hand the glasses over to Marquand.

STEVE: I see. You know it's funny, Paul, but, well, I've suspected Darwin all along, and yet, somehow … well, he's always seemed such a 'nice' person. (*Suddenly; softly*) Oh!

TEMPLE: What is it?

STEVE: I've just remembered. You invited him to dinner!

FADE UP of music.

232

FADE DOWN of music.

SCENE 7:   A Quiet Restaurant

TEMPLE, STEVE, DARWIN and MISS FRASER are at a table, the meal is finished.

DARWIN: Well, thank you for a most excellent dinner, Temple!

FRASER: Yes, indeed – it's really been most enjoyable.

TEMPLE: Won't you have another glass of port, Miss Fraser?

FRASER: No ... No, I don't think so, thank you.

TEMPLE: Darwin?

DARWIN: No, thanks old boy. I've had more than enough.

FRASER: Well, I suppose we'd better be making a move. You look a little on the pale side tonight, Mrs Temple – aren't you feeling too well?

STEVE: Oh, I'm all right, Miss Fraser. I didn't sleep too well last night, so perhaps ...

DARWIN: That's not surprising! We had a ghastly evening, Miss Fraser! Perfectly ghastly! First of all a chappie by the name of ... *(He stops: suddenly)* By the way, I'd completely forgotten all about it, but you know what you promised me last night?

TEMPLE: What?

DARWIN: You promised to show me those spectacles.

TEMPLE: Oh, yes. Yes, so I did.

FRASER: Spectacles?

DARWIN: Mr Temple's got rather an unusual pair of spectacles, Miss Fraser. He was offered £10,000 for them.

FRASER: What? £10,000 for a pair of spectacles?

DARWIN: *(Laughing)* Yes.

FRASER: They must be very unusual ones, Mr Temple. What are they made of – platinum studded with diamonds?

TEMPLE: No, they're just a perfectly ordinary pair of spectacles.

FRASER: Yes, but £10,000!

DARWIN: (*Laughing: forgetting himself*) You see, you've even got the old girl – (*He checks himself*)

FRASER: Not so much of the <u>old</u> girl, Mr Darwin!

DARWIN: I beg your pardon! You see, Miss Fraser's just as curious as I am.

TEMPLE: (*Pleasantly*) Well, I suppose I've no alternative but to satisfy your curiosity. (*Feeling in his pocket*) … Now where did I put them … Oh, here they are.

TEMPLE passes the spectacles to MISS FRASER.

FRASER: Thank you.

Pause.

TEMPLE: Well – Miss Fraser?

Another pause.

FRASER: (*Apparently bewildered*) Well! They appear to be just an ordinary pair of spectacles. I can't for the life of me imagine why anyone should offer you £10,000 for them.

DARWIN: (*Slowly: politely casual*) May I, Miss Fraser?

FRASER: Oh, yes – I'm sorry.

DARWIN: (*Taking the glasses*) Thank you.

A pause.

TEMPLE: (*Unsurprised: pleasantly*) Well, Mr Darwin?

DARWIN: (*A laugh*) I'm afraid I agree with Miss Fraser. If anyone comes along and offers you anything over a fiver, old boy, I should jump at it!

MISS FRASER laughs.

TEMPLE: What's your offer, Mr Darwin?

DARWIN: My offer? They're not a bit of use to me, old boy.

STEVE: (*Apparently amused*) It looks to me as if you've
           missed the bus, darling.
TEMPLE: I'm beginning to think so!
They all laugh.
DARWIN: Here you are, Temple – and take my advice. If
           you get …
DARWIN suddenly drops the glasses on the floor.
DARWIN: Oh, dear – I've dropped them!
*MISS FRASER and STEVE start to move their chairs away
from the table.*
FRASER: I'll move my chair over.
DARWIN quickly stoops beneath the table.
DARWIN: It's all right – it's all right, Miss Fraser …
TEMPLE: Have you got them?
DARWIN emerges from under the table.
DARWIN: Yes – yes, I've got them.
STEVE: Are they broken?
DARWIN: No, they're as right as rain. Sorry, Temple.
TEMPLE: That's all right: no harm done.
DARWIN returns the glasses to TEMPLE.
DARWIN: There you are.
TEMPLE: Thank you.
A pause.
FRASER: Well, I suppose we'd better be making a move.
DARWIN: (*Brightly*) Yes. And thank you again, Temple –
           for an excellent dinner.
TEMPLE: I'm glad you enjoyed it, but I'm sorry you were
           disappointed in the spectacles.
DARWIN: (*Laughing*) Oh, that's all right.
TEMPLE: I'm afraid you're going to be even more
           disappointed when you get home.
DARWIN: What do you mean?
TEMPLE: I mean: when you examine the spectacles more
           closely.

235

DARWIN: But how can I examine them more closely? You've got them in your hand.

TEMPLE: On the contrary: you've got them in your pocket.

DARWIN: (*Apparently astonished*) I've got them! Are you crazy?

TEMPLE: You did the switch-over very neatly, my friend, but I'm afraid it won't get you anywhere.

DARWIN: What do you mean?

TEMPLE: These glasses – the ones you've got in your pocket – are just as valueless as these. The real glasses – the ones that Joyce Raymond gave me – were handed over to Sir Graham Forbes and Commandant Hakim first thing this morning and by this time they –

DARWIN, intensely angry, overturns the table.

DARWIN: Why, you cunning devil!

There is general consternation in the restaurant.

STEVE: Paul, look out!

MISS FRASER speaks quickly, with authority, and with no Scots accent.

FRASER: Drop that revolver, Darwin.

DARWIN: What – what the devil do you mean?

A tense silence.

FRASER: You heard what I said – drop that revolver.

DARWIN: (*With a laugh*) Do you think you can scare me with that damn thing? Why it's loaded with peppermints! You showed us that revolver last night when you dropped your handbag!

FRASER: You think so, Mr Darwin? You think so?

MISS FRASER fires and DARWIN utters a cry of pain as the bullet hits his hand. Several women in the restaurant scream.

FRASER: Do you still think it's loaded with peppermints?

DARWIN: Who are you? What do you want? Are you … after the spectacles?

236

STEVE:	(*Also bewildered*) Who are you, Miss Fraser?
FRASER:	My name is Nicholson. I'm from Scotland Yard.

FADE UP of music.

FADE DOWN of music.

SCENE 8A:	The Flying Boat Passenger Cabin
STEWARD 1:	Can I get you anything, sir?
TEMPLE:	Yes, we'd like something to drink. What would you like, Miss Fraser?
FRASER:	(*No Scots accent*) Nothing for me, thank you, Mr Temple.
TEMPLE:	Are you sure?
FRASER:	Yes, quite sure, thank you.
TEMPLE:	Steve?
STEVE:	No, thank you, darling.
TEMPLE:	Sir Graham?
FORBES:	I'd like a whisky and soda.
TEMPLE:	Good. Have you any beer?
STEWARD 1:	Yes, sir.
TEMPLE:	Well, a whisky and soda and a beer.
STEWARD 1:	Very good, sir.
TEMPLE:	(*Laughing*) I'm afraid I keep calling you Miss Fraser, Miss Nicholson. I'm terribly sorry.
FRASER:	(*Laughing*) That's all right. As a matter of fact I simply can't get used to speaking without an accent. (*With her Scots accent*) It's a most distressing condition to be in, I can assure you!

They all laugh.

STEVE:	Miss Nicholson, why did you go down to Bournemouth in the first place?
FORBES:	We sent Miss Nicholson down to Bournemouth to keep an eye on Armstrong.

	We knew he was working for Marquand and we had a suspicion that Marquand was mixed up in the Monton robbery.
FRASER:	(*No Scots accent*) When I got down to Bournemouth, however, I spotted Darwin, became suspicious of him, and decided to take rather an interest in the young man.
STEVE:	I see. Well, what happened that night at the Hotel Karamet?
TEMPLE:	Marquand, Schreider and Quinn knew that Darwin was after the spectacles and …
FORBES:	And declared war on him!
TEMPLE:	Exactly! The night we dined at the Karamet Quinn tried to murder Darwin, but Darwin was too quick, turned the tables on him, shot him, and placed him in his car. He then fixed up with Valkerie, the waiter, to deliver the note to us and while we were outside searching for Quinn's car, Valkerie went out onto the terrace and fired a revolver to give the impression … that Quinn had only just that moment shot himself.
FORBES:	Of course the most interesting aspect of the … (*He breaks off*) Yes, what is it?
STEWARD 2:	I beg your pardon, sir – the wireless officer has just received this message.

The STEWARD passes over a message slip to FORBES.

FORBES:	Oh, thank you.

A pause as FORBES reads the message.

TEMPLE:	Well?
FORBES:	It's from Commandant Hakim: they've found the collection.
FRASER:	Oh, good!
TEMPLE:	That's good news, Sir Graham.

FORBES:	It certainly is.
STEVE:	Well, this looks like the end of the Sullivan mystery, darling.
TEMPLE:	Yes. Y-e-e-s.
FRASER:	What are you going to do when you get back to London, Mr Temple?
TEMPLE:	What am I going to do? I'm going to write a book, and when I've finished the book, Miss Nicholson, I'm going to sit back with my feet on the mantelpiece and think of nothing more important than the temperature of –
STEWARD 1:	(*Briskly*) Your beer, sir!

They all laugh.

SCENE 8B: The Cabin, Later

Several people are gently snoring. The STEWARD speaks softly not wishing to disturb anyone.

STEWARD 1:	I beg your pardon, sir.
TEMPLE:	Yes, steward?
STEWARD 1:	The gentleman in C cabin would rather like to have a word with you, sir.
TEMPLE:	Which gentleman?
STEWARD 1:	The tall thin gentleman, sir – you can see him through the door, smoking a cigarette.
TEMPLE:	Oh. What's his name?
STEWARD 1:	Delaney, sir.

A moment.

TEMPLE:	All right. Tell him I'll meet him on the promenade deck.
STEWARD 1:	Now, sir?
TEMPLE:	Yes, now.
STEWARD 1:	Thank you, sir.

SCENE 8C: The Observation Cabin on the Promenade
Deck

The door opens and TEMPLE enters.

DELANEY: Mr Temple?

TEMPLE: Yes.

DELANEY: I'm dreadfully sorry to disturb you, sir. My
name is Delaney.

TEMPLE: What can I do for you, Mr Delaney?

DELANEY: Well, I'm given to understand that you are
travelling through to England – to London, in
fact.

TEMPLE: Yes.

DELANEY: That was originally my own intention, but
unfortunately I've been delayed and I've got
to stay two or three days in Augusta.

TEMPLE: Well?

DELANEY: I have a book, Mr Temple – a present for my
daughter, my little girl – it's her birthday
tomorrow, and – well, I was wondering if
you'd be good enough to deliver it for me?
You see, if I post it in Augusta, she won't
receive it until the end of the week, and …
There'll be no inconvenience for you, Mr
Temple. I'll send my wife a cable and she'll
meet you at Waterloo.

TEMPLE: (*A moment: watching DELANEY*) What …
sort of a book is it, Mr Delaney?

DELANEY: (*A little surprised by the question*) It's a copy
of Alice in Wonderland. (*Smiling innocently*)
It's just a perfectly plain ordinary book, Mr
Temple.

TEMPLE: (*Faintly embarrassed*) I'm afraid …

DELANEY: (*Amazed*) You mean … you won't?

TEMPLE: (*Shaking his head: emphatically: not at any price*) No thank you, Mr Delaney! No thank you!

FADE UP of music.

THE END

It Began With a Pair Of Spectacles

Paul Temple returns to the air in the Light Programme on Monday. His creator, who has hitherto made a point of never telling how he thinks of his plots, here breaks his rule and describes the incident that suggested *The Sullivan Mystery*.

One evening, about two months after the broadcast of my last serial play, I telephoned Martyn C. Webster, the producer of the Paul Temple plays, and suggested an idea for a new Paul Temple adventure.

He seemed to like the idea and a little while later I completed the first instalment of *Paul Temple and the Sullivan Mystery*.

When he had read the first episode Martyn said: "I like the story very much but it seems quite different from the usual Paul Temple adventures. Whatever made you think of the plot?"

I said: "I never tell people how I think of my plots; you ought to know that by now!"

Five weeks later, just when I had reached a point in Episode 3 when a certain Colonel Marquand was pointing a revolver at Paul Temple and saying "I'm going to give you five seconds, Mr Temple, to tell me exactly where those glasses are," the Editor of the *Radio Times* telephoned.

He sounded polite and friendly but like all editors he had a strange note of determination in his voice. He said: "We want an article on the new Paul Temple serial and we don't want any nonsense about going to the dentist and falling asleep."

I was quite enthusiastic. I said: "I know exactly the sort of article you want. You want me to write about the new Paul Temple film, about the success Paul Temple – alias Paul

Vlaanderen – is having in Holland, about my new Paul Temple novel which is …"

He said: "We don't want anything of the sort! We want a bright, gay little article on the new serial. And we want to know how you thought of the plot."

After I had put the phone down I started to think about the plot of *The Sullivan Mystery* and how, oddly enough, the idea for the story had actually occurred to me. It happened like this.

One night, at about half-past eight, I strolled into the Penguin Club, which is just off Curzon Street. Cecil, the bartender, was mixing a cocktail. He smiled when he saw me and came across to where I was sitting.

He said: "You're just the party I want to see!" As he spoke he took a pair of horn-rimmed spectacles out of his pocket and put them down on the small table.

I said: "You're just the party I want to meet, Cecil. Mix me a dry martini."

Cecil said: "You consider yourself a bit of a Sherlock Holmes. What do you make of these?" He pointed to the spectacles.

I said: "You're confusing me with another guest. I've never considered myself a bit of a Sherlock Holmes."

He said: "But you're the chap that writes those 'ere Paul Temple plays."

I said: "Yes, Cecil. I also drink dry martinis."

When the bartender had departed I picked up the spectacles and examined them. They were a perfectly ordinary pair of horn-rimmed spectacles.

As Cecil put my drink down on the small table he said: "It's an extraordinary thing about these glasses. A man left them here last night. He telephoned this morning and told me to put them on one side for him. He telephoned again just after two o'clock and told me to take particular care of them. I've been expecting him to call all day."

"Has he called?"

Cecil shook his head. "No, but blow me if another man didn't telephone about a quarter of an hour ago. He said that if I'd keep them for him until Friday he'd give me fifty quid for 'em."

I said: "Fifty pounds is rather a lot of money for just a perfectly ordinary pair of spectacles."

Cecil nodded. "That's what I thought! I'm beginning to wonder whether they are just an ordinary pair of spectacles."

I picked up the glasses again and turned them over.

There was no doubt about it, they were just an ordinary pair of horn-rimmed spectacles.

"Cecil," I said, "this sounds like an awfully good beginning to a mystery story."

"That's what I thought," said Cecil. "Pop in on Friday and I'll tell you what happened."

I popped in on Friday and Cecil told me.

He was quite right, it was an awfully good beginning to a mystery story. I hope you'll think so too when you hear the first instalment on Monday.

Francis Durbridge